I0589625

# Miracle in Cade County

By

Larry Buege

**Gastropod Publishing**
Marquette, Michigan

This book is a work of fiction. Names, characters, places, and incidents are used fictitiously. Any resemblance to actual events or persons, living or dead, is entirely coincidental.

## Other books by Larry Buege

Cold Turkey (Political Satire)

Bear Creek (Humorous)

Super Mensa (Techno-Thriller)

William Goodman: Civil War Horse Solder

Chogan and the Grade Wolf (Native American)

Chogan and the White Feather (Native American)

Chogan and the Sioux Warrior (Native American)

Chogan and the Winnebago Merchant

Published by Gastropod Publishing, Marquette, Michigan
Copyright © 2013 by Larry Buege

Library of Congress Control Number: 2013939447
ISBN: 978-0-9892477-2-6

# Miracle in Cade County

## 1

Eric Kampe awoke from a deep sleep, and peered into the darkness. His shoulder muscles tensed, and his heart heaved forcefully against his ribs. A patina of sweat spread across his palms. Had it been a bad dream? He waited for the sensation to pass. Gradually his rapid pulse regressed toward normal, and his muscles began to relax. He wiped his sweaty palms on his pajamas, but his hands remained moist and clammy. This wasn't the first time he had awakened in a panic attack. Five years of maximum-security had turned him into a light sleeper with the slightest noise transferring him into a defensive mode. In prison that had been a necessity—a matter of survival. Fight or flight. He wondered if that would continue now that he was on parole. He lay quietly in bed listening for unusual sounds, but the silence of the room only magnified the sound of his breathing. His bedroom furnishings, illuminated by the dim light from the digital clock on his dresser, cast faint shadows on the bedroom walls. He had been home just over a week. Unlike the first few nights, the shadows were now catalogued and committed to memory. A cursory exam revealed all shadows present and accounted for. Perhaps a passing car had awakened him. Eric relaxed his taunt muscles. He needed to control his emotions before he began searching for gremlins under his bed like a common grade-school boy. He looked at his clock: it was just past two-thirty.

False alarm. Eric closed his eyes and began to relax—until a scratching noise renewed his anxiety. The duration was too short for his senses to fully analyze, but it came from outside, somewhere by the bushes in front of the house. Perhaps a raccoon or skunk was digging for grubs beside the foundation, or the wind could be scraping a branch against the house. Either way it offered no harm.

Eric fluffed his pillow and turned on his side. Adjusting to life outside prison was proving more difficult than he had anticipated. Unpleasant as it might be, prison offered security. Once the guards had locked his cell door for the night, not only was he locked in, but predators were locked out. Without his cell walls, he felt vulnerable.

Eric debated the merits of investigating the noise. It would be a waste of time, but it might assuage his anxiety and allow some sleep. That in itself would make the task worthwhile. The sound of shattering glass terminated further debate—someone was in his house. His heart again pounded against his chest while survival instincts honed by years of prison life took command. He began searching for a weapon, any weapon. He found a black baseball bat in his closet. He hadn't used the bat since Little League. His team was the Black Panthers, and he had painted it black to conform to their black shirts and caps. They must have returned the bat to his parents after the trial. A cardboard tag was still attached to the bat. He knew what the tag would say: *Exhibit Eight*. The bat would have to do.

Eric edged toward the front of the house. Judging from the noise, the intruder entered through the front door, although he was sure he had locked the door before retiring. He didn't bother with lights. His eyes were accustomed to the darkness, and it was his house. He knew where the shadows were lurking, giving him an advantage over any intruder. He wasn't looking for a fair fight. Those who fight fairly don't always win.

Eric crouched low as he advanced toward the living room. He had to be ready in case he needed to spring at his assailant or perhaps make a hasty retreat. He had to be prepared for the unknown. The unknown was the unpredictable variable so frequently responsible for one's demise.

Eric inched along the edge of the hallway, blending his silhouette with the wall. He paused and listened for noise while he scanned the hallway for unusual shadows. When he found none, he proceeded into the darkened living room.

A draft of cold air blew against his cheek. Any other time it would have been imperceptible, but with his remaining senses diminished by darkness, the draft was immediately obvious. He searched for its source and found the curtain by the picture window waving in the breeze. Shards of broken glass under his bare feet confirmed his suspicions. Eric backed away. He didn't need cut feet. A weathered brick lay on top of the broken glass. He reached down and picked up the brick. It was rusty brown with smooth, fire-glazed edges, a popular style for warehouses built in the 1920's. Duct tape strapped an envelope to the back of the brick. Throwing a brick through his window was hardly a friendly gesture, but neither did it present eminent danger.

Eric turned on the lights and waited for his eyes to adjust to the light. There were no markings on the envelope. He opened the envelope and held the single sheet of paper up to the light. The writing was computer generated and printed in a large, bold font.

*Rapist, get out of Cade County and don't come back. We don't want your kind here.* Eric placed the letter in the breast pocket of his pajamas. He had suspected something like this would happen; but now that it had, he needed to consider his options. He wasn't inclined to run. If he left Cade County, it would be on his terms, not because some vigilante ran him out of town. If he were to leave, where would he go? Most states required sex offenders to register with the local authorities. It wouldn't be any different in a new community. He would still be a rapist. He had served his time, five years in prison, but that didn't make him a free man. He was still on parole.

There was little Eric could do before morning. As he turned toward his bedroom, it felt like a sledgehammer slammed into his chest, squeezing the air from his lungs. Simultaneously a wave of hot gas seared across his skin, singeing his eyebrows and curling the hair on his upper forehead. Eric couldn't remember if he had been thrown to the ground before or after the sound of the blast reached his ears; he only remembered the excruciating pain in his ears.

3

* * *

How long had he been unconscious? He assumed it was seconds, minutes at most. He awoke coughing. Acrid smoke filled his lungs, his body ached with pain, and it felt like someone had kicked him in the groin. Eric forced himself to his knees. He had to escape. He needed fresh air. He was a dead man, if he remained in the house. Adrenaline increased his head pain but provided strength to crawl to the door. He reached up and forced open the door, allowing sweet air to fill his lungs. It felt like a dream where he was holding his breath underwater and swimming in slow motion toward the surface. But now he had reached the surface; now he could breathe. Eric lay hyperventilating in the doorway until his strength returned. He climbed to his feet. Apart from the aching pain, all movable parts remained in working order.

The front of his house was undamaged except for the broken window, but black smoke curled upward from the rear of the building—his house was on fire. Eric ran barefoot toward the back of the house, fearing the worst. He was not disappointed: Several small fires, insatiable in their hunger, licked greedily at a gaping hole in his rear entryway. Fortunately, there was more smoke than fire. But fires grow exponentially. If left un-extinguished, the fire would consume the house.

Eric found a garden hose attached to a spigot protruding from the foundation on the east side of the house. His mother used the hose to water her flowerbeds. He turned the knob and water gurgled through the hose—at least he had water pressure. Eric pulled the hose toward the back of the house; it was barely long enough to reach the fire. He sprayed the largest fires first and then worked his way toward the smaller ones. It didn't take long to extinguish the fires, but he continued soaking the smoldering wood to ensure it wouldn't rekindle. The bomb had ripped the back door from its hinges and blown out the windows. Tangled debris littered what remained of the entryway floor. Only a fair size bomb could have created such extensive damage.

Other than the entryway, which the bomb had gutted, there was minimal damage to the house. It would be livable once he opened the windows and aired out the house. The lights still worked; the phone was functional. Eric dialed 911.

The fire department arrived twenty minutes later, one of the middle-of-the-night drawbacks of an all-volunteer fire department. Pagers had to be activated. Men had to dress and drive to the fire station. Kampe's Korner was a ten-mile drive from the fire station in Tamarack. Considering the circumstances, twenty minutes was a remarkable response time for Cade County. But if Eric had waited for the fire truck, his house would have burnt to the ground.

The five firefighters who responded quickly set about their task. They parked the fire truck near the rear of the building and pulled two black hoses from spools on the truck. Without fire hydrants, the only available water came from the water tank built into the rear of the fire truck, seriously limiting the department's effectiveness in a prolonged fire. The garden hose had essentially extinguished the fire; still they poked and probed at the structure, squirting water here and there like dogs marking their scent on trees.

"Mr. Kampe?"

"Yes?" Eric assumed the man in his late forties was the fire chief, although his uniform bore no insignia that differentiated him from the others. He wore the traditional black fire hat without distinguishing mark or rank. The edge of his pajamas protruded from under his black raincoat; he had not bothered to dress.

"I checked the house. The fire's out, but you had a few live electrical wires. I switched them off at the panel box. The other circuits are good. Except for your entryway, I can't find any structural damage. I think it's safe to stay in the house tonight." The fire chief walked over to the phone and lifted the receiver to his ear, listening for a dial tone. "Your phone still works, so you can give us a call if the fire should rekindle."

How did the fire chief think Eric called him the first time, Eric wondered. And sleeping somewhere else was out of the question; he had nowhere to go.

"Also," the fire chief continued, "we'll be sending an investigator around in the morning. We found evidence of arson."

The entryway was blown apart, a brick was thrown through his window, and he *thinks* this may have been arson? Eric was sleepy, his entire body ached with pain, and his patience was wearing thin. It wasn't the fire chief's fault, he reminded himself. He was only doing his job.

The firemen were packing their equipment when Eric heard the siren and saw the red and blue flashing lights coming down the road. The noise from the siren was sufficient to arouse the hardiest of sleepers—and there weren't many of those. A crowd of bystanders in pajamas and hair curlers gathered around the house, all straining for a better view. The gossip mill would be working overtime by morning.

The police cruiser parked next to the fire truck, and Deputy Sheriff Cory Kramer stepped out, flashlight in hand. At five feet five inches, he stood on the short side of average but supported a slender, muscular frame. Kramer placed a Smoky-The-Bear hat over his sandy-blond hair, raising his stature another three inches. All he needed was a pair of mirrored shades to play the role of Hollywood cop. Kramer's testimony at the trial had been crucial to Eric's conviction. Kramer graduated from high school three years ahead of Eric. Eric hadn't liked him then either.

Kramer paused to confer with the fire chief before walking past Eric and stepping uninvited into the shell that had once been Eric's entryway, leaving little doubt as to who was now in charge. This was now his investigation; he would decide who needed to be interviewed and when. The pecking order needed to be established. Kramer was a deputy sheriff. Eric was an ex-con, a sex offender at that. Nothing more needed to be said. Kramer poked through the debris as if Eric were non-existent. No words were exchanged. Eric's presence was neither needed, nor encouraged.

Eric stood shivering amongst the debris, not knowing if the shivering was due to nerves or the cool evening. With heavy dew covering the grass, he assumed the latter. He was barefoot and wearing thin pajamas. The adrenaline rush of earlier was beginning to wane making the lack of creature comforts more obvious. If Kramer didn't need him, he could at least retire to his bedroom for slippers and a bathrobe. Eric headed toward his bedroom. Like the rest of the house, the bedroom had a pungent odor of smoke, but it was livable. He would air out the house in the morning when the outside temperature was warmer. Even with his robe, it still felt cool.

Eric walked to the kitchen and checked the cupboards for coffee. All he had was instant. He might pay dearly for the caffeine this late at night, but the warmth and stimulation offset any disadvantage. Eric found a mug on the counter, rinsed it bachelor-clean, and then filled the mug with hot tap water. At least the water heater was functional; he would need a shower in the morning. Eric placed the mug in the microwave and nuked it for thirty seconds. When the microwave dinged, he retrieved the mug of steaming-hot water and added a healthy amount of instant coffee, preferring his coffee black. He took his coffee into the living room, collapsed into a recliner, and propped his feet on the glass coffee table. The curtain still shimmied in the breeze flowing through the broken window. Fixing the window would have to be one of his higher priorities. He needed to call a glass repairman first thing in the morning. Eric sipped his coffee and stared at the wall. The shock of the evening was wearing off and reality was setting in. Hopefully, this wasn't typical of his future in Cade County.

"Kampe, did you have any plastic pipe in the rear entryway? Any plumbing fixtures?" Deputy Sheriff Kramer stood at the edge of the living room, his soot-covered boots firmly planted on the clean carpet. In his right hand was a mangled piece of PVC pipe.

"The water from the well comes through the east side of the building, and there's no bathrooms or sinks in the back of the house. There shouldn't be any plumbing back there."

"Didn't think so," Kramer said, well pleased with his find. "It appears it was a pipe bomb. From the smell, I'd say gunpowder."

"Gun powder? I would've expected something easier to make like a Molotov cocktail."

"A Molotov cocktail uses gasoline. If someone had thrown that into your house, you'd have had a nice bonfire. Gunpowder creates more explosive force, but not as much fire."

Eric set his coffee down on the end table. "Who has access to gunpowder? I wouldn't even know where to buy it."

"About ten percent of the local population. Sportsmen use it in their muzzleloaders; some even reload their own rifle shells. The stuff's not hard to come by. I've got some back at the house." Kramer paused to let his words sink in. "I don't suppose I need to tell you why this happened. Rapist was spray-painted on the side of your house."

Eric listened in silence, assuming any form of rebuttal would be counter-productive.

"A lot of people don't take kindly to having a rapist in the community. Can't blame them. I don't like your kind either, not that I condone what they did. I expect to see more of this until you leave town."

If this had been a prison conversation, Eric would have thrown the hot coffee in Kramer's face. But this wasn't prison. He was on parole, and nothing would please Kramer more than an excuse to send Eric back to prison. He wouldn't provide Kramer with that satisfaction. The truth was Kramer's sentiment was hardly a minority view. There would be others with similar views. He had better get used to it.

"You need to sell this place and move on. There's nothing for you here anymore—now that your parents are dead. They were good people. Hardly the kind I would expect to produce a rapist."

Eric could tolerate criticism. He had expected that. But what he had or hadn't done had nothing to do with his parents. They had supported him throughout the trial, a trial that had been equally stressful on them. They had visited him in prison twice a month for five years. They had been good parents. Kramer had no right to criticize them, even if he was a deputy sheriff. Eric clinched his fist but suppress his anger.

"Well that's all we can do tonight. Remember, this is a crime scene. No cleanup or repairs until it's cleared. Got that? We'll have a guy take pictures in the morning."

Eric watched the deputy drive off into the night. He couldn't do any more tonight either. He headed for the bedroom. As tired as he felt, the caffeine wouldn't be a problem.

Eric awoke the following morning with little men inside his skull beating on his brain with sledgehammers like the headache commercials. It was worse than a hangover. His circadian clock had aroused his physical body before his brain had fully recovered from the previous night's activities. He looked at the clock on the dresser: it was five past eight. He had been shortchanged three hours of sleep. Sunlight was streaming through his bedroom window as if it were just another day. Eric forced himself to a sitting position on his bed and massaged the sides of his head.

It took a moment for his mind to clear. Once it did, he became aware of sounds coming from the rear of the house. Some were indecipherable voices; others were mechanical in nature. Eric looked out his bedroom window and discovered three police cruisers parked on his lawn. He threw on a bathrobe, slipped into some slippers, and headed toward the noise.

"Good, you're up." Levi Stone, county sheriff, gave some verbal instructions to a man taking photos before returning to Eric. "We need to get your statement. Kramer didn't get one last night because of the lateness of the hour. Said you looked exhausted." Stone grabbed the clipboard he had laid on a ledge. "Do you mind if we step inside?"

Eric led the sheriff into the living room where the sheriff picked an overly stuffed recliner, but kept it in the upright position to maintain formality.

"Tell me about last night," Stone said.

"Not much to say. About two or two-thirty, I heard some noise. I went to the front room to investigate and found the window broken and a brick lying on the floor." Eric took the note from his pocket. "This note was attached to the brick." He passed the note to the sheriff.

Stone studied the note for a moment and then stuffed it into his pocket. "We'll hang on to this for you. What happened next?"

"About thirty seconds later, a minute at the most, I heard an explosion in the back. The back entryway was as you see it now, except for lots of smoke and several small fires. I went out the front door, turned on the garden hose, and put out the fire. Then I called 911."

"Did you see or hear anything else, any cars or people? Hear any voices?"

"No, whoever did this was gone by the time I got outside."

"This doesn't give us much to go on."

"I'm not expecting any justice from Cade County. The people responsible for the bombing are, no doubt, pillars of the community. The mayor's probably preparing citations to recognize their community service as we speak."

Stone ignored the sarcasm. In his line of work, people with chips on their shoulders were often the norm. Stone had become inured to their frustration over the years. In most cases it wasn't personal, only a venting of anger.

"Kampe, let me level with you." Stone leaned forward in his chair to emphasis his statement. "I'm not happy with what happened last night. People can't take the law into their own hands...not in my county. You committed a very repulsive crime. People are angry. That's understandable. But you paid for that crime as prescribed by law. Not as much as I would have liked, but that wasn't my call. You're young. If you think you can straighten yourself out, I'll see that Cade County gives you that chance. That means no drugs. No using drugs...no pushing drugs. That's what did you in last time. You do that and I'll do my best to find the people responsible for this and make them pay for their crime just like I made you pay for yours.

"That being said, let me make this perfectly clear. If you go near or even think about Sara Higgins, all promises are void. I will personally see that you are prosecuted—no, make that persecuted—for any indiscretion no matter how trivial. Because of you, Sara Higgins has suffered far more than any human should ever have to suffer. But despite what you did to her, she's pulled her life together. She worked her way through college, got herself a teaching degree, and has earned the respect of the community, all while raising a five-year-old daughter. You will not cause her any further grief. Do I make myself clear?"

Eric glared at Stone with palpable hatred in his eyes. The police chief was asking him not to think about Sara Higgins. Sara Higgins was all he thought about for five years—five stinking years. Her testimony sent him to prison. Hers and that Cory Kramer's. Five years in maximum-security. This was about getting even. This was about exacting revenge. But it would come at a time and place of his choosing. He was a patient man. He could wait until the timing was right, and no country sheriff with a clipboard was going to stop him.

"Do I make myself clear?" Stone repeated.

"I think you can say we understand each other." Eric smiled, his gaze unfaltering.

Stone picked up his clipboard from the floor where he had placed it and returned his pen to his breast pocket. "I'm serious about finding the people responsible for this," he said as he forced himself out of the plush recliner. "I'll find my own way out."

Eric walked him to the door anyway. The investigators were gone, and only Stone's police cruiser remained. He waited at the door until Stone started his car and backed out of the driveway.

2

"Sara, the police chief is here to see you."

Sara sat transfixed behind her wooden desk and stared at her grade book. The pen in her hand ceased writing in mid-sentence. She had been expecting him. She closed her eyes to force old memories from her mind, but the thoughts still seeped through like the runoff from a summer rain. Her pen fell from her hand, and her knuckles turned white as she clinched her fist. It was merely a gesture, as she was not by nature a violent person. What was it now? Had it been five years? Sara picked up her pen, opened her grade book to the entry of Isaac Bedford, and added a note in the log. *Isaac continues to display aggressive behavior and does not play well with other students.* She needed to schedule a meeting with his parents.

"Well...? I have to tell him something. He's waiting in the teacher's lounge."

Sara looked up at Holly Sutherland's sympathetic eyes. Holly, senior to Sara by two years, had taken Sara under her wing when Sara arrived the previous fall to find her youthful idealism no match for the unruly kindergartners and apathetic parents. If it hadn't been for Holly, Sara would have quit after two weeks. But Holly's cogent advice had transformed teaching into a pleasant experience. It was now May, and with Holly's help, Sara had gained the confidence of a seasoned professional. But now she questioned her ability to finish the day. A little voice deep within pleaded with her, suggesting she run screaming from the classroom, never looking back. It was a tempting suggestion until rational thought superseded panic. Sara lowered her gaze to her desk where her trembling hands fumbled with her grade book. The scribble she had just entered in her grade book was only vaguely readable—not the smooth-flowing penmanship for which she was noted. She closed the grade book and clasped her hands together as if their mutual comfort would allay the tremors. She had no desire to talk to the chief—not today, not tomorrow, not ever. She already knew what he would say.

"Holly, there's no way I can talk to him now. I still have ten minutes of class, and then I have to get the kids to their buses."

Nineteen kindergarteners hunkered over their small desks, totally absorbed in their projects. Each student, with crayon in hand, was drawing pictures of spring flowers, a project guaranteed to keep them busy until the bell rang.

"The music teacher's with my kids. I can watch your class."

"Thanks, but my students will need help with their coats." Was she really that indispensable or was it merely an excuse to avoid the Chief. Sara stared off into space as she considered her options. Eventually, she would have to talk to him. She couldn't avoid him forever. "Ask him if he can wait fifteen minutes."

"Not a problem. He's discovered the coffee pot and some two-day-old donuts. That'll keep any cop busy."

Holly lingered in the doorway until Sara looked up. "Sara, if you need someone to talk to…"

"Thanks, Holly. Really, I'm fine." Sara placed her hands in her lap to hide the tremors. If she were to maintain her façade of self-control, she would need to have them under control before she saw the Chief.

Holly closed the door as she left, and the classroom became quiet, except for the occasionally soft sound of crayon scratching across paper. Ignoring the susurrations, Sara resumed her far off stare while her mind replayed distant events in the starkest of detail. The images were as vivid as yesterday's memories.

"Ok, kids, let's put your crayons in your desks," Sara said when the bell rang signaling the end of school day. It was a welcome distraction. "You may take the pictures home to show your parents."

In unison, the nineteen kindergartners returned the crayons to their boxes and neatly tucked them inside their desks; Miss Sara expected them to be neat. The students then migrated toward the door where jackets and caps hung on hooks. Stenciled above each hook was a child's name.

"Miss Sara, my coat feels funny." Lily Rasmussen stood helplessly by the coat rack, awaiting adult intervention. Her coat was buttoned two holes off center and the coat hunched up over her left ear. She was close to tears.

Sara zipped up Nathan's jacket, patted him gently on the butt, and turned her attention to Lily.

"Lily, you have it buttoned wrong again." Sara knelt down to look at Lily eye-to-eye, a gesture she had learned from Holly. "If you want to understand the kids, you have to see them at their level," Holly had told her on the first day of class.

"Let's unbutton it and start over." Lily puckered her lower lip in self-imposed dejection until a gentle poke of an index finger into her belly brought forth unrestrained giggles. "Always start at the bottom. Count up one buttonhole and one button. Then work your way up."

With the recalcitrant buttons under control, Lily headed toward her bus, and the room became quiet. It was a welcome silence. Sara closed her eyes and breathed deeply to recompose herself. She couldn't break down and cry...not now. She wouldn't give anyone that satisfaction, not even the Chief. Once she had a semblance of composure, Sara opened her purse and pulled out a mirror. She never had been big on cosmetics, but what make-up she did have was still in place. Satisfied with her make-up, she ran a brush through her shoulder-length brown hair. Long bangs covered the scars on her forehead. The scars had faded with time, but Sara knew they were still there, glaring out at her every time she looked in the mirror. Unable to procrastinate any longer, Sara headed toward the teacher's lounge. She forced a smile as she opened the door to the lounge.

"Hello, I'm Sara Higgins. Holly said you wanted to speak with me?" Introductions were superfluous since they had met multiple times during the months following the incident. Still, Sara felt the formality necessary. She was relieved to find no other teachers in the lounge. This was not surprising for a Friday afternoon; teachers were as eager to vacate the premises as their students.

They called it a lounge, but in reality, this was where teachers corrected papers, prepared lesson plans, and hid from students. Bookshelves laden with out-of-date textbooks and magazines lined the side walls. On the far wall, a row of windows faced the playground, the lower half frosted, preventing inquisitive eyes from peering in, but allowing the taller teachers to look out. A five-foot-long counter of chipped Formica extended out from the corner near the windows. This was where the teachers used their drugs, where they got their fix. This was where they paid homage to the almighty coffee pot. And it was indeed a habit. Many of the teachers were non-functional without their caffeine fix, even though the coffee was invariably old and stale. Next to the coffee pot was an assortment of dirty coffee mugs and tarnished spoons. Occasionally, even cookies or donuts found their way to the countertop, all of which were considered fair game by the denizens of the lounge.

The police chief was sitting at the large conference table in the center of the room, his massive left hand wrapped around a coffee mug he had commandeered. He had the remnants of a donut secured in his right hand. A pile of soggy tissue paper that the Chief had had been using to soak up spillage suggested he had been dunking the donut into his coffee to counteract the donut's staleness. He was engrossed in an article from an old *Weekly Reader* but pushed it aside when Sara entered the room.

The police chief stood up, wiped the donut crumbs on his pant leg, and extended his right hand. "I'm Levi Stone. I believe we've met." Levi Stone was the Cade County sheriff, but everyone called him Chief; Cade County was not noted for its formality. With the aid of his nine deputies, Stone was responsible for patrolling the entire county with its large, sparsely populated, woodland area garnished with clusters of part-time residents congregating around the numerous lakes. The only major city in Cade County was Tamarack, the county seat, with a population of five thousand, hardly a metropolis.

"Won't you sit down?" Stone gestured toward one of the chairs. "Can I get you some coffee? The donuts are a bit dry." The chief waited for Sara to take her seat before returning to his chair.

"No thank you. I'm not much of a coffee drinker." Sara found it awkward for Stone to be playing host in her lounge, but if she remembered right, he always had been a take-charge individual. Stone was a quiet man, an intense listener noted for being slow to pass judgment, one of the reasons he was re-elected year after year. But as the saying goes, still waters run deep, and Sara assumed an underlying intelligence that would seldom miss a subtle nuance or inflection in any conversation. He was all of six feet one, Sara estimated, and well over two hundred pounds. He could dominate any conversation if he so desired, but he spoke softly and had the eyes of a teddy bear. He reminded Sara of her father, one of the best compliments she could give.

"I assume you know why I'm here."

"Yes, I suppose I do."

"They granted Eric Kampe a parole." Stone paused to let the full impact of the statement sink in. "How the state can parole him after five years is beyond me. You'd think rape would earn a stiffer sentence. Apparently with plea bargaining, good time, and the motor vehicle accident that killed his parents last month, some bleeding-heart liberal felt sorry for him. Anyway, as a sex offender he's required to register, which he did, and I'm required to notify you that he's in the area."

"Thanks, but I've already heard."

"You realize this could place you in danger. No telling what he might do, but I'm hoping he'll have enough sense to leave you alone. Just the same, we'll keep an eye on him. He'll eventually screw up his parole, and then we can send him back to prison where he belongs."

"I'll be ok." Sara forced a smiley face and then wondered if the Police Chief could see through her façade. That didn't represent the way she felt. The Chief had informed her of Kampe's return to Cade County. Why didn't he leave it at that?

"Sara, your testimony put Kampe behind bars. He wouldn't be the first ex-con to seek revenge. Five years in prison can do strange things to a man."

"I appreciate your concern, but, really, I'm fine. I'll keep my doors locked."

"One other thing. I wasn't sure I should mention this, but rumor has it Kampe came into some money with the death of his parents. I know teaching isn't the highest paid profession, and you probably have difficulty making ends meet, trying to raise your daughter and all." Stone paused again to let his words sink in. "I'm not an attorney and hardly in a position to offer legal advice, but he is the biological father. You could hit him for child support if you wanted."

"Thanks, but I prefer to keep our lives separate."

"Makes sense." Stone rubbed his chin, as was his wont when in deep thought. "I suppose he could use that to harass you, possibly seeking visitation rights. Although, I doubt protective services would allow that. These days you never know."

"I'd just say he wasn't the father. I could have been pregnant before the incident."

"That'd be difficult to prove. You dated him all through high school. He'd still be the presumed father. A simple DNA comparison would confirm it."

"They can't obtain her blood without my consent."

"A good lawyer with a subpoena would circumvent that. I doubt it'll come to that, but it's probably best to consult a lawyer before trying to garnish any of his income."

"Will that be all? I have to pick up my daughter at the sitter's."

"I guess that's all I have to say. If you have any questions or concerns, give me a call."

\* \* \*

Sara turned left onto M-28 and headed west. Other than a blue SUV with a luggage rack following a hundred yards behind her, the highway was deserted. That wasn't unusual. M-28 was one of two main conduits across Michigan's Upper Peninsula; even so, traffic was minimal this time of year. The summer crowd had yet to return from Florida, Arizona, and other warm places, and the local residents had already arrived at their homes and were preparing for dinner.

Sara turned on the radio, hoping for a pleasant distraction, but her mind refused to yield—always returning to the night of the incident, forcing her to relive the what if's, as she had done so many times before. Ways she could have prevented the incident. No matter how many times she went over them, it never changed reality. It never assuaged the pain or reduced her guilt. If only she hadn't walked to her friend's house. If only she had brought change for the pay phone, she could have called her father for a ride. She could have prevented the incident. She now feared the demons would return to torment her sleep. Only in the last two years had she been able to keep them at bay.

Sara returned her focus to the road. It was early May, and the light green leaves of the aspen lining the highway were beginning to unfurl. Three-petaled trilliums formed patches of white among the green ferns on the forest floor. She assumed the specks of yellow were buttercups. She had forgotten the beauty of springtime flowers. Perhaps she should take her daughter for a walk in the woods after dinner. They could both use the fresh air. With the recent rain, they might stumble on some morel mushrooms.

Sara checked her rearview mirror; the blue SUV was still a hundred yards behind her. She was a slow driver in a remote section of the state where drivers considered the speed limit an insignificant recommendation, not a binding statute. Most people would have left her chewing their dust. It was just a car she told herself. Any other day she would have ignored the vehicle, but not today. She considered pulling off the road and allowing the car to pass, but that would be childish. She couldn't live in fear. There would be other cars. She couldn't stop for all of them.

Sara drove two miles farther down the highway and then turned left onto Beaver Lake Road. The U-shaped road serviced the seasonal cabins on the south side of Beaver Lake before winding back to rejoin M-28. It was out of her way, but the road traversed through a hardwood forest noted for trees that arched over the road forming a tunnel of green. It was a picturesque drive well worth the detour; at least that was the lie she told herself.

Sara checked her rearview mirror, expecting the SUV to continue down M-28, but the vehicle slowed almost to a stop and then turned onto Beaver Lake Road. It could still be coincidental. At this time of year, people would be returning to their cabins on the lake to prepare them for summer. Just the same, Sara flipped the switch to lock her doors.

The SUV lost no time closing the distance between the two vehicles. The car was similar to the myriad other Sports Utility Vehicles that populated Michigan's Upper Peninsula. In the U.P., there were two choices for transportation: pickup trucks and SUV's. Only a wimpy schoolteacher like Sara would drive a Ford Taurus. Sara checked the SUV for markings, but a brush guard obscured the front grill making it difficult to identify the make or model. Brush guards were standard equipment in the Upper Peninsula. In theory, the metal lattice protected the vehicle's grill from brush damage when driving to that elusive fishing hole, but most people bought them to avoid the two thousand dollar repair tab incurred when colliding with a dim-witted deer. Hitting deer without a brush guard made for expensive venison.

Sara turned off the radio. The only available station was hosting a talk show. With the SUV tailgating her, she lacked patience for such prattle. She chided herself for allowing the minor irritation to annoy her, but the vehicle didn't belong to anyone she knew, and the driver wasn't trying to get her attention. Nothing explained the driver's erratic behavior. A bluish tint obscured the upper third of the SUV's windshield, and sunlight reflecting off the sloped windshield made the driver a vague image at best. Sara stepped on the gas to separate the vehicles. The speed limit in rural Michigan was fifty-five miles per hour, although on a winding trail like Beaver Lake Road, forty-five was more appropriate. Sara leveled off at fifty-five. That was as fast as she was willing to go before she reached M-28. The SUV was still hugging her tail, but if she didn't make any sudden stops, that shouldn't be a problem.

Sara applied gentle pressure to the brake at the beginning of a half-mile straightaway. If he wanted to pass, she would provide the opportunity. Her speedometer slipped to fifty and then to forty-five. Sara glanced at the mirror; the SUV remained five feet behind her. The driver had no intention of passing.

Sara slowed further until her car shook violently as if it had run over a dead animal or perhaps hit a pothole. Then the car began to accelerate. Sara slammed on her brakes, but that locked her wheels causing the car to skid out of control. Even with the brakes, she was unable to slow the car. The SUV was using its four-wheel drive to push her.

Sara eased off the brake to reclaim steering control. Her speedometer now registered seventy miles per hour. There was no way she would negotiate the approaching curve. He was forcing her into the trees. It could be hours before anyone found her on this road. She would surely be dead by then. Sara braced herself for the impact. She considered turning off the motor. With the electrical power severed, there was less chance of a spark causing an explosion—at least that was what she had read in some magazine. But with the ignition turned off, she would lose power steering, and the steering wheel would lock up. She decided against it.

Twenty-five yards from the curve, her car began to slow. She touched her brakes, and the car slowed further, allowing her to enter the curve at a reasonable forty-five miles per hour. She checked her rearview mirror; the SUV was turning around. He had been toying with her. Her three minutes of terror had been someone's idea of quality entertainment. Sara coasted to a stop and let the tears flow. Crying wasn't constructive, but it was therapeutic.

Sara parked on the shoulder of the road with her doors locked until she convinced herself it was only a random act by some anonymous teenager looking for a cheap thrill, but her trembling hands belied that assumption. She grabbed the steering wheel with both hands to control the tremors and pulled out on the road. She would feel safer once she was back on the highway, she told herself. When she reached the intersection with M-28, she scanned the highway in both directions, expecting to find the SUV waiting for her as her paranoid imagination had suggested. The road was void of vehicles. She turned left on M-28 and continued west.

Sara eased off the accelerator as she approached Kampe's Korner. It was little more than a crossroads, too small for city or even village status; although, it did have a cluster of houses skirting the south shore of Harley Lake. Squeezed among the houses was a small Presbyterian church. She knew the church well. Her father had been pastor there for twenty-six years. He would like to retire if they could find a proper replacement.

Sara turned left and headed north past Kampe's two-pump gas station and convenience store. Ward and Diane Kampe owned the gas station; at least they did until a drunk driver broadsided their car. They were members of her church, and she had felt obligated to attend the funeral.

Sara checked her gas tank: It was down to a quarter tank. She needed gas, but a quarter tank would get her to Tamarack in the morning. It was unlikely Eric Kampe would be working at the station; still, she did not wish to risk a confrontation.

Sara eased her car to a stop at the third house north of the corner. The two-story house was squat and square and, like the other houses in Kampe's Korner, had the look of the fifty's. Cedar shakes in dire need of staining covered most of the house—except for the white, open porch. Sara parked her Ford Taurus in the driveway and walked toward the porch where Nancy Johnson, a silver-haired woman in her late fifties, sat on a swing reading to a five-year-old tomboy wearing blue jeans and a red flannel shirt. Long blond braids hung half way down the child's back.

"Hi there, Twinkle Toes. You ready to go?"

"Hi, Mom. Can we finish this story first?"

"I suppose so, if it's not too long." Sara collapsed on a porch chair with an audible sigh. "Sorry I'm late, Nancy."

"You okay?" Nancy asked. "You look a little down in the dumps."

"Just tired. It's been a long day."

Nancy was almost family. Sara was eight when her mother died. Don Higgins tried to be a good father, but the loss of his wife left a hole in his world too. That was when Nancy stepped into Sara's life. When Sara contracted chicken pox, Nancy was there reassuring her that the sores would go away and Sara would still be beautiful. When Sara was stricken by the woman's curse, Nancy was there, explaining it might be inconvenient and it might be messy, but hardly a curse. After the incident Nancy camped beside Sara's hospital bed, praying incessantly, beseeching God for mercy. She refused to leave until the doctors had removed Sara from the critical list. Now she waited like a seasoned psychiatrist for Sara to vent her thoughts.

"I've been doing a lot of thinking the last day or two." Sara stared into space, as if talking to herself. "I've never thanked you for everything you've done for me."

"Sara, you did more for me than I ever did for you. My life was unbearable when Herb died. You may not be aware of it, but I even considered suicide…just to be with him again. You gave me reason for living."

"But sometimes I think I'm taking advantage of you. I don't know where I would have found a sitter for the school year."

"Hogwash! Your daughter is just what an old lady like me needs to stay young. I'm going miss the little tyke when school's out." It was now Nancy's turn to stare into space. "Kampe's Korner is getting old. We don't have kids running around the neighborhood anymore. I miss them. This is such a great place for kids. You and that Kampe boy used to have so much fun playing down by the lake when you were young. The two of you were always getting into trouble of one form or another. Your parents were fit to be tied that summer you guys went skinny-dipping. If I remember right, that was your idea. What were you…seven at the time?"

"We were six, and it was by mutual consent."

Nancy, lost in her memories, swayed quietly on her porch swing. At her age, memories were a precious commodity.

"Nancy?"

"Yes?"

"If something were to happen to me, would you take care of my daughter?"

"Is that what this is all about? Eric Kampe's out on parole, and now you're worried? If he harms you in anyway, you just let me know. I'll go after him with my broom. He doesn't scare me in the least." Nancy paused, and then added, "It's kind of sad. He used to be such a fine boy."

"I'm serious. My father may be too old to care for her. I don't have any other relatives."

"I'm only eight years younger than your father; but yes, between the two of us, we'll see she gets a good Christian upbringing."

"I had always hoped you and my father would have gotten together. You would've made a great stepmother."

"Your father is a dear and precious friend, but he's still in love with your mother, and I'm still in love with my Herb."

"Can you guys stay for dinner?" Nancy asked when it was obvious Sara had nothing more to say.

"It's tempting, but I have work to do. We'll have to take a rain check." Sara would have enjoyed the company, and no one cooked better than Nancy; but in her current state of mind, she wasn't sure how long she could control her emotions. She needed time to deal with this new situation privately, where she could cry without embarrassment.

It was a quarter past six when Sara turned her Ford Taurus into her driveway, five miles north of Kampe's Korner. It felt good to be home. Better than that, it was Friday; she had two days off.

Her two-bedroom house was small but more than adequate for her limited needs. The nearest neighbors were Sam and Elena Carlson, an elderly couple who lived a mile farther down the road. That had been a major selling point when Sara purchased the house the previous fall. She had relished the seclusion, a safe retreat from the social life in Tamarack. After nine months, she was still unsure about her acceptance in the community. If it hadn't been for her father, she never would have returned to Cade County.

Sara brought the Taurus to a stop by the back door and placed it in park. She immediately regretted it. Why hadn't she stopped at the end of her driveway to pick up the mail? It was only a thirty-yard walk to the mailbox, but it required more energy than she currently possessed.

"Hey, Twinkle Toes. Can you get the mail for me?"

"Okay, Mom."

Her daughter took off in a run. Why do they waste so much energy on the young, Sara wondered as she watched her daughter remove the mail from the mailbox. Sara was thawing frozen sloppy joe in the microwave when her daughter returned with a fistful of mail. Sloppy joes and oven-baked Tatter Tots. Not very elegant, but quick and simple with minimal clean up—an essential combination if they were to have an after-dinner walk in the woods. With Daylight Savings Time, there should be plenty of light. She hoped it wouldn't be too cold. Evenings in May can get chilly.

"Just put the mail on the table, honey."

The overly energetic five-year-old scattered a dozen letters on the table and headed for her room. Apparently, she had other projects in mind.

There were far too many letters with windows mixed in with the usual junk mail. But that was not what caught Sara's attention. All the letters had her address neatly typed on the envelope—all except one. One had the address carelessly printed across the envelope as if done by a child. There was no return address. She had seen that printing before. More ominous was the lack of postage. He had personally placed it in her mailbox. Sara set the letter on the counter. She didn't need to know its contents…at least not now.

After dinner, Sara cleared the table, leaving the dishes in the sink. She would wash them later. The overcast skies of earlier in the day had cleared, and the wind had subsided. If she wished to go for a walk in the woods, she needed to go while there was still daylight.

"Hey, Twinkle Toes, you want to go for a walk in the woods? We can pick some wild flowers." Sara couldn't remember when she first started calling her Twinkle Toes. Her daughter didn't seem to mind, and the moniker had stuck.

"Coming." Forty-five pounds of youthful enthusiasm bounded out of her bedroom and headed for the door.

"Don't forget your jacket. It's going to be cool outside."

Built in the 1930's, the farmhouse, barn, and surrounding four acres were all that remained of someone's dream. Most of the farm's original acreage had been sold off during the depression. Aspen and jack pine had quickly retaken the inactive land. The single-story farmhouse constructed from fieldstone was the only structure that had weathered well. The previous owners had remodeled it several times over the years. They replaced the wiring, bringing it up to code; and added new insulation to make the cold, Upper Peninsula winters tolerable. The windows were still single paned and needed to be replaced. Before summer, she would have to cover the bedroom windows with screens to keep out the insects.

The barn, ignored since the demise of the farm, now lay weathered and gray and sloping at a forty-five degree angle. It was useless as a structure and presented a safety hazard. Several boards were missing from the side leaving diagonal slats of darkness. It was too dark for Sara to see into the barn where a man watched Sara through his binoculars. She couldn't hear him curse softly under his breath, as he watched mother and child head into the woods as if they hadn't a care in the world. The man watched his quarry disappeared into the woods.

Outside the barn where the cloud cover had dissipated and the wind had subsided, the sun provided unseasonable warmth. Sara was beginning to regret wearing a jacket until they entered the woods where the aspen canopy blocked the sun.

It was early spring, and there was minimal undergrowth to impede Sara as she strolled through the woods. She was in no hurry, unlike her daughter who ran from one intriguing object to the next like a housebound puppy set free in a city park. It reminded Sara of her youth when she and Eric had explored the woods leaving no rock unturned or hollow log unexplored.

"Look, Mommy, a baby deer."

No more than twenty-five yards ahead of them, a fawn foraged on the spring grass. White spots covered its back; it couldn't have been more than a few days old. The fawn stopped to graze on a patch of grass—oblivious to their presence. It was the size of the fawn Sara and Eric had rescued years before.

They had found that fawn hiding in the weeds near Harley Lake. Wasted away to skin and bone, the animal had lain motionless in the grass. The fawn's eyes were matted shut, and flies swarmed around the small head. Sara had wanted to leave the fawn to die. It was not that she was cold-hearted, but it looked so hopeless. At Eric's insistence, they moved the fawn to a storeroom in the church basement where they fed it from a bottle they found in the church nursery. Sara wanted to name it Annika after a girl in a story her mother had recently read to her, but Eric said it was a "boy" deer. Even at age seven, Eric knew about such things. They decided to name him Tiger. Tiger lived in the church basement until an inquisitive Sunday school teacher discovered him. Sara's father explained that God likes deer, but he likes them outside.

That was the year Eric first saw Tarzan in the movies. Tiger following Eric everywhere, convincing Eric he had Tarzan's powers. A rope hanging from a tall oak tree provided an improvised vine; and Tarzan, with Jane at his side, spent much of the summer swinging from tree to tree in their make-believe jungle while Tiger playfully tagged along. This ended one day when Tiger showed up with a hunter's arrow lodged in his abdomen.

Eric and Sara sought out Sara's father—he could fix anything. But Tiger could not be fixed, her father explained. Tiger was quietly dispatched with the help of a neighbor. Eric wept openly. Sara saved her tears for her pillow.

"Look, Mommy, another deer."

A doe had stepped into the clearing. She stared at the onlookers for a moment, and then ushered her fawn into the brush and disappeared.

"Mommy, what's this?"

Never underestimate the shortness of a child's attention span. Sara bent down to see what had now captured her daughter's attention.

"That's a jack-in-the-pulpit," Sara explained after studying the piece of vegetation proffered. "See Jack sitting there in the center of the pulpit?"

Sara and her daughter investigated the strange as well as the mundane objects found in the woods. Each one was a learning experience, giving Sara the opportunity to share knowledge from her college biology classes. It was approaching dusk when they headed back toward the farmhouse under the watchful eyes of the clandestine observer.

The letter was still waiting for Sara when she returned to the farmhouse. Eventually she would read it, but not now. She would wash the dinner dishes first, maybe watch some TV. The letter could wait until her daughter was in bed. It was still lying on the counter when Sara put the last of the clean dishes in the cupboard.

"Mommy, can I have a glass to put the flowers in?"

Sara searched the cupboard and settled on a plastic cup. It was unbreakable. Her daughter was precocious, but still a five-year-old. Next year she would start kindergarten. That could be awkward. Maybe she and Holly could switch classes for the year. She would have to discuss that with Holly before fall.

Her daughter was growing up too fast. One day she would be gone. Sara couldn't imagine life without her daughter. She was what Sara lived for. She was also part of the conflict that tore at Sara's soul. If there had been no incident, she would have no daughter. Out of the pain and agony of rape came a wonderful blessing. A part of her wanted to rejoice and be thankful. Another part of her was tormented by the deep-seated memories it created.

The two incompatible feelings dominated her waking hours. At one time, she had considered seeking professional help, but who could understand the way she felt?

How would she tell her daughter? She would surely hear about it once she started school. How do you explain rape to a five-year-old who doesn't have the emotional capability of understanding the passion of sex? She would postpone that conversation as long as she could. Eventually, she would tell her. At least some of it. Part of it could never be told. That was the part of the incident she hadn't told the police. That was why she couldn't seek their help. That was the part of the incident that caused the most pain.

"Mommy, does that look pretty?"

"That looks gorgeous. I couldn't have done better myself." Centered on the kitchen table was a plastic cup with an assortment of buttercups, trilliums, and wild violets. Protruding from the middle was a mangled jack-in-the-pulpit.

"I think it's bedtime."

"Okay."

What? No argument? Her daughter must be really tired, Sara decided. That shouldn't be surprising. The walk in the woods had worn her out also.

"Mommy, read me a story."

"I'll be right there. Pick out a good book...not a real long one." Sara stared at the letter on the counter for a moment and then headed toward her daughter's bedroom. Twinkle Toes was already in her pajamas, lying on her bed. She was eagerly holding *The Cat In The Hat*.

"How did I know it would be *The Cat In The Hat* again?" Sara lay down on the bed, placed an arm around her daughter, and began to read. She had read the book hundreds of times. Her daughter probably had it memorized. No matter how many times she read it, her daughter still enjoyed it.

"Bed time," Sara said when she had finished the book. She gave her daughter a kiss and turned off the light. Maybe she would go to bed early herself. Sara picked the envelope off the counter and headed for her bedroom. She opened the top drawer of her dresser. In the right-hand corner, next to a stack of envelopes, was a bottle of sleeping pills. There were twenty-one pills inside; she had counted them many times. Sara took out a fresh set of pajamas and shut the drawer.

Sara again looked at the printed address. It had been several years, but she had seen that printing before. The letters were block style, formed from a series of small, straight lines. She opened the envelope and read the contents of the letter: *This afternoon was just a warning. Leave town and don't come back or I will have to hurt you and your daughter.* With an outwardly stoic expression, Sara placed the letter back in the envelope. No one would ever harm her daughter; she would not allow that to happen. He was leaving her no choice: she would have to kill him. Sara opened her dresser drawer, added the letter to the other letters, and crawled into bed.

# 3

Eric awoke to pain in muscles he hadn't known existed. He had squandered the previous day lying in bed, but that had only increased his pain and stiffness. Eric forced himself out of bed and headed for the shower. At least the water heater was functional. That was one of the few positives. The house still reeked of smoke, and mosquitoes had free access to his blood; fixing the broken window would have to be high on his priority list.

Eric turned on the shower and dialed the temperature just shy of intolerable. He wasn't fond of cold showers or even lukewarm showers. That had been standard fare in prison. Today he intended to utilize all the hot water. He stepped into the stream and let the heat sink into his aching muscles. The stimulating heat performed its chore, and his tense muscles began to relax. Eric had always been muscular, lettering all four years of high school. While in prison he had lifted weights—not for recreation, but in self-defense. Weak inmates fell prey to strong inmates. Given a choice he preferred the latter group.

Other than minor bruises, he remained in adequate shape considering the abuse his body had endured. He could no longer use his injuries to justify lying around in bed. It was time to plan his short-term future. Professionals would have to replace the window, likewise the wiring. He had no expertise in those areas, but rebuilding the structural portion of the entryway he could do himself.

Eric's parents retired when Eric's case came to trial, and Bob Thompson, a long-time employee, now managed the gas station and convenience store. He deposited the profit directly into the Kampe's bank account. He didn't need Eric's assistance, and the less people saw of Eric, the better business would be—no one wants to associate with a rapist. Even more reason to repair the house himself. If nothing else, it provided an alternative to gainful employment. No one would hire him even if he wanted a job.

Eric toweled himself dry and slipped into work clothes. He had to demolish what remained of the entryway before he could begin repairs. The way he was feeling, a little violent destruction would be therapeutic.

Eric commandeered a sledgehammer and crowbar from his father's workshop and set about his task. As he expected, he found the work deeply gratifying. No one outgrows the pleasure of destruction. He felt the same thrill he experienced when destroying block towers as a child. Putting his back into the work, the blocks began to fall. The sky was gray and the air humid. After two hours of therapy, Eric was shirtless and sweating. He ignored the sweat; sweat was not a deterrent—it augmented the experience. Five years of anger and hatred provided an endless source of energy that transcended creature comfort. He ripped boards from their studs with the crowbar and then smashed the studs with the sledgehammer. He visualized Cory Kramer's face in the charred wood as he swung the sledge. When Kramer's face was thoroughly demolished he switched to Sara Higgins. Someday he would destroy more than boards.

Eric's house sat adjacent to the convenience store and, like the other houses at Kampe's Korner, the backyard bordered the bike path encircling Harley Lake. Eric's generous lot was typical of homes in Michigan's Upper Peninsula where land was cheap, but the debris still accumulated into a pile covering a major portion of his back yard. He could burn most of debris, although safety concerns dictated moving it farther from the house. Eric grabbed several large pieces of semi-burned debris and dragged them toward the bike path. Since the county now owned the bike path and lake, he selected a spot five yards shy of the asphalt path for his fire pit; he didn't need further encounters with the sheriff's department.

Eric dropped the debris into the newly designated fire pit and was about to return for another load when movement in the tall grass caught his eye. The movement was subtle—just a small patch of yellow that blended with the tall, dry weeds. It was only twenty-five feet away, but he would have overlooked it if not for the movement. Surrendering to curiosity, Eric walked over to investigate.

A yellow dog lay motionless in the grass. Without the twitching tail, Eric would have assumed the dog was dead. Ribs rippled the dog's skin, and putrefied lacerations on the back and scalp drained pus onto the fur. Maggots infested some of the cuts, and thick exudates drained from the eyes.

Eric knelt beside the dog. "Looks like you've seen better days." Multiple healed scars crisscrossed the dog's back between the open sores. Eric wondered if the dog *had* seen better days. Someone had whipped the dog more than once. The dog's eyes were glazed and fixed. It was as if the dog were looking through Eric in the *thousand-yard stare*. "We need to get you to a vet." Eric scooped the dog into his arms. The dog offered no resistance.

Eric placed the dog on a tarp in the backseat of his car and strapped him in with the seatbelt. The belt was a superfluous gesture, but it made Eric feel better just the same. The dog's breathing was shallow and labored, and each breath appeared to be its last. The dog survived the transfer to the car, but Eric wondered if it could survive the ten-mile trip to the veterinarian in Tamarack.

It was almost noon when Eric walked through the clinic doors. The last patient of the morning, a small, curly-haired dog named Muttly, was being discharged; and the owner was receiving last minute instructions from the veterinarian's assistant while the rest of the office personnel geared down for lunch. Eric carried the dog up to the reception desk. "I'd like to have the vet look at this dog."

The receptionist was about to ask if he had an appointment but after looking at the dog, changed her mind and led them into a vacant exam room. "You can lay him on the table if you want. The vet will be with you shortly."

"That's okay. I'll hold him."

The room was no different than a doctor's office. A Formica counter with a small stainless steel sink extended across one wall. Several stainless steel canisters squatted on top of the counter, all neatly lined in a row. Eric assumed they contained tongue blades, Q-tips, and other medical paraphernalia. A stainless steel cabinet with glass doors hung from the wall above the counter. Eric could see more stainless steel tools inside the cabinet. The only difference between a doctor's exam room and this was the absence of a padded exam table. In its place was a stainless steel platform resting on a stainless steel pedestal. Everything was stainless steel. It made the room feel cold and sterile. Eric felt a chill even though he knew the temperature was well into the comfort zone.

Doc Hansen entered the room without knocking and closed the door behind him. He wore the customary white lab coat with exam equipment filling the pockets. A black stethoscope draped around his neck. Eric estimated him to be in his mid-fifties. A horseshoe of peppery-gray hair surrounded an otherwise bald scalp. But what he lacked on top was compensated by a generous beard, also peppery-gray in color. He held a clipboard in his left hand; his right hand curled around a ballpoint pen. Hansen stuffed the pen in his breast pocket and offered his hand.

"Hi, I'm Dr. Scott Hansen."

Eric laid the dog on the exam table and shook the offered hand. "I'm Eric Kampe."

Hansen held his grip on Eric's hand as the name sank in. He appeared momentarily confused. He obviously had heard about Eric's parole—everyone else in Cade County had. No doubt he expected rapists to have an unsavory appearance, a cocky demeanor, or at least an antisocial attitude. Eric was sorry to disappoint him. All he had was a dog in need of medical care.

Hansen quickly regained his composure. "And what can we do for your dog today?" He did not wait for a reply but began a gentle exam with his hands. The dog, for the most part, lay unresponsive. "Is this your dog?"

"No, I found him in my back yard this morning. I have no idea where he came from."

"This dog's been beaten, and from the looks of the scars, I'd say more than once." Hansen listened to the heart and lungs, then gently palpated the abdomen. "I don't understand how anyone can take pleasure from beating such a beautiful creature."

Dr. Hansen draped his stethoscope around his neck after completing the lung exam. He did not appear pleased with his findings. "This is such a waste. He must have been a pretty dog…a golden lab, possibly purebred." Hansen looked in the ears, and then the mouth—the teeth appeared in good shape, and the dog was not old. "It wouldn't surprise me if someone paid good money for this pup."

Hansen stepped back from the exam table and gave a sigh. "I'll put him down for you."

Eric stared at veterinarian in disbelief. "I didn't come here to have you put him down. I came here to have you fix him."

"You don't seem to understand. This dog's dehydrated; he's suffering from malnutrition; and he's got God only knows how many infections brewing. It would take several hundred dollars to treat him, and he'll probably die anyway. If he were to live, he won't make much of a pet. The dog's been beaten. He'll either have no spirit and hide under the bed all day with its tail between its legs, or he'll be mean and vicious."

"I'm willing to take that chance. I'll pay whatever it takes."

"What's this dog to you?"

"Life's dealt him a bad hand. I think he deserves a second chance."

"You willing to put in the time required to nurse this dog back to health?"

"Doc, I'm sure you know who I am and what the community thinks of me. I'm as popular around Cade County as this dog. We have a lot in common. I'll do whatever it takes to pull him through…and I'll see that you get your money."

The determination and forcefulness of Eric's demand appeared to catch Hansen by surprise, as if he thought Eric had made the request in jest, but he quickly regained his professional demeanor.

"Okay. Let's see what we can do to get this dog of yours back to good health." Dr. Hansen pushed the *speak* button on the intercom mounted on the wall. "Cindy, can you get me an I.V. setup with a liter of D5 in normal saline? We'll also need an amp of vitamins and I.V. penicillin."

Moments later the assistant arrived pushing a tall I.V. stand. Swinging from the top was a plastic bag filled with five percent dextrose in normal saline. "I've already added the antibiotics and vitamins." Cindy attached some plastic tubing to the I.V. bag and allowed the fluid to drain through. After flushing all the bubbles from the tubing, she attached it to the needle Dr. Hansen had inserted into the dog's leg. "How fast do you want it to run?"

Dr. Hanson studied the dog for a moment. "He looks pretty done in. I think we need to be aggressive. Why don't we run it at 100 cc per hour?"

Cindy attached the tubing to an I.V. pump, set the rate for 100 cc per hour, and then added some notes to the chart. "Mr. Kampe, this seems so impersonal. Most of our patients have names. Is there any name you have in mind for your dog?"

"His name's Tiger."

Eric had planned to drive over to Jeremy Watson's glass repair shop while the vet treated Tiger, but the window repair would have to wait. Tiger needed him here. It was amazing how quickly Tiger responded to rehydration when fluid refilled his veins. Although still looking sick, he now appeared aware of his surroundings. His eyes tracked Eric's movements, following him wherever he went. Eric sat on a stool by Tiger's head and gently massaged his scalp while Dr. Hansen cleaned and dressed the wounds. Tiger occasionally flinched in pain but otherwise lay on the exam table in complete submission.

"Well, that's about all we can do for him here," Dr. Hansen said when the last of the I.V. fluid and antibiotics had infused into Tiger's vein. "The rest is up to you. If you can get him to eat and take his medicine, there's an outside chance he might pull through. My assistant has prepared a bag of medications along with some directions."

"Thanks, Doc."

"Don't thank me; you'll have to do most of the work. I just hope you know what you are getting into."

Eric gently scooped Tiger into his arms and wiggled a hand free to grab the bag of medicine. Maybe this was a bit over his head, but he had to try. Eric walked through the lobby, now filled with an assortment of animals and owners. He paused at the door. "Can you send the bill to my address at the store? It's in the phone book."

Hansen waved him off. "There's no charge. You aren't the only one with a compassion for animals."

It was late afternoon when Eric arrived home, too late for further work on the entryway. A heavy tarp separated the hole in the wall from the rest of the house, providing some protection from the cold and dust. Repairs to the house would have to wait. Tiger's recovery had a higher priority.

"Well, Tiger, I think the best place for you to convalesce is in the bedroom." Eric laid Tiger down on the bed, then folded an old army blanket into quarters and placed it on the floor near the bed. "This will be your bed for the foreseeable future."

Tiger watched with dispassionate indifference from his cozy spot on the bed. The infused fluids had instilled Tiger with a modicum of energy, allowing him to move slowly if he so desired; it was obvious he did not so desire. Eric picked him up and placed him on the blanket. Tiger made a few circles around the blanket then lay down for a nap. The following morning, when Eric awoke, Tiger was snoozing peacefully on the bed. Eric placed him back on his blanket and gave him some milk, which Tiger consumed with relish. The second morning, Eric awoke with Tiger's cold nose resting on his chest. After the third night, Eric, assuming it a lost cause, gave up entirely. Fortunately, he had a queen-size bed. Sometimes sacrifices have to be made for man's best friend, in Eric's case, his only friend. He had Sara Higgins and Cory Kramer to thank for that, as well as the hole in the back of the house. But their days were numbered. It was the persistent dream that maintained him through five years of prison.

# 4

"Over here, Chief."

Levi Stone climbed over the guardrail and cautiously made his way down the thirty-foot embankment toward the light blue Honda Civic with Illinois plates buried in the brush at the bottom of the ravine. It had apparently gone off the road just before the start of the guardrail.

"What ya got, Cory?" From Cory's phone message, Stone assumed this was more than a simple motor vehicle accident—with or without fatalities. Although unpleasant, they were too common to rouse up the county sheriff at five-thirty in the morning. From the lack of ambulances in attendance, Stone also assumed there were no survivors.

"We received a tip from an early-morning jogger who found the vehicle," Kramer said. "I don't think it would have been noticeable from the driver's seat in a passing car. The jogger says he runs past here every morning. The car wasn't here yesterday."

Stone wished he had energy to jog every morning at five-thirty. He looked into the front seat. Even with the limited early-morning light, he could see no bodies or bloodstains. The key was still in the ignition, but the air bag had deployed. "You think this was a walk-away?" It was not uncommon for an injured person—especially a drunk—to walk or hitchhike home after an accident. More troublesome would be a brain-injured individual who might wander into the woods. It had been a cold night; an injured individual could quickly succumb to hypothermia.

"I searched the area. No bodies were thrown from the vehicle. If you notice," Kramer pointed to the interior of the car, "the key is still in the ignition but turned off. The car is also in neutral—not drive. I don't think this was an accident. Someone pushed the car over the embankment."

"Did you run a make on the license plate?" The question was rhetorical. Kramer was a good officer and noted for his thoroughness. Stone had no doubt Kramer ran the plate before he called Stone.

"It's registered to a Michael Morrison, from Chicago."

"I guess we need to find Mr. Morrison and ask him a few questions."

"I think we found him," Kramer said, "but he won't be answering any questions. That's why I called you."

Kramer walked to the back of the car, and popped open the trunk; it was unlocked. Lying curled in a fetal position was a man, obviously dead, his hands tied behind his back. A pool of coagulated blood surrounded the head and neck, with a small stream of blood draining into the tire well. Someone had slit the man's throat and pulled the tongue through the cut like a necktie. A perfectly centered hole perforated the forehead, presumably made by a large caliber handgun. The bullet had blown out the back of the skull. Since blood hadn't splattered over the trunk, the execution had to have occurred elsewhere, and the bullet would never be recovered. Stone hoped the bullet wound came first.

"I didn't want to touch the body until forensics had a chance to take photographs and check the crime scene, but I'm willing to wager any I.D. found on the body will belong to Michael Morrison."

Stone had no desire to take Kramer's bet. This wasn't just a killing; it was an execution and a warning. A warning by organized crime bosses as to what can happen when individuals get out of line or talk too much. The warning was undoubtedly effective.

"Okay, Cory, what are your thoughts; what's your read on this?" Stone often sought the opinions of his officers. It raised their self-esteem and forced them to think beyond the obvious. Occasionally—not often—Stone obtained insights he, himself, had not considered.

"It's obviously an execution, gangland style. I think if we were to get Happy from the State Police K-9 unit up here, he would sniff out traces of drugs. Cocaine would be my guess."

"You may be right. The Feds suspect drugs are coming across Lake Superior from Canada. That wouldn't be difficult since the Coast Guard's more concerned with buoy tending, ice breaking, and small watercraft safety; they don't have the time or the resources to combat small-time dope smugglers."

"Chief, this is no coincidence. Kampe's trying to reclaim his position in the drug trade. We know he's capable of this kind of brutality. He's proven that. Unless he leaves town, there'll be more killings."

That thought had occurred to Stone. He had been hoping the Kampe kid would clean up his act and put the past behind him. That obviously was not the case. He wouldn't be the first ex-con to return to his old drug habits. Prison hardened criminals as often as they rehabilitated them. Kampe had to be tougher and wiser now than when he entered prison. They would have to increase their surveillance of Kampe. Maybe a stakeout at his house or a tail by an under-cover officer. With no relatives or friends in town, it was unlikely Kampe would have an alibi for the last twenty-four hours.

"I want to show you something else." Kramer walked around to the passenger side and opened the front door. Using a ballpoint pen, he lifted an empty soda can from the floor. "See this? It's a can of Barq's Root Beer."

"So? Last I checked, root beer is still legal in the state." Stone assumed the can had significance. He wished Kramer would just come out with it. He hated guessing games.

"I was on the track team with Kampe my senior year. He was fast for a freshman."

"You saying Kampe will give us a run for our money?"

Kramer ignored the Chief's sarcasm. "He had a fetish for drinking Barq's Root Beer before each meet—like he was Popeye and the root beer was spinach."

"Dust if for prints. If we're lucky, they'll match."

"You won't find finger prints. Ex-cons are too smart for that. Kampe knows the can has no forensic value. He left it as a calling card. He's toying with us."

Kramer could be right. Kampe wouldn't be the first criminal in Stone's career to leave a calling card, either out of arrogance or a subconscious desire to be caught.

"Doesn't look like anything more I can do here." Stone looked at his watch. "I think I'll head back to the office. Did you call forensics?" Another rhetorical question. Stone asked out of habit.

"They'll be here in about twenty minutes. I'll stick around until they get here."

"Don't you get off at seven?"

"An extra twenty minutes won't kill me."

If Kramer was trying to impress the boss, it was working, Stone decided. Kramer was a good cop. He enjoyed the power that went with the job a little more than Stone would have liked, but Kramer was young; he would mellow with age.

It was too late to crawl back into bed; he was fully awake. Instead, Stone stopped at the local IHOP for a breakfast of pancakes and sausage. If he had gone home, his wife wouldn't have allowed the sausage. It was an obvious case of withholding evidence. So he wasn't perfect. What his wife didn't know wouldn't hurt her.

It was just past eight when Stone arrived at the police station. Laura Weatherdon, his secretary, clerk, and all around Friday, was filing reports.

"Laura, can you get me the Higgins file?"

"It's on your desk, Chief. I read the morning dispatch and assumed you'd need it."

"Thanks." Stone wasn't sure if he should be thankful or irritated. Laura always knew what he wanted before he wanted it.

Stone sat down at his desk and picked up the thick file with Sara Higgins stenciled across the cover. It had been three and a half years since he had last seen it. He knew most of it by heart. Stone could never put a finger on it, but something in the case left a bad taste in his mouth. It's hard to beat a case where the victim, who had known the rapist all her life, can make a positive I.D. Kramer had no alibi and admitted to being in the area—running on the school track less than two blocks from the rape scene. It had been an open and shut case for the prosecutor. But what was the motive? According to the prosecuting attorney, just being an oversexed teenager was sufficient motive for rape. If that were the case, it would have been more likely on a formal date, not as a separate incident. There had to be other factors.

Stone turned to the sheet that summarized the events: *Sara Higgins (age 17) left Tamarack High School at approximately 20:30 hours after attending an Honors Society meeting. She was walking to a friend's house where she expected to phone her father for a ride home when she was accosted by Eric Kampe (age 18). He enticed her into an abandoned creamery building where he raped her and then viscously beat her with a black baseball bat. (Investigators discovered a black baseball bat in Kampe's bedroom during a search of the Kampe residence.) Higgins hid behind a stack of crates, but Kampe found her and continued his assault. He then left her for dead. At approximately 21:00 hours, Officer Cory Kramer drove by the creamery and discovered the door ajar. He went inside to investigate and discovered the Higgins girl lying in a pool of blood.*

Chief Stone sat back in his chair to rehash the scene in his mind. If Kramer hadn't arrived when he did, Sara Higgins would be dead. As it was, she still nearly died.

Stone took out five eight-by-ten glossies taken at the hospital. In his thirty years of law enforcement, he had never seen such brutality. Kampe had beaten in the side of Sara's face and her almost-detached right eye pointed aimlessly into space. Her broken nose, no longer centered over the face, protruded from the left cheek. The ER physician stitched up the facial lacerations prior to the photographs. She had looked even worse before the repairs. Other injuries included a fracture just below the right shoulder and multiple broken ribs. A chest X-ray confirmed a collapsed right lung.

As far as Stone was concerned, the doctors performed a miracle. The Higgins girl was comatose for three days and no one, including Stone, expected her to live. If she hadn't been such a fighter, she would have died.

She refused to discuss the attack in the beginning. Stone couldn't blame her for that—not after what she had been through. That was understandable. She also refused to see Kampe after she came out of her coma. That was not understandable—at least it wasn't until eight days after she returned home and discovered she was pregnant. That's when she fingered Kampe as her assailant.

Maybe that was what had been bothering Stone. Why had she waited so long to tell her story? Why had she waited until she got home to point the finger at Kampe? Stone never could understand why battered women protected their abusive boyfriends and husbands, often returning to the same abusive relationship. When presented with a choice between love and hate, they chose love nine times out of ten, always assuming their significant other would improve with time. They seldom did. At least the Higgins girl eventually came to her senses.

"Hey, Laura," Stone yelled out to the outer office. "Which emotion is stronger, love or hate?"

"No doubt about it, Chief. Love always wins out. It feels better than hate."

"It didn't win for Eric Kampe," Stone replied.

Stone returned to the Higgins report. She described hiding behind wooden crates. There weren't any crates mentioned in Kramer's report. The building was empty when he arrived—another conflict in the story. Kramer normally wrote very detailed reports. With the extensive head injury, a few discrepancies in the victim's report had to be expected.

Stone sorted through the papers until he found what he had been looking for. He pulled out a two-page document labeled *Eric Kampe: a psychological profile*. He knew what it would say but needed to read it again for his own piece of mind. Stone skipped down to the summary: *Predictability for violence is low*. At the bottom was a small footnote: *could become violent under the influence of drugs*. That footnote did Kampe in. Kampe was drug free when arrested, but they had taken the blood sample a week after the incident—long after any drugs would have cleared his system. They found traces of cocaine and methcathinone in the warehouse, providing the motive for Kampe's violent behavior. That was the missing piece to the puzzle the prosecutors needed to seal the case—a motive for his behavior.

Was Kampe back into drugs? Stone couldn't overlook that possibility. The evidence was skimpy, but Judge Ed Madalinski had little tolerance for drug dealers. He had tried the Higgins case. Perhaps he would authorize a monitoring device on Kampe's car. An unmarked police car could then follow him from a mile away.

If Kampe were meeting with drug dealers, they would know when and where.

5

Sara looked up at the dense, azure-blue sky. The color was so intense it gave a surreal appearance as if someone had painted acrylics on a sky of canvas. She could almost see the brush marks in the otherwise perfect sky. In contrast, large puffy-white clouds formed animated objects that constantly changed before her eyes. One looked like a horsy with legs that slowly moved as it trotted across the sky. Sara watched as the horsy morphed into a white ducky.

Six-year-old Sara Higgins waded along the shallows of Harley Lake with Eric Kampe. The water was smooth and clear and reflected the images of the white birch along the shore with the same intensity as the objects themselves. The water was neither hot nor cold. Sara couldn't even feel the water pressing against her feet; though she could see her feet disappear into the water with each step. From the tops of spruce trees, agitated chickadees scolded the children with their persistent "chick-a-dee-dee-dees." Sara ignored the chickadees and focused her attention on a squadron of dragonflies skimming across the surface of the lake. They darted here and there and then hovered momentarily in mid-flight for reasons known only to them before zooming off to another location.

Eric and Sara were like Adam and Eve in a modern-day Eden, oblivious to their nakedness, knowing no shame. The day was hot even for summer, and skinny-dipping in Harley Lake offered the logical escape from the sweltering heat. Sara pushed her foot into the lake bottom and let the sand oozed between her toes. Life didn't get any better than that.

They spent most of the morning in knee-deep water along the shoreline where they built sand castles and dug holes, trapping water with barricades of sand to form pools of water. It was a time of innocence and one of Sara's favorite summers.

Eric found a tennis ball floating among the cattails, and they moved into deeper water to play catch. But Eric had a strong arm, and when he threw the ball to Sara, it sailed over her head, landing far from shore. Sara immediately swam after it. She was a good swimmer and had no fear of deep water. She had almost reached the ball when she felt the current. It was gentle at first but then it picked up speed, swirling her in a wide circle. She had entered a maelstrom, a large funnel of water that slowly pulled her downward where the circular speed increased. Where was Eric? Eric would help her. She called out to Eric, but no sound resonated from her vocal cords…She tried swimming out of the whirlpool, but the current was too strong. She sank deeper…deeper into the depths of the funnel. She was spinning faster and faster.

Slowly the water obscured the sunlight, and it became dark. Day became night. It took a few minutes for Sara's eyes to adjust to the darkness, but when they did adjust, she noticed a door in the side of the whirlpool. Someone was calling her from behind the door, beckoning her to enter. Was it Eric? She couldn't tell. She opened the door and stepped inside. The door slammed shut behind her. It was eleven years later, and she was now seventeen. She was still naked. A man in black had ripped off her clothes, but the age of innocence had passed, and she now knew shame. This was no longer Eden. The serpent had arrived, and she had been banned from the Garden. She now saw her nakedness for what it was: evil. She tried to cover her nakedness with her arms, but the man in black pulled her arms away. He was dressed in black pants and a black leather jacket. His hair was also black, but his face was featureless, as if purposely blurred by computer graphics. No eyes, no nose, no mouth.

Sara hid behind a stack of wooden boxes, but he came after her, beating her with a baseball bat—a black baseball bat. The bat hit her right forearm, when she tried to deflect the blows. The pain was intense. She could see a deformity in the bone.

The man in black continued hitting her...in the head...in the face...in the ribs. Sara fell backward to the floor, her nude body oblivious to the coldness of the concrete. She could no longer fight back. She lay there on the cold concrete in total submission, naked, waiting for him to come to her and have his way with her. She could feel beads of sweat dripping down her forehead.

Sara sat up in bed. The beads of sweat on her brow were real. Was it just a dream, or was the man in black lurking somewhere in her bedroom? Sara pulled the covers to her chin. Even though she wore pajamas, she felt the shame of nakedness. She needed to ensure she was covered.

She thought she had conquered her nightmares, and she had for two years. Now they were back. This was the third dream in a week. Each one was different, but they contained the same theme. They began with carefree days of childhood, mostly with Eric, and ended with that faceless monster in black. The hatred on the face of the rapist was too intense even for a nightmare.

Sara looked at her clock; it was half past five, too early to get up, but she was too frightened to sleep. She turned on the nightstand lamp and retrieved a novel she had been reading. A bookmark identified page 130.

* * *

The alarm clock awoke much too cheerfully for Sara's tastes. She whacked at the snooze bar and the noise stopped. Sara looked over at the clock: it registered eight o'clock as she knew it would. She had gotten an extra two hours sleep. Her book lay beside her, opened to page 132; she had read two pages before falling asleep. With her throbbing headache, further sleep seemed impossible. The attack on the snooze bar had been in vain. She might as well get up and start breakfast, she decided. She had big plans for the day.

Breakfasts on weekdays were hectic since Sara had to drive her daughter to the sitter's and make it to work by eight. Cold cereal was the usual fare. Sara tried to make up for it on weekends with a hot breakfast. Today would be French toast, her daughter's favorite.

"Mommy, can I take this book with me?"

Sara was washing the last of the breakfast dishes but looked over at her daughter. Not surprisingly, she was holding *The Cat in the Hat*. "As long as you don't pester Aunt Nancy to read it all day long." Sara felt guilty about leaving her daughter with Nancy on a Saturday. She normally reserved Saturdays for her daughter, but her daughter was as excited about staying with Aunt Nancy as Sara was about getting out of the house.

Holly had invited her on a shopping spree in Marquette. She even offered to spring for lunch.

Sara had nothing she needed to buy, but the thought of spending an afternoon with an adult and talking in other than short, simple sentences was enticing. Holly had suggested the outing the previous evening, very atypical for Holly who normally planned her life two weeks in advance. Fortunately, Nancy was willing to baby-sit, even at such a short notice.

"Don't forget your hat in case you play outside."

"Come on, Mom, let's go." The overly eager five-year-old pulled her knit stocking cap over her braids and headed out the door.

"I'm coming." Sara snatched her purse from the kitchen counter and stepped outside. The sun was shining, suggesting a warm day, although there was a strong breeze from the west. Maybe her daughter wouldn't need her hat.

"Can I take my kitty to Aunt Nancy's?"

Sara's mind was still on the *Cat in the Hat* as she locked the back door. She mentally catalogued her daughter's books, but couldn't remember another kitten book. Her daughter must be referring to one of the new library books. Sara was about to give permission when she turned to find her daughter holding a half-grown cat.

"Whoa! Where did the cat come from?"

"I found him yesterday. He was hungry, so I gave him something to eat."

"I suppose that explains the empty bowl by the back door?" Until now the bowl had escaped Sara's notice. Her daughter always did have a soft heart for stray animals big or small.

"I gave him some milk. He likes milk. He's my kitty now."

Sara inspected the kitten. It appeared healthy, although somewhat underweight. The kitten was obviously too young to fend for itself. The kitten's fur was mostly black except for the white paws and a white stripe that extended down from under the chin to the kitten's chest. The loud purring confirmed that the animal was quite content in her daughter's arms. The feeling appeared mutual.

"Honey, the kitten has a collar."

"So?"

"It belongs to someone."

"No one lives around here. He's my kitty now."

Her daughter did have a valid point; the nearest neighbors were the Carlson's a mile down the road. As far as Sara knew, they didn't have a cat. The cat was obviously lost—or abandoned.

"We'll have to see if we can find the owner." That wasn't the answer her daughter wanted to hear.

"If we can't find the owner, can we keep the kitty?"

"We'll see." Having a pet during the summer wouldn't be bad, but during the school year there would be no one home to care for the cat.

"I think the kitty's hungry."

"I suppose we can spare some milk, but we need to hurry. We're going to be late." Sara quickly refilled the cat's bowl with milk and returned the milk container to the fridge.

Sara reached into her pocket searching for her house keys, so she could lock the back door for the second time. When she pulled the keys out, she also pulled out the note containing Holly's cell phone number. It was for Nancy to use in case of an emergency. Someday she would have to get high tech and buy a cell phone of her own. The small slip of paper caught the wind and sailed down the driveway.

"I'll get it, Mommy."

Sara walked past the car toward her daughter who had snagged the paper in midair with the skill of a Labrador retriever chasing a Frisbee and was returning at full trot.

"How many times have I told you not to leave your bicycle in the driveway!" A small bike lay just under the rear bumper. Sara wouldn't have seen it in her rearview mirror. If the wind hadn't blown away the note, she would have backed over the bike, destroying the bike and perhaps taking out the muffler of her car. It could have punctured the gas tank.

"I didn't leave the bike there, Mommy."

"Someone left it there."

"It wasn't me, Mommy."

The bike had been placed behind the car after Sara parked the car the previous afternoon. Sara tried to remember if her daughter had recently ridden her bike. She played outside for a short time before supper, probably with the kitten. Sara couldn't remember if she rode her bike. Her daughter didn't normally lie, although she was still a five-year-old and capable of lying in her own defense.

Sara picked up the bike. Beneath the bike's frame lay a crumpled Barq's Root Beer can.

"Come on, Twinkle Toes. Hop in the car. Hurry."

Sara backed out of the driveway and headed toward Nancy's house. She felt safer once she was heading away from the farmhouse. First the nightmares—now she was seeing boogiemen behind every tree and hiding in every closet. Anyone could have left the root beer can in her driveway. Was she losing touch with reality? The reality was that he was definitely out there and definitely after her. The hard part was separating reality from imagination.

* * *

Marquette was a two-hour drive from Tamarack but well worth the time for the serious shopper. Being the largest city in the Upper Peninsula, it was the regional shopping center with two malls and outlets for all the major large-chain department stores. It was approaching noon when Holly and Sara arrived.

"Let's do lunch first," Holly said. "Where do you want to eat?"

Not only was Holly willing to spring for lunch, she was letting Sara pick the restaurant. It was an easy decision.

"How about the Bonanza Family Restaurant? I like their service and it has one of the largest soup and salad bars in the U.P."

"The Bonanza it is."

"Take the bypass through town."

Holly turned west at the roundabout on the outskirts of Marquette and followed the bypass to the restaurant.

After a quick perusal of the menu, they both settled for the salad bar and took their trays to the enclosed sunroom, where a table in the corner offered both sunlight and privacy. By evening the restaurant would be crowded, but the lunchtime crowd was thin.

"Okay, Sara, spill your guts. What's on your mind? You haven't said two words during the whole trip. That's not like you."

"I didn't get much sleep last night," Sara confessed. "Probably too much caffeine." She forced a smile.

"You were probably up late watching one of those scary movies."

Holly obviously wasn't sold on the caffeine theory, but she let the subject die when Sara declined to elaborate.

"What about you? You've been talking non-stop during the entire trip. I couldn't have gotten two words in even if I had wanted to...and it's not like you to impulsively decide on a major shopping spree."

"I have to buy a few things and needed your input."

"Okay, where do you want to go, and what do you want to buy?"

"Well, I'm not sure what I want yet, but I thought we could start at Bethany's Stork Shop."

"YOU'RE PREGNANT?" An elderly couple three tables down look up in surprise. "It's okay: she's married." The elderly couple chuckled and returned to their lunches. "You're pregnant?" Sara repeated in a whisper.

"YES!" Holly replied, not caring if the elderly couple heard. I haven't seen a doctor yet. It was just a home pregnancy test, but it lit up like a Christmas tree."

"That's fantastic. I'm so happy for you. I know you've been working hard trying to get pregnant the last several years."

"We've been trying for three years, but I can't say the work was that hard."

"When did you find out?"

"I was a week overdue on my monthlies, so I suspected it, but I didn't get the courage to test myself until yesterday. I wanted so badly to tell you, but I had to tell Aaron first. He called from Montana yesterday evening."

"What did Aaron say?"

"He said, 'Take Sara and the credit card to Marquette and buy whatever we need. Money is no object.'"

"I'm so excited I can hardly eat, and I'm not the one who's pregnant."

"I think Aaron's excited too. He called two hours later from a truck stop in North Dakota. He's already bought cigars. Two boxes: one says 'it's a girl' and the other says 'it's a boy.' He also decided to give up the long-distance truck driving and get a logging job. It'll mean a cut in pay, but he'll be home every night."

"You and Aaron will make great parents."

"Aaron will be home on Monday and has a week off. We're thinking of having a small celebration on Friday. Just a few close friends, but we want you there."

"I wouldn't miss it for the world."

"We thought we might go to a fancy restaurant for a quiet dinner and then go bowling."

"I'm not very good at bowling. I'll probably make a fool of myself in front of your friends. How many people are going to be there?"

"Just a few."

"How few?"

"Well, there will be you, me, Aaron, and maybe one of Aaron's friends."

"Are you talking about a blind date?' Sara sat up straight in her chair, the excitement of the day momentarily lost.

"He's not blind. I don't think he even wears glasses."

"Holly, I know you mean well, but I'm not ready for another relationship."

"Sara, you've gotten a bad deal in life—had some bad experiences, but not all men are bad. Unless you force yourself to open up, you'll never be ready for another relationship. Sara, life is passing you by. You aren't getting any younger."

"I know you and Aaron have a wonderful relationship, but Aaron is special."

"Sure, Aaron's special, but so is your father; so is my father. There're lots of special men out there. We just have to find them. You don't know what you're missing. You don't know what it's like to crawl into bed with your lover and lay your head on his shoulder while he holds you tightly in his arms. You don't know what it's like to confide your most intimate feelings while he runs his fingers through your hair. I tell Aaron things I'd never tell you, and you're my best friend. Aaron and I sometimes spend an hour or more holding each other while we share our innermost thoughts. It's a wonderful feeling. And I'm not talking about sex—although it frequently deteriorates into that. That's dessert. You don't know how good it can feel."

But Sara did know how wonderful it felt having a lover hold her for hours while they shared their most intimate thoughts. She once had such a relationship, a relationship she fully expected to last a lifetime—but it ended prematurely; it ended with the incident.

"I suppose you've already told this blind date I would be there?"

"This man with exquisite eyesight had his heart set on meeting you, but he's an adult. I'm sure he can handle rejection."

"So now we try the guilt trip?"

"Sara, if you really don't want to, I can cancel it. I'm sure he'll understand. I don't want you to do anything that makes you feel uncomfortable. I just thought the two of you might hit it off."

"What's his name?"

"I know you'll like him."

"I didn't say I would do it."

"His name's Cory Kramer."

"The deputy sheriff?"

"You know him?"

"We've met."

"Is that good or bad?"

"I guess he saved my life."

Holly poked at her salad with her fork, preparing to pursue the topic no further. The conversation was moving into areas they both tacitly had agreed to avoid.

"Okay, I'll go on one condition: I don't want you and Aaron sitting in the front seat doing some serious necking and petting while we're in the back seat discussing the weather." Sara smiled, and they both broke into laughter like two teen-age schoolgirls. The elderly couple looked up and smiled at them.

"It's a deal. Although I won't vouch for our behavior after we drop you two off."

# 6

Eric awoke ten minutes before his alarm clock. The sun was streaming through the bedroom window, displaying far more enthusiasm for the new day than Eric could muster. Previously he had used his minor injuries to justify his laziness, but that excuse no longer held merit. His aches and pains had all resolved within four days of the injury. It was now time he got out of bed and did something strenuous. As usual, Tiger was sleeping with his chin firmly ensconced on Eric's chest and occupying far more space than a dog's share of the bed ought to be. One of the first priorities of the day might have to be some discipline training. Two weeks had passed since he found Tiger wasting away in the grass. The honeymoon period was over. It was time to assert some authority over this dog he had inherited—no more pampering. Eric reached over and scratched Tiger behind the left ear. Tiger momentarily rolled his eyes upward to give Eric his best pathetic-dog look before resuming his nap.

Tiger was a pleasant companion, although the dog displayed limited understanding of the master/dog concept, preferring to do whatever he pleased, whenever he pleased while taking full advantage of his master's easy going disposition. At least the previous owner had housebroken Tiger, a fortuitous blessing since Eric was not skilled in the art of potty training. Judging from the scars on Tiger's back, the training sessions had not been a pleasant experience. It was no secret Tiger was staying with Eric, and since the previous owner hadn't bothered to claim the dog, Eric assumed

Tiger was his to keep. If the owner had appeared, Eric would have turned him over to the humane society. He was sure Dr. Hansen would make a formidable witness.

Tiger's skin infections had responded to the antibiotics; and after a week they were no longer tender, but the scars would remain forever, a constant reminder of man's inherent capability for cruelty. And with Tiger's voracious appetite, it hadn't taken long for the malnutrition to self-correct. The weekly dog chow expense far exceeded Eric's food budget such that Eric had facetiously considered claiming Tiger as a dependent on his income tax. It was inconceivable any dog could consume that much food. Eric scratched Tiger's belly, finding the beginning of love handles. Maybe it was time Tiger had a more prudent diet as well as an exercise program. Tiger didn't appear concerned.

The alarm irrupted precisely at eight. Eric swatted at the clock, hitting the off-button on the second try. "Time to get up, you lazy dog." Eric pushed Tiger out of the way and crawled out of bed. He would postpone his morning shower until later. Instead, he slipped into jogging clothes. "Up and at 'em, Tiger. We need to see what kind of shape you're in." Tiger, making no effort to relinquish his spot on the bed, responded with an inquisitive look.

Eric had always enjoyed running, lettering in cross-country and track in high school. During his five years in prison, a five-mile run in the prison yard had been a daily routine. Running provided an ecstasy only a long-distance runner can appreciate. It was time he returned to his previous routine.

Eric strapped on his running shoes and headed toward the back door. Not willing to be left behind, Tiger followed out of idle curiosity. Eric pushed aside the tarp that separated the house from the back entryway. He had hung the tarp to keep the burnt smell out of the house. Although the burned and unsound structure was now gone, the tarp still discouraged all but the most persistent mosquitoes from gaining access to Eric's veins. Eric had initiated a modest amount of repair, completing the sub-flooring and the frame for one wall. At the rate he was going, it would be several weeks before the house would again be mosquito proof. Some of Cade County's self-righteous citizens had also contributed to his project. Spray-painted on the floor in red paint was "rapist." At least it was not destructive. Vinyl tiles would eventually cover the sub-flooring. But as his mother used to say, "It's the thought that counts."

Eric shuffled through the construction zone and stepped out into his back yard where a partially overcast sky now concealed the sun. The weather channel had predicted the temperature would reach the high seventies by afternoon, but the morning remained cool—perfect weather for running. Eric paused to stretch his muscles when he reached the asphalt bike path. Warm up exercises were an obsession, a vestigial habit left over from his high school track days. Unless chased by a man wielding a knife, he would never consider running without his warm up exercises.

Eric's warm up exceeded Tiger's attention span, and Tiger began searching for other sources of entertainment, which he found in the form of a hapless toad that had the misfortune to cross Tiger's path. Encouraged by his new coach, the toad leaped into the tall grass. Tiger tracked the toad's scent to the new hiding spot where a subtle nudge from Tiger's cold nose sent the toad jumping again. The game was more exciting for Tiger than it was for the toad.

"Come on, Tiger. Let's go for a run." Eric headed down the bike path, first at a slow jog and then at a faster pace as his muscles limbered up. Although officially designated a bike path, more joggers and walkers used the six-foot wide asphalt trail than bikers. Today, Eric had the trail to himself. Any early-morning, before-work joggers who might have used the trail had come and gone, and since school was still in session, there were no kids on bikes. The most he could expect would be an occasional housewife with a Walkman.

Eric stretched out his legs, further increasing his pace. Any concerns he had about Tiger's physical conditioning quickly dissipated. Once Tiger understood the concept of the new game, he ran ahead, pausing now and then to sniff a log or mark a tree with his scent while waiting for Eric to catch up.

Except for the cluster of houses along the south shore, the path around the lake was rustic. Eric ran under sprawling oaks that arched over the trail forming a virtual tunnel of green. Large vines hung down from the taller trees, reminding Eric of his Tarzan days. In some areas the trail meandered closer to the lake where the trees were sparser. Park benches alongside the water's edge offered refuge with a view of the lake to weary walkers during the day, and at night provided a haven for serious lovers. These areas were more open, and the offshore breeze offered a welcome respite from the damp woods.

Eric slowed to a more moderate pace when he entered a thickly wooded area carpeted with ferns and spring flowers. The verdant grandeur brought back pleasant memories of his childhood. As pretty as it was now, Eric preferred the way it had been—before it became commercialized. When he was a child there hadn't been a bike trail, only a few well-beaten paths left by fishermen seeking perch or largemouth bass. The lake was too small to warrant a boat ramp. Most fishermen fished from shore or waded out into the sandy-bottomed lake.

He and Sara had waded along those same shallows, searching for frogs, pollywogs, or any other object of interest to young children exploring the world. He had fond memories of those days, including that hot summer afternoon when he and Sara were six. They had doffed their clothes for a refreshing swim in the lake—it had been Sara's idea. When their parents caught them, Sara received a lecture—he got a whipping. That was Eric's first introduction to the equality of the sexes. He and Sara had been friends then, inseparable, but that had since changed. He still thought of her. Every day he thought of her—but they were no longer pleasant thoughts.

The circular bike path measured slightly over a mile in length, making it a favorite trail among serious joggers. Eric finished the first lap in just under seven minutes; he expected to do four more. The rest of the laps would be at a faster pace. Eric stretched out his legs and pushed himself until his lungs ached and begged for relief. He finished his five laps winded and sweaty. The three weeks of inactivity had taken its toll; he was out of shape. Finding a large oak tree alongside the trail, he collapsed on the freshly cut grass in view of the lake. The county periodically mowed the grass around Kampe's Korner, giving it a park-like appearance. He loved the smell of new-mown grass. Added to the fresh smells of spring, it was almost intoxicating. Tiger, not yet winded, ran from tree to tree. His energy was endless. Although fully-grown, he still had a puppy mentality that forced him to explore the new surroundings with puppy-like vigor.

Except for a girl bouncing a tennis ball on the bike trail, the area along the south shore was currently deserted. The girl's tattered jeans complemented a well-worn flannel shirt, and the two long braids of blond hair extending down her back gave her a tomboy appearance. Eric guessed she was four or five. It was unfortunate there weren't more kids her age in the neighborhood to play with, but most of the residents had raised their brood and were looking forward to retirement. Eric couldn't remember any families who might have a daughter her age; but a lot can change after five years in prison.

The girl's ball bounced against a stone on the pavement sending the ball careening into the grass. That provided all the incentive Tiger needed. He tore after the ball, catching it on the bounce. After playing with his newfound possession for a moment, he proudly returned to the oak tree, dropping the ball at Eric's feet.

"Hey, that dog stole my ball!" The girl glared at Eric, as if he had been personally responsible for the theft.

"Sorry, he's a retriever. That's what they do." Eric picked up the ball. "I'd throw it to you, but I'm afraid he would just go after it again."

The young girl walked over to the oak tree where Eric was sitting. "What's a retriever?"

"That's a kind of dog that brings things back. Watch this."

Eric threw the ball, and Tiger took off in a flash, overshooting the ball in his enthusiasm. He pounced on it, gave it a shake or two with his head, and then returned, dropping it at Eric's feet.

"Hey, that's neat. What's your doggie's name?" The girl cautiously rubbed the back of Tiger's neck. Tiger responded with a lick to her face.

"His name's Tiger."

"That's silly. He's not a tiger."

"That's his name just the same."

"Will he fetch the ball if I throw it?"

"Try it and see."

The girl threw the ball, and seconds later Tiger had the ball at her feet. The girl rewarded Tiger with a hug. Tiger reciprocated with another lick to the face.

"What's your name? You live around here?"

"My name's Rory. I stay with my babysitter while Mommy works. My babysitter lives over there." Rory pointed to a large gray house. "What's your name?"

"You can call me Eric."

"My Mommy says it's not nice to call adults by their first name. I have to call you Mr. something."

"That's okay. I'm just a kid who's big for his age."

"No, you're not! Mommy says it's not nice to lie."

"If you call me Mr. something, it'll make me feel like an old man. When I was a kid, I always wanted to be called Tarzan."

"What's Tar Zan?"

"It's African. Tar is similar to mister. It connotes a lot of respect."

"What's connotes?"

"It means someone's important."

"Okay, Tar Zan. I guess I can call you that."

Tiger nudged Rory's hand, trying to get at the tennis ball.

"I think Tiger wants to play. Why don't you throw him the ball?"

Rory threw the ball, and Tiger catapulted out at full speed, showing no fatigue whatsoever from the five-mile run. Rory ran after him, straining to keep up. Watching the two of them run made Eric feel his age. He wished he had their energy. The five-mile run had left him exhausted. Eric repositioned his back against the oak tree and stretched out his legs. They were beginning to cramp. He had planned to work on the entryway, but that could wait. He had until fall to finish the repairs. Watching Rory and Tiger play on the grass was relaxing. It brought back memories of his childhood. They were pleasant and carefree memories. At that time his future had appeared so bright and promising. He had expected to eventually marry and raise a family, perhaps have a child like Rory. But that would never happen now. How could any respectable girl introduce him to her parents? "This is my friend, Eric," she would say. "He brutally beat and raped his last girlfriend and spent five years in prison, but he's otherwise a nice guy." Eric's criminal past would follow him wherever he went.

Exhausted after twenty minutes of running around on the grass, Rory and Tiger returned to the oak tree and collapsed next to Eric. Even Tiger was willing to rest.

"I like your doggie." The feeling was obviously mutual; Tiger rolled on his back, begging to have his stomach rubbed. Rory accommodated the request. "Do you live around here?"

"I live in that brown house, three doors down." Eric pointed out his house. "It's the one with the back torn apart."

"Do you have any children?"

"No, I'm not married."

"Do you have a girlfriend?"

"I used to, but not anymore."

"Why not?"

"What is this, twenty questions…?" Eric would have been offended if anyone else had posed such questions, but Rory asked with the innocence of a child. "Something happened years ago, and now I hate her, and she hates me. It's as simple as that."

"My Mommy says it's not nice to hate."

"Your mother's never met my old girlfriend."

"Maybe you and your girlfriend will get back together someday."

"Never happen. I wouldn't take her back even if she were on her knees begging. And after what's happened, there is no way in hell she would come begging, if you will excuse the language."

"My Mommy says there is no such thing as never."

"Your mother seems to have all the answers. Is your father that smart too?"

"My father died."

"I'm sorry. That must have been tough."

"My Mommy says he died before I was born."

"But she must be a good mother."

"Yes, but she needs a boyfriend…I think she'd like you."

"You playing cupid now?"

"What's cupid?"

"That's a little boy who runs around naked shooting arrows at people."

"You're being silly again."

"Trust me; if your mother knew who I was, she wouldn't like me." Eric stood up and dusted off his running shorts. "I have to get to work. Tiger and I'll be running again tomorrow morning. Maybe we'll see you again."

* * *

The following morning was again partly overcast but a bit warmer when Eric headed for the trail. The humidity was low, unlike the hot, sticky days he would experience later in the summer. Eric touched his toes a few times, and then methodically stretched-out his hamstrings. Tiger waited patiently by his side. He had more enthusiasm now that he understood the drill.

"TAR ZAN! TAR ZAN!"

Eric paused in mid-stretch. Rory was running toward him at full gallop, her long braids flopping in the wind. She clutched a tennis ball in her right hand. "Hi, Rory."

"Can I play with Tiger?"

Tiger assumed it was a rhetorical question. In his mind the answer was clear. He ran circles around Rory, trying to nudge the tennis ball from her hand.

"I'm running five laps around the lake. If he wants to miss all that fun and excitement, I suppose that'll be his loss."

"Thanks, Tar Zan." Rory threw the ball into the grassy area and raced after it, hoping to beat Tiger to the prize. It was a lost cause. Tiger was several paces ahead of Roy when he claimed his trophy. Instead of returning the ball, Tiger decided a game of keep away was in order. Eric would have to make his run without a running partner.

Eric finished his stretching exercises and started down the trail. He gradually increased his speed, pushing himself harder than the day before. He clocked his first mile at six minutes, fourteen seconds. Rory and Tiger were still playing fetch when he passed them on his first lap. Lost in their own little world, they were oblivious to his passing. After the third lap Rory and Tiger were nowhere in sight. Eric hoped the two of them had enough combined sense to stay out of trouble. Eric finished his five miles twenty-five seconds faster than the day before, but also more winded—he was definitely out of shape. He wiped the sweat from his brow and sat down by the oak tree to catch his breath. Fresh beads of sweat quickly replaced the old. Eric closed his eyes and leaned back against the tree until his breathing returned to normal. Only then did he notice the objects pressing against his spine.

Eric reached behind him and pulled out a pair of small sneakers and a tennis ball; the sneaker's owner had apparently decided to go barefoot. A quick visual search of the area revealed Rory with pant legs rolled up, wading in the water. The water had still managed to reach her pants, which were now darkened with water stains two inches above the rolled edge. Rory's mother would not be happy about the wet pants. If he remembered correctly, he and Sara hadn't always pleased their parents. Skinny-dipping immediately came to mind. Tiger, with no parents to please, was completely drenched. He looked smaller with his hair wet and matted down. Parents or no parents, Tiger would be staying outside until he dried off.

With his breathing now back to normal, Eric walked over to the water's edge. Rory and Tiger, engrossed with their mission, ignored his presence. "What are you guys doing?"

"Trying to catch a frog." Rory didn't bother to look up. Her eyes remained focused on a small patch of reeds in knee-deep water where the elusive frog had disappeared. Tiger, also focusing on the spot, but with far less patience, plunged into the water with his front paws, spraying water in all directions. At the current rate of inundation, Rory would be drenched by the time the big-game hunt was over, and it did appear to be over. Despite Tiger's pawing at the sandy bottom, no frog materialized.

"Looks like he got away." Rory surveyed the surrounding area but found no evidence of their quarry. The frog had made its escape in the muddy water Tiger had stirred up.

"There should be plenty of frogs by the end of the summer. Look at all the baby frogs." Eric pointed to the numerous pollywogs swimming about in the water.

"Where? I don't see any."

"See all those little black balls swimming around."

"Those aren't baby frogs. Those are pollywogs."

"Yes, but they grow up to be frogs."

"No they don't. You're lying again. My Mommy says it's not nice to lie."

"I think we've already established your mother's position on lying, but this isn't a lie. Pollywogs grow into frogs. When I was a kid, my ex-girlfriend and I caught some pollywogs and kept them in a pail of water all summer until they turned into frogs. Their back legs grew first, then their front legs. Eventually, as they got bigger, their tails disappeared. Someone told me the frogs ate their tails, but I think that's a fairy tale."

"Can we do that?"

"What? Eat their tails?"

"No, silly. Catch some pollywogs and watch them turn into frogs. We could keep them in this jar." Rory held up an old Mason jar she had found at the edge of the lake. The edges were chipped and the glass frosted from water and sand. At one time it probably held someone's fishing worms. It had been Rory's intention to secure a frog in its confines, but she was now willing to settle for a few pollywogs.

"I think we can do better than that. I have an old ten-gallon aquarium in my garage. If it doesn't leak, we could use that."

"What's aquarium?"

"It's a large glass container that we can put a piece of the lake into."

"How big of a piece of the lake can we put into it?"

"Ten gallons worth. That's why they call it a ten-gallon aquarium."

"Cool. I'll catch a pollywog." Rory scooped at the water with her Mason jar but came up empty.

"My ex-girlfriend and I used our mothers' strainers to catch pollywogs, but that didn't make our mothers very happy. I don't suppose mothers have changed over the years."

"I think you still like your girlfriend."

"Why is that?"

"You keep talking about her."

"So now you're Ann Landers?"

"Who's Ann Landers?"

"Don't worry about it. She's dead anyway."

"My Mommy says it's not nice to make fun of dead people."

"Is there anything your mother does think is nice?"

"I bet she would like pollywogs."

"I suppose anything's possible. My old girlfriend did."

"See! You're talking about your girlfriend."

"Ex-girlfriend. Let's forget her and catch some pollywogs."

Eric took off his shoes, rolled up his jogging pants, and waded into the water. The water was cold; but then, it was only May. It would warm up by June and July. Despite the sandy bottom, a small amount of silt clouded the water around his feet. Eric waited for the water to clear. Several pollywogs swimming close to the surface came into view. Cupping his hands just below them, Eric slowly raised his hands, allowing water to filter through his fingers.

"You got one!" Rory held out the Mason jar for Eric to place his trophy catch. "Let's catch another one."

"See if you can catch one." Eric stood behind Rory, holding her cupped hands together just below several pollywogs. "Now slowly lift your hands...not too fast or the water will wash the pollywogs away."

"We got two of them!" In her excitement Rory raised her hands too quickly, allowing one pollywog to slip through her fingers. "One of them got away."

"You still have one." Eric held up the Mason jar. "See if you can put it into the jar."

Despite Tiger's assistance, they added six more pollywogs to the jar.

"Look, Tar Zan. There's a crayfish. Can we put a crayfish in an aquarium?"

"If we can catch it."

Eric knelt down on his knees. His jogging pants were already wet. A little more water wouldn't hurt. "They have pincers, so we have to be careful." Eric slowly eased his right hand into the water behind the crayfish. "Hold on to Tiger. We don't need his help on this one." Eric grabbed the crustacean just behind its head. The crayfish's front claws flared up but were unable to reach behind to attack Eric's fingers. "One crayfish for our aquarium." Eric added the reluctant crustacean to the Mason jar.

"That's neat. What else can we put in the aquarium?"

Twenty minutes later the contents of the Mason jar included eight pollywogs, two crayfish, one clam, four water bugs, and a small painted turtle.

"Well, Rory, they look a bit crowded. I think it's about time to see if my old aquarium holds water."

The old aquarium was dusty, but after they washed and cleaned the aquarium, it still held water. Eric placed a layer of beach sand on the bottom along with a few choice stones in a cavelike arrangement, providing shelter for the crayfish. He then anchored a few aquatic plants in the sand for scenery before adding the new tenants.

"We'll keep the aquarium outside on my patio table. That way you can check on them anytime you happen to be at your sitter's. In a month or two, you should see the pollywogs change into frogs."

Rory, with hands pressed against the glass, peered into the aquarium with all the enthusiasm of an inquisitive child.

# 7

"Follow me."

Holly maneuvered the foursome through the crowded lounge toward the bowling lanes. Friday nights were open bowling at the Tamarack Lounge and Lanes. The leagues had completed their seasons in April, but with little else to do on a Friday night, it was not surprising the lanes were full. Excess bowlers waiting for open lanes filled the lounge. A steady flow of beer and pretzels made the wait tolerable.

Sara surveyed the bar with unveiled disgust. A smoky haze lingered over the tables like the morning mist over a mountain lake but smelled like dragon's breath, and the staccato coughing of the chronic lungers did nothing to dissuade the smokers from their nicotine fix.

The smoke-filled bar was inconsistent with Sara's Presbyterian upbringing, and she found such environments intolerable. At least the people were happy. Except for an occasional boisterous argument that permeated above the normal din of the crowd, everyone was in good humor. They drank their beer, ate their pretzels, and smoked their cigarettes.

"I'm glad you called ahead for reservations." Sara mentally thanked the Lord for small favors. "I don't think I could have survived a wait in the lounge."

"Don't I always take care of you?"

Holly led the group toward lane three on the far side of the bowling alley. It was smoke-free but still retained the odor of sweat, dirty socks, and other locker room smells of human activity. Sara sat down on a bench to slip into her rental shoes. It had been an enjoyable evening, much to her surprise. She had accepted the blind date as a favor to Holly. Now she was glad she had. They had just finished a candlelight dinner of fillet mignon in a fancy restaurant where obsequious waiters pampered them while soothing music played in the background. She wasn't a normal patron of such restaurants. Normal fare for her was either McDonalds or Burger King, depending on which restaurant had the best promotional gift with the children's meal. Best of all, at the end of the meal, Aaron and Cory fought over the honor of picking up the tab. Cory won, arguing the gathering was in honor of Holly and Aaron's pending parenthood. Aaron left the tip. That's the way life should be: men arguing over how to pamper women.

Cory sat on the bench beside Sara to put on his non-rental bowling shoes. Sara assumed the bag beside him contained his personal bowling ball.

"Bowlers who own their own ball intimidate me." Sara gave Cory a coy smile. "Bowling isn't my best sport. I may turn out to be an embarrassment."

"Don't worry. We got you covered. We're teammates. It's you and me against them. We're combining the scores."

"Now we'll both lose."

"Actually, I'm not as good as you think. Without my lucky bowling shirt, I'm as formidable as Sampson with short hair."

Sara hadn't wanted to say anything, but Cory's colorful shirt would have made any self-respecting Hawaiian feel self-conscious. She should have suspected it had something to do with the typical male athlete's mental aberration. Men tend to be highly superstitious and ritualistic when it comes to their sports. In high school Eric had a similar fetish for Barq's Root Beer.

"The only reason I bought my own ball is because it's difficult to find a left-handed bowling ball around here."

Sara wasn't sure if Cory was pulling her leg. She would have placed left-handed bowling balls in the same category as left-handed hammers. "So you're a southpaw?"

"Got something against us lefties?"

"No, except it's more work teaching them to write, and they still develop deplorable penmanship."

Cory offered no rebuttal—only a smile. It was a friendly smile and went well with his blue eyes and sandy-blond hair. She could learn to like him.

"The entire world discriminates against left-handers. When I was a kid, I couldn't play on the Little League team because none of the stores in town sold left-handed gloves. Even my service pistol is made for right-handers."

"I wouldn't think that would make a difference."

"The safety lever is on the left side and is meant to be thumb activated. It's more of a nuisance than a true liability."

"How long have you been a deputy?"

"It'll be six years in June."

"I never did thank you for saving my life. The doctors said I would've died if you hadn't found me when you did."

"Hey, forget it. It's part of the job. Now let's go show Holly and Aaron how to bowl."

Despite several gutter balls, Sara eked out a 97 on the first game. That wasn't bad for someone who hadn't bowled in four years. She did better on the second game with a score of 105.

Left-handers may have poor penmanship, but it didn't hinder Cory's bowling skill. The fluid motion of his approach and delivery was almost poetic, producing one strike after another. If Holly had picked bowling to allow Cory to impress Sara, it was working. Sara assumed he could have done well with a right-handed bowling ball right off the rack. With Cory's scores of 212 and 240, they easily surpassed Holly and Aaron's combined scores.

"Cory and I are going to get something to drink. Do you girls want something?" Aaron asked. "As official loser, the treats on me."

"I'll have a Pepsi. No alcohol until the baby's born."

"Diet Pepsi for me," Sara said.

As soon as the men left, Holly gave Sara her *Well, what do you think* look. Sara, feigning ignorance, smiled back, forcing Holly to take a more verbal approach. It was a little cat-and-mouse game they often played when one had information the other was dying to know.

"So? Spill your guts, girl. Do you like him?"

"He's okay."

"He's okay? He's good looking, he has a steady job, he's courteous, he has good manners; and all you can say is, 'He's okay?' I'll bet he'd even put the toilet seat down for you, which is more than I can say for Aaron."

"I really do like him. It's been fun, and I've had a good time—thanks to you and Aaron. I'd forgotten what it's like to have fun."

"Don't forget to thank Cory."

"I won't. Any more questions you're supposed to ask?"

"One more. I'm supposed to ask if you would accept a date with Cory if he were to ask."

"Unless he comes back with a big booger hanging from his nose, the answer would be yes."

"Define big."

"Anything over a half inch."

"Good, I'll tell Aaron that—verbatim."

"Don't you dare!"

Holly waved at Aaron and Cory. They were lingering at the counter, feigning interest in a new bowling ball design while they waited for the *all clear*.

"Here are your drinks, ladies." Cory passed a Diet Pepsi to Sara, and Aaron gave Holly her regular Pepsi.

Holly scrutinized Cory's face. "Well, Sara, it looks like you won't need that measuring stick after all."

"Holly!"

"We missing something here?" Aaron asked.

"I'll tell you later," Holly replied.

"No you won't!" Sara countered.

Cory assuming the private joke was on him decided it was time to change the subject. "How about another game?"

"One more game, and then I need to rescue a babysitter from a five-year-old," Sara said.

It was a quarter past ten when Aaron pulled into Nancy Johnson's driveway, where Sara had left her car. It made little sense to drive home after dropping off her daughter. Cory raced around the car to open Sara's door. It reminded Sara of her senior prom, but it quickly became awkward when he walked her to the door. It had been a fun evening, although she preferred not to end it with a kiss—not with Holly and Aaron watching from the car. Sara rang the doorbell, hoping Nancy would come to her rescue.

"Well, Cory, I want to thank you. It's been an enjoyable evening."

"Maybe we can do it again sometime."

"I'd like that. Maybe next time we could try something different like tennis. I'm better at tennis. That's assuming you can find a left-handed tennis racket."

"You making fun of us lefties again?"

"I'd never do that, but tell me: do they actually make left-handed bowling balls?"

"It's subtle, but the fingering is slightly different."

Nancy turned on the porch light and opened the door. "You two want to come in for some coffee and cookies?" Nancy had a never-ending supply of fresh-baked cookies.

"Thanks, Mrs. Johnson, but no. They're waiting for me in the car. I hope I didn't keep Sara out too late."

"Shucks no. My date for the evening fell asleep on the couch at quarter to nine, halfway through the *Cat In The Hat*. I was just catching the end of the ten o'clock news."

"Thanks again, Cory." Sara stepped inside, carefully closing the door to avoid awakening her daughter.

"I put her things in a bag." Nancy picked up a brown grocery bag. Protruding from the top was *The Cat In The Hat*. "I'll carry it to your car for you. I'm afraid your daughter is too heavy for me to carry."

Sara scooped her daughter off the couch, blanket and all. "Come on, Twinkle Toes. It's time to go home."

# 8

Sara flipped on her wipers to remove the fine mist accumulating on her windshield. It was only a sporadic drizzle, not a hard rain, but it still forced Sara to use her windshield wipers. Normally, Sara would have found the hypnotic *whop, whop* of the wipers agitating—little things like that irritated her—but not tonight. Nothing could ruin her romantic evening that began with a candlelight dinner at a fancy restaurant with linen napkins and obsequious waiters and then ended with three relaxing games of bowling. Life didn't get any better than that.

She had been apprehensive about bowling in the beginning. Bowling never had been her strong suit, but when they added her score to Cory's, they creamed the competition. Sara approached her driveway feeling more upbeat than she had in years. Cory had all but accepted her suggestion to play tennis.

Cory was a pleasant surprise. When she had first seen him in his starched uniform at the trial, he appeared cold and professional, not the type of person she would like to antagonize, but neither was he someone she would care to befriend. She wondered at the time if he were physically capable of smiling. Tonight he was warm and charming. Dressed in his blue jeans and his lucky Hawaiian bowling shirt, no one would have guessed he was a cop. Without much effort, she could easily learn to like him.

Sara was about to turn into her driveway when she noticed the upright flag on her mailbox. She must have nudged the flag upright earlier in the day when she picked up her mail, but deep inside she knew she hadn't. Sara pulled up to the mailbox and rolled down her window. She pushed down the flag, and then after some hesitation opened her mailbox. A lone letter lay on the floor of the mailbox as she had feared.

Sara examined the front of the envelope, hoping for a canceled stamp in the corner. She would have been happy to find an envelope with a window. A utility bill would have made her ecstatic. Instead, she found her name boldly printed in stick letters on the envelope—it was him.

Sara opened the letter but not before rolling up her window and locking her doors. He had written many letters in the past and nothing ever happened. She tried to convince herself tonight would be no different. She shouldn't let his letters intimidate her, but they always did. She knew what he was capable of doing. He didn't need to remind her. Sara held the letter up to the car's dome light.

*Your bowling score was pathetic. Even a grade-schooler could have bowled better than your 97 and 105. Since you haven't left Cade County, I will now have to kill you, and your deputy friend can't stop me. Perhaps I will kill you tonight—or then, maybe I will wait until morning.*

He had been in the lounge watching her bowl. Sara closed her eyes and tried to visualize the people in the lounge, but the lighting had been too dim; and with the thick smoke, Jack-the-Ripper could have been lurking in the shadows and she wouldn't have noticed. He didn't mention the score on her last game. He could have left early to stuff her mailbox and was now miles away. The alternative—that he left the same time she did and stuffed her mailbox minutes ago while she was picking up her daughter—was unsettling. She had spent no more that fifteen minutes at Nancy's house. That would have given him time. Sara looked around for parked cars and found none, but there were many places to hide a car. The overcast sky was deep and dark, and the drizzling rain severely limited visibility. He could be hiding anywhere. She considered spending the night at her father's house. That would provide safety, but he would ask too many questions—questions she preferred not to answer. Eventually she would have to return home. She couldn't hide forever.

Sara drove down the driveway and parked next to her house. She waited several minutes, hoping any stalker would lose patience and make his presence known, but no one jumped out of the shadows. She interpreted that as a good sign. She turned off the ignition and rolled down her raindrop-covered window for a better view. The silence was almost absolute. She heard nothing more than the heavy breathing of her daughter sleeping in the back seat. Occasionally a raindrop dripped off the roof and splashed onto the garbage can lid. The resulting noise seemed sinister and out of place amid the silence.

Sara wished she had the foresight to leave a light on in the house. That would have given her courage. Nothing is darker or more foreboding than an overcast night sky in the country. She could barely see the outline of the house, and the house was no more than thirty feet away. Someone could be standing next to one of the shrubs and she wouldn't notice.

Sara restarted the car and then angle parked so her headlights flooded the backdoor. Bolstered by the headlights on the house, Sara quietly exited the car, locking her daughter inside. If he came after her daughter, the locked car door wouldn't stop him for long. Still, it made her feel like a protective mother.

Sara walked toward the backdoor with her thumb hovering over the red panic button on her key chain. Pushing it would be a useless gesture. No one would hear the car's horn, unless by chance they happened to be driving by. At this time of the night, that was an unlikely scenario. She picked up the gardener's hand trowel she had left beside the house two days earlier when she had been working the flowerbeds. The hand trowel would also be useless unless she could poke him in the eye. She hoped she would never again get that close.

The backdoor was locked just as she had left it. Sara began to relax. A cursory walk around the house revealed no signs of forced entry. Although with her house, it wouldn't require much force; she didn't have any locks on the windows. Her bedroom window was partially open, but then, she remembered cracking open the window in the morning to admit some fresh air. Sara stared at the window for a moment and then tightened her grip on the gardener's trowel; the window was now open more than a crack. Had she opened it that far? She couldn't remember. The opening was still too small for a man to crawl through. Paranoia was overcoming common sense.

Sara returned to the backdoor and keyed it open. She flipped a switch, and an overhead light flooded an empty kitchen. Nothing was out of place. That should be reassuring, but it did nothing to assuage her fear. Irrational fear can be difficult emotion to overcome.

She was alone, but her intruder—if he was actually in the house—wouldn't know that. For all he knew, she could have a deputy sheriff with her—an armed deputy sheriff.

"Cory, can you carry in my daughter for me?"

No villains scurried toward the nearest exit at her suggestion of an armed deputy. The house remained silent. Sara walked through each room of the house while conversing with her imaginary bodyguard. Only after she had meticulously searched each room and every closet did she proclaim the house safe— except for the basement. There was no way she was going to check the basement in the dark. The hook and eye screw latch remained in place near the top of the door. No one could have gone into the basement and then locked the latch behind him. That was close enough. She proclaimed the basement secure. Sara laid the hand trowel on the kitchen table and returned to her car.

"Come on, Twinkle Toes; time to get you into bed."

Sara scooped up her daughter and pushed the car door shut with her butt. Despite the shuffle from car to house, her daughter continued sleeping. She could sleep anywhere.

"Tonight you sleep in your clothes," Sara told her slumbering daughter.

Sara wasn't up to the hassle of getting a sleeping zombie into pajamas, and her daughter didn't seem to care. Sara tucked her daughter into bed and turned on the nightlight in case she needed to make an emergency trip to the bathroom. If that were to happen, it might be time to reconsider the pajamas.

Sara turned off the excess lights and locked the doors. She left the kitchen light on to warn any prowler that someone in the house was awake. Sara re-read the note. The message was quite clear. Tonight was only a threat, but one of these days, he would act on his threats. She considered shredding the note and flushing it down the toilet where it belonged. Instead she added the note to the others in her drawer. She grabbed clean pajamas from the open drawer; her daughter could sleep in her street clothes but Sara would sleep in soft pajamas.

Sara slipped into the pajamas, and then, feeling a chill, walked over to shut the bedroom window. As she closed the window, she noticed a weight at the end of the curtain's drawstring. She pulled on the cord—a dead black and white kitten hung from the end of the cord.

9

Matt Pippin opened the window of his Ford pickup and crushed his cigarette stub on the truck's rusted-out frame. With a flick of his finger, he sent the cigarette butt into the brush alongside the trail. It had rained the day before, and the ground was still damp, eliminating any threat of fire—at least that was how he rationalized his behavior.

The trail—two parallel ruts through the woods—led north off M-28 into the Hiawatha National Forest. It no longer provided any commercial value and was used only by hunters and dirt-bikers—and then only rarely. Matt returned both hands to the wheel to fight through a section of ruts that made steering difficult. Four-wheel drive was not obligatory, but few people ventured down the trail without it. The high ground-clearance of the pickup, however, was mandatory to avoid the protruding rocks.

Matt reached over and relieved Jennifer of the paper-bag-wrapped bottle. He didn't know if it were true, but he had heard cops couldn't bust you for "in possession" unless they could see the bottle—not without a search warrant. He raised the bottle to his lips and took a swig.

"Take it easy on that stuff," Jen said. "This isn't the best road to drive drunk."

"Relax; I'm just drinking enough to mellow me out. I have no intention of getting drunk…stoned, maybe, but not drunk."

Matt passed the bottle back to Jen who took a sip and then wedged the bottle between her thighs to free both hands. She placed her left hand behind Matt's neck and let her fingers creep up into his dark brown hair. She took a drag on the cigarette held in her right hand and coughed out white smoke. She had not yet become accustomed to smoking. Matt eased off the accelerator when he came to a puddle in the road left by the previous day's rain. It was about ten feet across, hopefully not deep. It wasn't necessary, but Matt punched the pickup into four-wheel drive. He stepped on the gas, gunning the truck across the water.

"How much farther is it?" Jennifer asked.

"It's twelve miles from the highway. We got about a mile to go." Minutes later, the trail opened into a clearing.

"That's it," Matt said.

Grass, grown wild over the years, covered most of the clearing. Here and there, half-buried iron pipes, rusty flywheels, and remnants of old steam engines protruded from the sod. A tall structure framed with thick timbers and covered by gray, weathered planks rose almost fifty feet from the center of the clearing. It housed the shaft of the Sage Iron Ore Mine.

Built in the early twenties, it had never turned a profit and was abandoned after five years of operation. Iron ore was abundant in many areas of the Upper Peninsula—this was not one of them.

Matt drove around the structure to ensure they were alone, and then parked behind the building under some trees.

"Looks creepy," Jen said. "Are you sure it's safe?"

"Been up there several times, and it hasn't fallen down yet." Although not intoxicated, Matt had reached that mellowness he had been striving for. He placed the bottle of wine in his school backpack along with a cheap digital camera. "Come on, let's go. It's a beautiful view from up there. Maybe we can get some good pictures. In an hour or so, there should be a decent sunset."

A rusty, nineteen-twenties padlock secured the door to the structure. It was a needless gesture. Matt led Jennifer to a section of the wall where several boards were missing. They stepped inside and waited until their eyes adjusted to the dim light. The inside was dark and damp and smelled of mold, but enough light leaked through the cracks between the wooden planks to outline the remaining carcass of the old mine hoist. The county sealed the mineshaft years ago for safety reasons, but left intact the iron girders and pulleys that raised and lowered the ore carts. They still reached up to the top of the fifty-foot structure.

"There's a small room at the top." Matt took Jennifer's hand and led her to a set of wooden stairs without risers that switch-backed up the far wall. Normally, Jennifer would have been reluctant, but she had also mellowed out on the wine and followed Matt up the creaking stairs without comment.

When Matt reached the top, he pushed up on a trap door providing entry to a twelve-by-fifteen-foot room. Rusty beer cans and broken wine bottles were testimony that they were not the first individuals to use the room.

Matt pushed open two swinging doors, and sunlight flooded into the room. Jennifer backed away. Even with a modest amount of alcohol running through her veins, she had sufficient prudence to shy away from the fifty-foot drop. "They used these doors to bring in heavy equipment," Matt said. "It's a pretty view, isn't it?" The leaves on the trees had unfurled their spring plumage revealing rolling hills of green for as far as they could see. Matt opened his backpack and had a sip of wine, and then he took several pictures from the open doorway.

"Not so close to the edge, Matt. You make me nervous."

Matt stepped back from the door and removed the rest of the backpack's contents. He looked admiringly at a Ziploc sandwich bag with some white crystals at the bottom. He had paid a good sum of money for those crystals. Another bag contained brown, shredded leaves.

Jennifer took a sip of the wine. "That's it?" she asked as she examined the bag of white crystals.

"Twenty grams of high purity methcathinone, the big Cat."

"How long does it last?" Jen asked with mild interest.

"Depends on how you use it. A needle gives you the best rush but doesn't last long. Snorting provides a milder high that lasts a little longer."

"I'm not using any needles."

"Don't have to. We're going to mix it with the marijuana and smoke it."

"How do you know so much about drugs?" Jen asked.

"The Internet—the *Partnership for a Drug-Free America* has a good website."

"What does it feel like?"

"I've only tripped a couple of times, but it gives you a feeling of euphoria, almost like a mental orgasm. You feel like you're floating in air. It gives you endless strength."

"Is it dangerous?"

"It'll make your heart race. People with heart problems have died, but it's safe if you're young and healthy."

"It's still sounds creepy. What if I have a bad trip?"

Matt mixed some of the Cat with the dried marijuana and wrapped it in cigarette paper. "We'll go one at a time. I'll let you go first. I won't take a drag until I know you're not having a bad trip."

Matt raised the supercharged cigarette to his lips and held a match to the tip. He inhaled slowly until the tip glowed red. Then he passed it to Jennifer. "Here, just suck slowly on this and hold your breath as long as you can. It'll give the drug more time to enter your system."

Jen took a drag on the cigarette and held her breath as suggested. After three inhalations, a warm sensation swept through her body. She sat back and giggled. "I feel weird."

"Do you like it?"

"It's sort of neat. But everything is blurry."

"That's because the drug dilates your pupils."

Jennifer closed her eyes, eliminating the blurred vision, which she found pleasantly irritating. She could see much better with her eyes closed; her imagination filled the voids. "I could do this all day."

"Unfortunately, this is all I have. That stuff's not cheap."

"Where'd ya get it?"

"Don't ask. Let's just say I have a friend who can supply all the cocaine, Cat, and marijuana I'll ever need."

"I have ways to make you talk," Jennifer giggled. With eyes still closed, she stood up and began spinning around the room with arms out to her sides like a ballerina. Exotic music, seemingly coming from nowhere, flowed effortlessly from synapse to synapse in the depths of her brain. The beat was intense, constantly increasing in tempo and rhythm. They were playing her song. In a state of ecstasy, she danced around the ballroom, swaying from side to side, while admiring peasants threw rose petals at her feet.

"Careful you don't waltz out the opening," Matt said. "It's a long way to the ground."

"I don't care."

Matt pushed her back when she got close to the opening. After five minutes, Jen's high began to taper. Finally, the music withered and died. Jen sat down in the far corner of the room, a smile still on her face. "That's neat stuff. Can we do it again?"

"I'm next." Matt took a drag on a cigarette heavily laced with Cat. "I'm going to see if I can get a stronger high." He felt a rush but continued inhaling the fumes. This would be his best high yet. After several minutes, the cigarette fell from his hands. The euphoria was overwhelming. He had reached a level he had never before obtained. His feet were weightless, and he floated effortlessly across the room. His energy was without limit. He could leap over tall buildings in a single bound. He was faster than a speeding bullet. Nothing could stop him. He was Superman. He could fly!

Then he heard it: voices. "Someone's coming!"

"I don't hear anyone," Jennifer said.

"Can't you hear the voices?" Beads of sweat clung to Matt's forehead; and his eyes, now fully dilated, had a glazed appearance.

"Stop it, Matt. You're scaring me." But Matt was no longer listening—not to her.

"We got to get out of here."

"Okay, let's go back to the truck." Jen took Matt's hand, pulling him toward the staircase.

"No, not that way. We can't go that way. They're coming up the steps. Don't you hear them? They're coming after us. We need to get out of here. We have to go out this way." Matt headed toward the opening.

"No, Matt!"

"We can do it. We can float to the ground. We can fly."

"Matt, no!"

Matt spread his wings and soared through the opening, flying all the way to the ground. Jennifer heard no scream or cry for help, only a thud like a bag of feed hitting the ground.

\* \* \*

"I wouldn't bother taking off your coat, Chief." Laura didn't look up from her computer where she was typing a report.

"I know I'm a little late for work, but that's no reason to fire the boss."

Laura had been with Stone most of his tenure as County Sheriff. Their constant banter belied the deep mutual respect, which had developed over the years. But today the levity was lost on Stone's secretary. She was not smiling and obviously not in possession of good news. Bad news always meant more paperwork. Stone had sufficient paperwork already sitting on his desk with the recent homicide. He didn't need anything new on his plate.

"Okay, what's up?"

Laura paused in her typing. "Just got a call from Dr. Gillespie at Tamarack Memorial. She has a hysterical patient in the ER who says the Pippin boy killed himself."

"Matt Pippin?" Stone knew him only by reputation. He was one of the best running backs ever to come out of Tamarack High, earning a full scholarship at Michigan State.

"That would be the one."

"Suicide?"

"Depends on your definition. According to the girlfriend, he was doing drugs and decided to jump off the top of the Sage mine shaft building. Thought he could fly."

"They should burn that damned building to the ground." Stone assumed this would take the better part of the day—and not a pleasant day at that. "I suppose the parents haven't been notified?"

"Not yet."

Much as he hated that job, he wouldn't feel right delegating that responsibility to one of his deputies. That's why the county paid him the big bucks, he told himself.

"Dr. Gillespie says there's a chance it's a false alarm, but she's not optimistic. The girlfriend is a basket case. She couldn't force herself to take the truck keys from Matt's pocket—apparently he's a mess. Instead, she walked all night to reach the highway twelve miles away. She's being admitted for psychiatric observation."

"We got anyone on the scene?" Stone asked.

"Not yet, Cory Kramer's on his way there in the Search and Rescue van and should be on site in fifteen minutes. He said he'd call in when he gets there. If you're heading out there, he wants you to bring the camera."

"Doesn't Kramer get off at seven?"

"Koski's tied up with a finder bender on the east side of the county, and Kramer was already patrolling in the Sage Mine area. I asked him to put in a couple hours of overtime. He jumped at the opportunity. Apparently, dating the Higgins girl has placed a dent in his budget."

"I'll never make it out to the mine shaft in my wife's Subaru," Stone said in his most pathetic voice. "My car's at the repair shop. You wouldn't know anyone with a Jeep Cherokee I could borrow?"

Laura pulled a key ring from her purse and tossed it at her boss. "Just don't scratch the rust. That's all that's holding the car together."

"Laura, you're a doll. Remind me to double your Christmas bonus."

"The county doesn't give us a bonus."

"Well, I'm going to double it anyway. I don't know why Lois isn't jealous of you. Maybe she thinks no one will have me just because I'm old, bald, and highly irritable before my morning cup of coffee."

"Personally, I think Lois is a saint for putting up with you for—what is it now—forty years?"

"It'll be forty-two next August, but who's counting." Stone headed toward the door. "I won't have access to a radio, so you get to hold down the fort until I return."

"Chief?…the camera…you forgot the camera." Laura walked over to the counter and pulled a black canvas bag from the cupboard. "You remember how to use the Polaroid?"

"Hey, I'm just a police chief. I never claimed to be good at 'chinery."

"It's fully automatic. Take the cover off the lens and aim though the viewfinder. Push the red button when you're ready. The picture will pop out and develop on its own. I placed an extra box of film in the bag. Cory can show you how to change film."

"Am I excused now?"

"Go on; get out of here."

The Cade County Ambulance was on scene when Stone arrived. Dr. Gillespie was in a huddle with Cory Kramer and one of the paramedics. No one was in a hurry. Stone didn't find that surprising. There's little you can do for a person who falls fifty feet other than scoop up body parts. This was now a crime scene, and no one could even remove the body parts until cleared by the appropriate authorities.

Dr. Gillespie was present as county medical examiner. She would have to authorize the release of the body to the funeral home. In this case she would request an autopsy. Stone pitied the pathologist who would get the job.

Carrie Gillespie was one of the few students who returned to Cade County. Most of the smarter kids who left for college never looked back. Cade County had nothing to offer. All the high paying jobs were downstate. Smart kids followed the opportunities, and Cade County wasn't one of them. Stone assumed Dr. Gillespie could have had a more lucrative practice in the big cities, but there had never been any doubt in Dr. Carrie Gillespie's mind as to where she would reside following her family practice residency. Home was home, and she had no desire to practice elsewhere. Now in her fifth year of practice, she was a great asset to the community.

Stone pulled the black camera bag from the back seat of the Cherokee and walked over to join the conference. On the ground in front of the mineshaft building, he could see what had to be the corpse. A white sheet stained red in several places covered the body.

"Here, Cory." Stone passed the camera bag to his deputy. "I'll let you take the pictures. You're better at it than I am." Stone had no desire to look at the body. There had to be some advantages to making the big bucks. "What do we have so far?"

Cory placed the strap of the camera bag over his shoulder. "It appears it happen like Jennifer Wilkins described to Dr. Gillespie. We found two bags of drugs. One looks like marijuana. The other one had some white crystals. My bet is Methcathinone. I checked the room at the top. No bloodstains or evidence of trauma. There was a bottle of wine, which was almost empty. Want me to show you the room?"

Stone looked up at the loft at the top of the old, weathered building. "That's okay. I'll look at your pictures."

"How do you identify the body in a case like this?" Carrie asked. "He landed face down. There's no facial features left. Even his dental records will be useless."

"Just before I left the office, Matt's parents declared him missing; we have an eye witness who saw him jump; and I'm sure the plates will confirm it's his truck. If we can find I.D. on the body, we'll call it close enough for Cade County."

"I'll still order an autopsy," Carrie said. "The gross exam won't show much, but the toxicology report should be interesting. What about Jennifer Wilkins? Is she going to face charges?"

Stone looked over at the corpse. Cory had removed the sheet and was taking pictures. "No, unfortunately, there's no law against stupidity. We could get her for a few minor charges like 'minor in possession.' That would be all. If you can get her into a good rehab program, I'll talk the prosecuting attorney into dropping the charges."

"I think she just graduated from a very painful rehab program, but she's still going to need help."

"We can't do much for Matt Pippin," Stone said. "If we can turn Jennifer Wilkins' life around, maybe we'll have earned a day's pay."

"Were you ever that dumb when you were a kid?" Carrie asked.

"No, I was dumber. A police officer once caught me doing something stupid. He could have thrown the book at me...sent me to reform school. But he didn't. Lord knows I deserved it. Instead, he gave me a no-holds-barred lecture. Put the fear of God into my soul. Then he took me under his wing. Watched me like a hawk for the next couple of years to make sure I went straight. I owe everything to that cop. He died about eight years ago."

"Sounds like quite a police officer. Who was he?"

"My father."

To avoid further embarrassment, Carrie looked away when Stone's eyes began to water.

"They don't make police officers like him anymore," Stone said.

"I think they still do," Carrie replied.

Stone felt a sudden chill. "If you'll excuse me, I think I'll get my jacket from the car. It's a bit chilly this morning."

Days like this made Stone hate his job. If he had control of the illicit drug trafficking, this wouldn't have happened. Two drug related deaths in as many weeks, far too many on his watch. Even more depressing was the lack of progress in the investigation. Forensics came up with zilch on the Michael Morrison murder. It was a professional job by someone with knowledge of forensic techniques, but that was what made them professionals. A background check on Morrison revealed nothing more than a valid Illinois driver's license. It was as if he didn't exist.

The only lead in the murder, if you could call it a lead, was Eric Kampe. Kampe had a documented history of drug abuse, and he had proven himself capable of such brutality; the photos of Sara Higgins left little doubt of that. Kampe was under surveillance, but it's difficult, if not impossible, to follow someone at night—not on rural roads where the headlights of the tailing car are the only other lights on the road. Maybe it was time to ask Judge Madalinski for a warrant to place a homing device on Kampe's car. With Pippin's death, he would likely approve it.

Stone slipped into his jacket and zipped it half way up. There were few clouds in the sky, and Stone assumed it would be warm by noon, making for another nice day, but not for the Pippin family; they would not have a nice day.

Matt Pippin's body, now re-covered by the sheet, lay motionless on the cold ground. An occasional breeze fluttered a corner of the sheet. Stone had seen similar scenes countless times over the years, each different, yet each the same, whether it be a gunshot wound or motor vehicle accident. He never could get used to it.

Stone walked over to the body. Cory was adding a new film pack to the camera. Apparently, he had sufficient photos of the corpse. "You got all the pictures you need?" Stone asked. It was more idle talk than a serious question and not motivated by any need to know.

"I got all I need of the body. I need to get some pictures of the loft."

"If you don't have any objections, I'm going to release the body to Dr. Gillespie for the autopsy." Stone turned to leave. "I'm heading back to the office."

"Chief, you might find this interesting," Cory held up a clear plastic bag. "It's his personal effects." Cory passed the bag to the chief.

"You found something of interest?"

"The wallet has the usual stuff: some folding money, a driver's license, an unused condom, and an old lottery ticket."

"So?"

"The lottery ticket has a phone number on the back. I called the office to have Laura run it down…It's Eric Kampe's."

"That won't hold much water in court," Stone said, "but it'll buy us a wiretap with Judge Madalinski." Stone reached into the bag and removed the condom. "Matt's personal effects will eventually be returned to his parents. I don't think they need to see the condom." Technically, it was tampering with evidence, but this would never go to court, Stone rationalized. You can't punish a dead man. "If you need me, I'll be at the office most of the morning, but right now I'm heading over to the Pippin place. Try to keep the news media away for another hour."

The Pippins lived in a small subdivision on the outskirts of Tamarack. Most of the houses in town were small and poorly constructed. The logging companies built them during the heyday of the logging years when family roots were shallow and people didn't expect to stay long. Since they built the houses on company land, lots were small, leaving little elbowroom between structures. People like the Pippins who had well-paying jobs shunned such areas, preferring to build in the newer subdivisions where lots were generous and houses spacious.

Stone was relieved to find two cars in the driveway when he arrived. Jack Pippin worked as a truck driver for a local logging company. With his son missing, he had apparently taken the day off. Stone preferred talking to both parents. They would need each other's support when he left.

Elaine Pippin was watching him through the bay window as Stone walked along the flagstone path toward the front door. An elevated stone flower box ran alongside the house terminating in the concrete steps leading up to the front door. Newly planted marigolds filled the flower box, some already in flower. The Pippins took pride in their home.

The front door opened before Stone could push the doorbell. Jack and Elaine Pippin stood in the doorway clinging to each other for support.

"He's dead isn't he?" Jack asked, hoping for a quick denial.

"May I come in?"

Neither Pippin responded other than to back away from the doorway, allowing Stone to enter their spacious living room. "Please sit down, Mr. and Mrs. Pippin. We need to talk." Jack and Elaine Pippin sat on a couch facing the soft-back chair Stone had chosen. Their faces were expressionless except for the tears cascading down Elaine's cheeks. They weren't going to make this easy. "Last night just before dark, Matt fell fifty feet from the top of the Sage mine shaft building. We didn't recover the body until this morning."

Elaine's head dropped into her hands and she wept openly. Jack tightened his fists into convoluted masses of muscle and bone. His stoic face faded as facial muscles tensed into a well-controlled rage. "It was drugs. He was on drugs, wasn't he?"

"It appears so. I'm very sorry."

"Sorry? You're sorry?" Jack stood up, his anger no longer controlled. "Sorry won't bring back our son."

"Please, Jack, he's only doing his job." Elaine pulled on Jack's arm, and Jack collapsed back into his chair. He, too, began to weep.

There's something devastating about a man crying, something that destroys the equilibrium of a person's soul. Stone sat back in his chair and let them cry. He had no words of wisdom. He had nothing to offer that would assuage their pain. They would have questions; but for now, they needed a few minutes to express their grief. It was déjà vu. How many times had he re-lived this scenario? He would allow them to cry, venting their grief. Once they were emotionally drained, they would pull themselves together forming a façade of strength for the benefit of visitors. Tonight, after all visitors and well-meaning friends left, the real grieving would begin.

"We told him those drugs would harm him," Elaine said, "but he wouldn't listen."

"Do you know where these kids are getting their drugs?" Jack asked.

"We don't know for sure. We have some leads," Stone said. "We'll get the pusher who provided the drugs. That's a promise." Stone wished he felt that confident. He had to tell them something; he had to give them hope.

"It was that Kampe boy, wasn't it?" Anger again replaced sorrow. Jack rhythmically opened and clutched his fists.

"We don't know that for a fact."

"He raped and almost killed the Higgins girl. What other facts do you need?" Jack's voice grew louder, augmented by his anger. "All he got was five years. Five stinking years. Scum like him don't change. He was into drugs before, and he's into them now."

Assuming it would be counterproductive to argue the point, Stone sat in silence, letting Jack vent his anger. Jack Pippin was a reasonable man. He would calm down in time. Stone wasn't sure he would react differently if it were his son lying in a morgue waiting for an autopsy.

"If you don't take care of Kampe, I'll get some of the boys together, and we'll take care of him ourselves."

Stone hoped it was only anger talking. "Sir, you have my word that I and everyone on my force will do everything possible to find the individual or individuals responsible for bringing drugs into Cade County." Stone stood up to leave. "Our office will keep you informed. If you have any further questions, call the office and ask to speak directly to me."

# 10

"Hello, Papa."

Don Higgins looked up from his desk. It was Saturday afternoon, the time he normally reserved for preparing his Sunday sermon. "Sara, this is a pleasant surprise. How's my favorite daughter?"

"Fine, thank you, but the compliment would be more flattering if I weren't your only daughter."

"How about my favorite granddaughter?"

"Your favorite granddaughter is over at my favorite babysitter's. Nancy said she'd watch her for an hour or so." Sara looked at the picture sitting proudly on her father's desk. It had been fifteen years since her mother's death, yet Ruth Higgins's portrait still commanded a place of honor on the desk, always watching as her husband wrote his Sunday sermons. Some marriages extended far beyond *until death do us part*. "It's such a nice Saturday afternoon; I was hoping you might be up to a walk around the lake. It's short sleeve weather, just like summer."

Pastor Higgins pushed aside the pad of paper on which he had been scribbling. "I'm sure this sermon can wait. If God gives us a day like this, it would be sacrilegious to waste it."

"It is, indeed, a gorgeous day," Pastor Higgins told his daughter when he stepped into the sun light. The temperature was in the seventies, and the slight breeze was more refreshing than chilly. The sun, now high in the sky, radiated down with such intensity that it would have quickly sunburned the pastor's bald head had it not been for his broad-brimmed hat. The black hat was his personal trademark, and few people ever caught the pastor on the streets of Cade County without it.

"Sara, I think a walk around the lake with a beautiful woman is just what an old man like me needs to stimulate the gray matter. Maybe it will provide inspiration for tomorrow's sermon. I'm afraid the sermon was starting to drag," Don confessed. "It wouldn't be the first time I've conjured up a spirited sermon while walking around Harley Lake. Sometimes I feel God placed the lake in our back yard just for me."

Sara walked quietly beside her father, letting him provide the bulk of the conversation. Like most pastors, he was good at one-sided conversations, although he could be a compassionate listener if the need were to arise. His conversations were always so upbeat, dwelling on the many wonders God had created just for him. The only time she had seen him sad was at the death of her mother. He could find no silver lining in that cloud. Even so, it never interfered with his church obligations. He delivered a stimulating Sunday sermon two days after her funeral. If Nancy hadn't stepped in when she did, Sara was sure he would have fulfilled the obligations for both mother and father.

"Sara?"

"Yes, Papa."

"I'm thoroughly enjoying this stroll around the lake, but I don't believe you invited me on this walk out of concern for my health. You have something on your mind, girl. What's going on in that highly educated brain of yours?"

"Well, I do something I wish to talk about." Sara stared at the path ahead of her, avoiding her father's eyes, which she knew were now focused on her. Her father was a good listener, but this would still to be a difficult conversation. She didn't know where to begin.

"You want to talk to Don Higgins, the father, or Rev. Don Higgins, the pastor?"

"Probably both."

"That's good. No matter which one you talk to, the other one always wants to listen in. And what, pray tell, is the topic of concern on this gorgeous Saturday afternoon?"

"I'm not sure where life is taking me, and it's beginning to scare me. I feel like I'm losing control of my destiny."

"I won't be much help there. I'm fifty-five years old, and I'm still not sure where life's taking me." Don paused, allowing his daughter to elaborate if she so wished; she did not. "Nancy tells me you've been dating someone."

"I've gone bowling with Cory Kramer. We played tennis a couple of times and seen a movie together. That's about it. Nothing serious."

"Isn't he the deputy sheriff who testified at the trial?"

"Yes, he's the one."

"He seemed like a pleasant fellow. And now you want to know if he's the right one for you?"

"No, I already know the answer to that."

"And that would be?"

"Cory's nice, but I don't feel attracted to him. I feel no emotion, no hot desire. That's part of the problem. I don't think I ever will...with anyone. Maybe I'm expecting too much out of a relationship."

"If you're not expecting much out of a relationship, you don't have much of a relationship. Sometimes even casual associations can develop into meaningful relationships with time. You and Cory might hit it off once you know each other better."

"Not with Cory. I don't think he likes my daughter. He hasn't come out and said it, but I can tell. Men don't like women who come with baggage. Any man I marry will have to marry both of us, and that'll never happen. But that doesn't bother me. I can survive as a single mom."

"Sara, there are many fish in the sea, some worth catching and others need to be thrown back. You might yet find your Prince Charming. But if you don't have your hook in the water, you'll never catch anything. And might I add you have excellent bait."

"Papa, you're talking in parables again, definitely the preacher in you coming out."

"So I am. Maybe I can work that into tomorrow's sermon. The Lord always was partial to a good parable."

"Do you have any parables to explain why a caring God would let bad things happen to me? I don't think I've been that bad."

"I could do an entire sermon on why bad things happen to good people."

"Can you give me the *Cliff's Notes* version? The bike path is only so long."

"You must remember; I'm only a country pastor. My interpretation of the universe may be less astute than that of the theologians in the big prestigious seminaries. Do you remember when you were learning how to ride a bike? You fell and broke your arm."

"Yes, Papa. I had a cast on half the summer and couldn't go swimming."

"As a parent, I could have prevented that by not giving you the bike. It hurt me almost as much as it did you when you came into my study with your forearm bent where it shouldn't bend. As soon as the cast came off, you wanted to get back on the bike. I wanted to protect you and not let you get back on the bike, but your mother—always the practical one—said we had to let you try out your wings. We had to let you fly. I think God gives us enough freedom so we can try out our wings, and sometimes we get hurt. He probably feels bad when we get hurt just like I did when you broke your arm. I think he only intervenes with a miracle or two in extreme cases."

Sara looked up at her father. He was so sure of his faith. Sara had tried to be faithful, but every now and then she wondered if God really cared about her. Was he really watching out for her or was he looking the other way.

"Papa, do you think God still does miracles? You don't hear of people turning water into wine anymore."

"Of course God still performs miracles. It's just that today's miracles are more sophisticated than in biblical times. Any second rate magician can turn water into wine."

"Okay, name one modern day miracle," Sara said.

"Fair enough. You may not know this, but your mother and I thought we would never have children. We went from doctor to doctor. We went to the best fertility clinics. They all said your mother was incapable of having children. Finally we had to face the fact that there would be no children in our life. We had to accept the collective wisdom of the best medical minds of the time. Your mother was devastated. It was even more painful for her knowing that there was nothing wrong with my sperm. She was to blame. We gave up on the doctors and fertility clinics, but we never gave up loving each other. Six months later she became pregnant. Sara, you are our miracle. Personally, I think God was showing off—just letting a simple country pastor know that it takes more than a man and a woman to create a baby."

"That's not fair. Why hasn't God given me any miracles? I could use a few miracles in my life."

"The doctors thought it was a miracle you survived that assault," Don said. "They thought you were going to die."

"I survived because of the excellent medical care. If God really wanted to perform a miracle, he could have prevented the attack all together."

"Would you be willing to give up your daughter?"

That was Sara's dilemma. She wasn't willing to give up her daughter. The nightmares, the threatening letters, and the constant feelings of paranoia were devastating. They were causing her to lose control of her life. Yet, as terrible as they were, her daughter had been worth all that pain. She wouldn't undo the assault even if she could. Would she really be happy if God had prevented it from happening?

"I still think God owes me a miracle."

"I'm not a great theologian, but I can tell you this: God is always good on his word. If he owes you a miracle, he'll see that you get it. But he'll choose the time and the place."

Momentarily devoid of thoughts, Sara walked silently along the bike path with her father. It was a beautiful day, and just walking in silence beside someone you loved was reward in itself. It was late May, and the leaves on the trees had fully unfurled. The spring flowers were approaching the end of their season and beginning to die, yet enough remained to paint a mosaic pattern on the forest floor. Tall trees arched over the trail forming a virtual tunnel.

The picture was hardly a still life. A pair of gray squirrels chased each other from tree to tree. Probably part of their mating ritual, Sara thought. And two teenagers on roller blades cruised down the pathway, their fingers intertwined. That, too, was a courtship ritual. Sara could remember when she and Eric had roller-bladed down this same pathway. They had been contemplating marriage. They would have had a lifetime of happiness if it hadn't been for the incident. Sara forced the thought from her mind.

"See those kids swinging on the rope?" Sara's father pointed to some kids swinging from a rope tied to an overhanging tree branch. It reminds me of when Eric and you thought you were Tarzan and Jane. You spent the entire summer swinging from a rope with that deer following you everywhere you went. What was the name of that deer?"

"Tiger."

"Yes, Tiger. That was one of the hardest things I've ever done, when I put Tiger down. I knew how much that deer meant to you and Eric. I felt like a murderer."

They again walked along the bike path in silence. They were passing the halfway point. If she were to discuss it with her father, she couldn't delay it any longer.

"Papa?"

"Yes."

"Which do you think is more important, the Old or the New Testament?"

"That's like asking if a nice, thick, juicy steak is better than an ice cream sundae. Each has its virtues. For me it depends on my mood and what I wish to get out of it."

Just ahead, the trail opened into a clearing. A park bench with legs imbedded in concrete looked out over the lake.

"Let's sit awhile on the bench. It provides one of the better views of the lake. I often come here to think, and you're asking questions that require some thought."

Sara sat down beside her father. It was indeed a beautiful view. A mallard duck with seven newborn ducklings played in the shallow water by their feet.

"I think I like the Old Testament for its literary value."

"Literary value?"

"Most people don't think of literary value when they talk about the Bible, but the Old Testament has some beautiful poetry people often overlook. My favorite is the twenty-third Psalm. It's best in the old King James Version. Close your eyes and just focus on the powerful imagery."

Sara closed her eyes.

"*The Lord is my Shepard I shall not want. He maketh me to lie down in green pastures. He leadeth me beside the still waters. He restoreth my soul.* Sara, can you see those green pastures beside the still waters? When I visualize it, the still waters always look like Harley Lake."

"I can picture it," Sara said, "but I don't think my picture is as pretty as yours."

"*He leadeth me in the paths of righteousness for his name's sake. Yea, though I walk through the valley of the shadow of death, I will fear no evil, for Thou art with me.* Walk through the valley of the shadow of death, now that's powerful poetry."

"That valley I can visualize," Sara said. "I've been through that valley more than once."

"*Thy rod and thy staff they comfort me. Thou preparest a table before me in the presence of mine enemies.*"

"I think I've also been at the table with my enemies."

"*Thou anointest my head with oil; my cup runneth over. Surely goodness and mercy shall follow me all the days of my life; and I will dwell in the house of the Lord forever.* I've never been one to memorize Bible verses feeling it was a form of Christian vanity, but the twenty-third Psalm is so beautiful, I had to memorize it."

"Papa, I don't know how you can always find something positive in everything. Whenever I hear the twenty-third Psalm, I think of old black-and-white James Cagney movies where someone is heading off to the electric chair...What about the New Testament?"

"My favorite section of the New Testament would have to be the Sermon on the Mount. That was one of the most magnificent speeches I've ever heard. *Blessed are the poor: for theirs is the kingdom of God. Blessed are they that mourn: for they shall be comforted. Blessed are the meek: for they shall inherit the earth. Blessed are they that hunger: for they shall be fed. Blessed are the peacemakers: for they shall be called the children of God.* That speech was so powerful it would make any present-day politician green with envy. But then Jesus had a good speechwriter—one of the best. Even if a politician came up with a speech like that, they'd never be able to deliver on the promises."

"What about the philosophies of the two testaments? They're so different. The New Testament is all about non-violence: thou shalt not kill, turn the other cheek, love your enemies. And in the Old Testament people are always killing each other out of jealousy, hatred, or revenge. Is killing someone always wrong?"

"That does present a dilemma. *Thou shalt not kill* is Old Testament, of course, being part of the Ten Commandments. Some theologians feel is one of the newer commandments."

"How can that be a newer commandment?" Sara asked. "Moses brought all ten commandments down from Mt. Sinai at the same time."

"True, but they had attorneys and legal beagles in ancient times who weren't above twisting the laws, even God's laws, just like present-day lawyers. Some people believe the original commandment was: *Thou shalt not murder.*"

"What's the difference?"

"Not much at all to the person who is killed. Murder is the taking of a human life when not sanctioned by law. In our society it is not considered murder when a police officer shoots someone in the line of duty or a man kills another in time of war. Stoning a prostitute was considered proper punishment in biblical days."

"Is killing someone in self-defense wrong?"

"Quakers would say it is, but most people would consider it justified. Sara, we've been beating around the bush for half an hour. Why don't you tell me what's bothering you?"

Sara looked down at her feet. Her fingers toyed with a small twig she had somehow come to possess. "Papa, please don't be angry with me, but last week I purchased a gun—a .38 caliber pistol."

"Do you even know how to shoot it?"

"Cory took me to the police range. I'm really quite good at it—at least at shooting targets."

"I assume this gun is not for shooting rabbits?"

"No, I could never shoot a rabbit...unless it was attacking my daughter. Maybe I could shoot over the rabbit's head and scare it away."

"Is that what this is about? Eric Kampe is out on parole, and you think he might harm your daughter?"

"Eric would never harm my daughter. I'm not sure, but I don't think he would even hurt me."

"If someone wanted to hurt you, he would be the logical person. Why would anyone else want to hurt you?"

Sara looked back at the ground. "I can't tell you that, Papa. When I was at college, I took a self-defense course for women. We learned how to break chokeholds and block knife thrusts. It was a lot of fun, but I don't think it would help me in real life. I'll probably never use the gun, but I sleep better knowing I have it."

"Sara, see that mother duck and her seven ducklings? Life would be a lot easier for her if she could just fly away and be on her own. But she stays with her ducklings. She hides them in time of danger and gathers them under her wing when the weather is cold. She will do whatever it takes to protect her young. A killdeer will fake a broken wing to lure a fox away from its chicks. That's the way it's been for eons. Mothers, and in some species fathers as well, do what they can to protect their young. That's God's way."

"Papa, would you have killed someone to protect me?"

"Don Higgins, the father, would do it in a heartbeat, but Rev. Don Higgins, the pastor, would live in guilt for the rest of his life."

Sara watched as the mother duck climbed up onto the shore. Her seven ducklings dutifully followed. "You know, Papa, the thing I remember most about when Mama was alive was how we used to come down to the lake and feed bread crumbs to the ducks. It's amazing how little things in life have a way of sticking in your memory."

"Your mother and I still feed the ducks, but she watches from above."

"I wish we would have thought to bring some bread."

Pastor Higgins removed his broad-brimmed hat from his head revealing a sandwich bag filled with crusts of bread perched on his bald head.

"Oh, Papa!"

"You didn't think I would walk around the lake and forget to feed the ducks, did you?"

For the next few minutes, father and daughter, absorbed in the mystic enchantment of Harley Lake, fed the ducks. Worldly problems were momentarily set aside as they watched the young ducklings run helter-skelter after the coveted morsels of bread.

"Sara," Don said when the last of the bread was devoured, "I don't understand all that is going on in your life, but your mother and I tried to teach you good Christian values. I think you know right from wrong. If your mother were here, she would say we have to let you try your wings. We have to let you fly and pray you don't get hurt. You have to use your best judgment—follow your heart. Whatever you do, whatever you decide, your mother and I are behind you one hundred percent."

"Oh, Papa." Sara threw her arms around her father's neck. "That's what I wanted to hear."

# 11

Eric shimmied a sheet of plywood onto the entryway's north wall and secured it in place with ten-penny nails. Repairing the entryway was taking longer than he had anticipated. A team of hired carpenters could have finished the job in five days. He had been working on it for three weeks, and it was only now taking shape. It wasn't that he was in a hurry; he had no plans for the future. Future remained a nebulous concept at best. No one in Cade County was about to hire a rapist, and the prospect of sitting around the house all day failed to excite him. At the moment, he didn't need a job. The revenue from the gas station provided a decent income—more than enough to cover his needs—as long as Bob Thompson was the manager. If Eric were to manage the gas station, the income would evaporate in no time.

"Hi, Tar Zan."

"Hi there, Rory." Eric firmly secured the plywood with two more nails and then climbed down from his stepladder. "Haven't seen you around for a couple of days."

"I only stay with Aunt Nancy on weekdays when Mommy's working. I came to see if the pollywogs turned into frogs."

"They aren't going to change that fast. It's only been two weeks." Eric walked over to the aquarium. Rory and Tiger followed closely behind. The three of them peered at the pollywogs through the aquarium glass.

"Can't see much from here," Eric said. "Let me get a strainer." Eric disappeared into the house and returned with a kitchen strainer. "Let's see if we can catch a pollywog."

Eric scooped up one of the pollywogs swimming near the surface and dumped it onto his palm. "See those small structures on the belly just in front of the tail? Those are the beginnings of hind legs."

"That's neat," Rory said. Tiger sniffed at the pollywog, but wasn't impressed.

"In two or three weeks, it'll begin to grow front legs, and the tail will shrink. Right now it can't breathe air so we need to return it to the water." Eric placed his hand into the water, and the pollywog took off to join the others. "We should check them once a week."

"So what do you think of my new entryway?" Eric stepped back to admire his work.

"It looks okay."

"Okay? It's just okay? I thought it looked pretty spiffy. I've spent a lot of time on it."

"I bet you could make a neat tree house."

"My ex-girlfriend and I made one when we were kids. It was a pretty decent tree house if I do say so myself." Eric had forgotten that tree house. He and Sara had built the floor from scraps of lumber and the walls from old cardboard boxes. It only lasted three weeks, until a hard rain came and destroyed the cardboard. That was the Tarzan and Jane summer. The tree house was an essential component of their childhood delusion.

Eric surveyed the pile of discarded lumber lying around his yard. "Tell you what. If I have enough lumber left over, I'll see if we can build a tree house." Eric pointed to a large, sprawling maple near the bike trail. "See that tree. The trunk's on my lot. We could build a tree house on the lower branches. Don't want it too high off the ground. If you fell and hurt yourself, your mother would have my hide."

"Cool, can we start today?"

"Relax," Eric said. "I didn't promise I'd do it. I said if I have enough leftover lumber. Right now, Tiger and I have to repair this entryway."

"Tiger's a dog. He can't help repair your house. My Mommy says it's not nice to lie."

"Where have I heard that line before?" Eric asked. "Tiger's a CAT"

"Is not," Rory said defiantly. "He's a dog."

"Not cat, C-A-T. It stands for Carpenter Assistant in Training. Watch this...Tiger, fetch the hammer." Tiger gave Eric a bored look, then walked over to the hammer, picked it up, and returned it to Eric. "Good boy, Tiger." Eric set the hammer down on top of a sawhorse and scratched Tiger behind the ear. "Rory, how's that for a good CAT?"

"Neat. What other tricks can he do?"

"I'll show you today's lesson. Tiger, fetch saw." Tiger walked past the saw, picked the hammer off the sawhorse, and returned it to Eric's feet. Eric rewarded Tiger with a pat on the head despite the poor performance. "We'll have to work on the saw. Maybe when you come back next week, he'll have the saw mastered."

"I might not be around next week," Rory said.

"How come?"

"School's almost out, and Mommy doesn't work in the summer."

"Tiger and I are going to miss you."

"I'll still stay with Aunt Nancy whenever Mommy plays tennis with her new boyfriend." Rory stuck her hands into the pockets of her jeans and kicked at a stone, her cheerful smile gone.

"Do I detect some problems with this new boyfriend?"

"I don't think he likes me." Rory stared at the ground, her hands still deep in her pockets.

"That does present a problem," Eric said. "We need to think this out." Eric couldn't remember seeing Rory without her ubiquitous smile. "You know, Rory, I do my best thinking over a bowl of ice cream. You think that would help?"

Rory nodded in the affirmative.

"I'll be right back." Eric entered the house and returned with a tub of ice cream and three bowls. He set the bowls on the patio table beside the aquarium and filled them with ice cream. Then he covered the ice cream in one bowl with chocolate syrup. "Tiger prefers his ice cream with chocolate syrup." Eric placed the bowl on the ground. "You want some chocolate on yours?"

Rory again nodded in the affirmative.

Eric squirted chocolate syrup on the remaining two bowls of ice cream and gave one to Rory. "You'll have to excuse Tiger's table manners. For some reason he refuses to use a spoon."

"You're being silly, dogs can't use spoons."

"Now that's the same thing Tiger told me. I thought he was lying."

Unable to control herself, Rory burst out in a giggle. "Tiger would never do that; it's not nice to lie."

"What makes you think your mother's boyfriend doesn't like you?"

Rory's smile immediately vanished. "He never talks to me, and he always makes me feel like I'm in the way."

"I suppose that would make anyone feel unwanted." Eric took a bite of ice cream. "Do you know Abe Lincoln?"

"No."

"He's the guy on the penny."

"You know him?" Rory asked.

"Not personally, but I've been told he had a plaque on his desk that said, *I don't like that man. I'll have to get to know him better.* Maybe it's too early to make judgments. Maybe your mother's boyfriend will like you after he gets to know you better."

"Maybe."

"Have you talked to your mother about this?"

"No...She's too busy with her boyfriend."

"I suppose now you have to share your mother. That can be tough. I'm sure she still loves you, but sometimes that kind of love isn't enough. As people get older, they need another kind of love. That doesn't mean she loves you any less. Your mother's boyfriend makes her happy and maybe fills a void in her life. She might even marry him some day."

"Yuck!" Rory scrunched up her nose. "Why would she want to do that? She doesn't have to marry him to play tennis."

"That part you won't understand until you get a set of raging hormones of your own. But if she does marry him, your life will change, perhaps for the better...Look at those pollywogs. They're swimming around doing their own thing. They all appear happy don't they?"

Rory nodded.

"They don't know it, but their lives are changing, and they have no control over it. Someday they'll be frogs. They'll no longer be able to breathe under water but will have to come to the surface for air. They'll jump around with their legs instead of swimming with their tails. Those are some serious changes in their lives. But who is to say the life of a pollywog is any better than that of a frog? Not that it matters; the pollywogs have no choice in their future.

"You're like one of those pollywogs. You're happy as you are, but life is changing, and you have no control over it. The only difference is, unlike the pollywogs, you can see the changes coming, and it's making you nervous. The change might be for the better. If your mother marries her boyfriend, you might wind up with two loving parents. That's the way it's supposed to be."

"I'd rather be a pollywog."

"Your mother won't marry him unless she thinks the change will be good for both of you."

"You're not married, and you're happy."

"I'm hardly the happiest pollywog in the pond." Eric replied. "You may not be aware of this, but right now you and Tiger are the only friends I have. In the next month or two I'll have to make some serious changes in my life, maybe leave town. I need to turn into a frog."

"You talk funny."

"I know... I'm starting to sound like Ann Landers," Eric admitted.

"You said she's dead."

"That she is, but her philosophies live on." Eric scooped up the empty bowls. "Why don't you and Tiger play? I have to work on the house. The sooner I finish, the sooner we can work on that tree house."

"Okay, Tar Zan. Thank you for the ice cream." Rory took off running with Tiger at her heels.

It took Eric two hours to cover the walls with sheathing and firmly nail them in place. He still had to install the windows and apply the aluminum siding. The roof was open, and would remain so until the lumberyard delivered the trusses. He didn't expect that until noon at the earliest, leaving an hour of free time. He considered fixing a sandwich and eating it at the patio table. If nothing more, he would have pollywogs for company.

Eric removed his carpenter's utility belt and slung it over a rung of the ladder, taking several pounds of weight off his hips. Finishing the sheathing was a major accomplishment. He was due for a break. He picked up a towel from the patio table and wiped the sweat from his forehead. The humidity was increasing, suggesting a muggy afternoon. Eric collapsed on a patio chair for a moment of rest. A crawfish peered at him through the aquarium glass as if it were actually concerned with Eric's welfare.

The aquarium had been the centerpiece of his bedroom when he was a kid. It sat on top of his dresser next to his piggy bank and Mickey Mouse alarm clock. He and Sara had spent hours watching its inhabitants swim, crawl, or burrow depending on the nature of their species. He never bought fish. Instead, he stocked it with whatever they could find in Harley Lake. They rearranging the stones and aquatic plants sometimes daily. In retrospect, it was like playing house. If he would have thought of it in that light, he would have been repulsed, but the turtles and crawfish made it socially acceptable. Like Rory, they had watched pollywogs change into frogs.

Eric was about to get up to fix lunch when he saw him. Don Higgins was walking up the bike path. Eric hadn't seen Higgins since the trial. He was wearing his black, broad-brimmed hat, which was his trademark. Eric couldn't remember ever seeing him outdoors without that hat. He waved at Eric. Eric waved back.

The backs of all the houses faced the bike path, and people used the path like a sidewalk to commute from house to house. Eric assumed Higgins was just passing by. Unless he had changed his ways, this was the time of day he visited shut-ins.

Higgins left the bike path proving the assumption wrong. He was heading toward the patio table where Eric was sitting. He held a brown paper bag in his right hand.

"Good morning, Eric," he said when he reached the patio table. "May I sit down?"

"Be my guest."

He sat down with a sigh. The Pastor Higgins Eric had known had been humble, but confident. This man appeared tired and hesitant. He had aged during the years Eric had been in prison.

Higgins set the paper bag on the table. "I saw you working on your house and thought you might need a break." He reached into the bag and produced two cans of ice-cold Barq's Root Beer. "If I remember right you prefer Barq's Root Beer. I made some chocolate chip cookies. I'm afraid they're not as good as what Ruth used to make." He removed a paper plate piled high with cookies from the bag.

Eric opened his can of root beer and took a swallow. He was thirsty, and the root beer was a welcome treat. He bit into a cookie. It was still warm from the oven and every bit as good as what Sara's mother had made years before. It had to have been the same recipe. "The cookies are excellent."

"I'm glad you like them. But that's not the reason I'm here. I came to apologize."

"Apologize?"

"You spent five years in prison and not once did I come to visit. You were one of my flock. As your pastor, I failed you. For that I'm truly sorry." There was sadness in the pastor's eyes that confirmed his sincerity. "I discussed it with your parents, and they thought it would be counterproductive, being Sara's father as well as your pastor. I'm afraid I was too quick to agree."

Eric had expected an awkward confrontation, but this came as a surprise. The State had sent Eric to prison for raping this man's daughter, and now he was begging forgiveness for not visiting him in prison? If Eric had been in the pastor's shoes, he would have demanded revenge—an eye for an eye and a tooth for a tooth—he wouldn't have been so quick to turn the other cheek.

"I didn't expect you to visit me in prison." Eric sipped his root beer, hoping this would not be an extended visit. He no longer had anything in common with Pastor Higgins.

"I've always felt something happened that night—something that never saw the light of day. I have no evidence to prove it," Higgins admitted, "Just a feeling. Yesterday, I had a long chat with Sara. She's a troubled woman. Something's tormenting her. Now, I'm more convinced than ever that the whole truth didn't surface at the trial."

"Maybe," Eric replied, "Nothing can be changed now."

"Whatever happened that night, whatever she doesn't want to discuss is eating away at her. It's like a festering wound that's constantly growing. She won't experience any emotional healing until that festering wound is lanced and the truth is allowed to come to the surface."

"It's too late for truth." It wasn't intentional, but there was anger in his reply.

"It's never too late for the truth. I think that same lack of truth is eating away at you. The Bible says, *The truth shall set you free*. I can't tell you what to do, Eric; but I'll give you the same advice I gave my daughter. You had good parents who gave you a good upbringing. You know right from wrong. Do what you feel is right. Follow your heart, Eric; follow your heart. If you do, the Lord will lead you down the right path."

With that Higgins got up to leave. "You're always welcome at my church, although I can understand if you prefer not to come." He then turned and headed toward the bike path. He walked like an old man. Until now, Eric hadn't realized how old this man had grown over the years. What he had to do to Sara, he had to do, but he regretted the pain it would inflict on her father.

# 12

Stone turned off M-28 and headed north on US-41 at the outskirts of Marquette. He looked at his watch. He had made the hundred-mile trip in an hour and a half—not bad for an old Ford. And better yet, no one stopped him for speeding. The traffic cops must have been working overtime at the donut shops. If a cop had stopped him, Stone would have accidentally flashed his badge while looking for his driver's license. That would buy a *get out of jail free* card from his fellow boys in blue.

Stone took the bypass across town. He had told his wife and secretary, he was going to the medical center for an eleven o'clock appointment with his ophthalmologist, but instead of turning north onto McClellan Street and heading toward the medical center, he continued a half-mile farther down the bypass, and then turned into the Bonanza Family Restaurant's parking lot. His ophthalmologist was expecting him the following week. When Stone returned to Tamarack, he would have to sheepishly admit he had the wrong date. Stone checked his watch again. It was eleven-ten, five minutes early for his meeting.

Stone normally didn't eat a large lunch, but his diet-conscious wife had prepared a skimpy breakfast. At least that was his excuse for ordering the seven-piece shrimp dinner as he passed through the serving line. He added a Diet Coke to his tray to ease his guilt, before presenting his selections to the cashier.

The cashier pushed a few buttons on her machine and rang up his bill. "You're not Levi Stone by any chance, are you?" she asked.

"Guilty as charged." Stone wondered if someone had stenciled his name across his forehead. This was to be a secret meeting.

"Your friend's waiting for you in the back room."

"Thank you." Stone had assumed he was first to arrive—apparently that was not the case. He carried his tray into the back room normally reserved for parties and conferences. It took Stone a moment or two to adjust to the light in the dimly lit room.

"Levi, over here."

"Marshall, you old dog, you look as ugly as ever." Stone placed his tray on the table and shook hands with Marshall Peterson. The room was otherwise empty. Stone rightly guessed this was not by accident. "So, what's with all this cloak and dagger stuff? The FBI getting paranoid?"

"Sit down, Levi. What's it been…a year since I last saw you?"

"At least." Stone looked over at Peterson's tray. He had also ordered a full dinner. "I see your wife has you on a diet too."

"I've put on a few too many pounds, she says. There's a sack of carrot sticks in the car you can have if you want."

"No thanks, I'll pass."

Both men wore sport coats and ties. Peterson's coat had a slight bulge just below his left shoulder. Stone seldom carried a weapon, finding it more of a nuisance than an asset.

"How's the family, Levi. I haven't seen your kids in years."

"Kelly just graduated from law school. She took a job with a law firm in Washington. David's married with two kids—lives in California."

"My kids all left the area too. No jobs in the U.P."

Stone and Peterson spiced their dinners with social chatter, as they exchanged notes on their important and some not so important family milestones. Even trivia is a cherished morsel between close friends.

"Well, Marshall," Stone said after he finished his shrimp dinner and chased it down with a chocolate sundae topped with nuts, "I assume you have a reason for this clandestine meeting."

Marshall took a sip of his coffee and set the cup back down on its saucer. "I understand you had several drug-related deaths over the last couple of weeks."

"A Mike Morrison was murdered—probably a drug dealer. And we had the accidental death slash suicide of Matt Pippin. He thought he could fly off a fifty-foot-tall building. Hardly as interesting as a bank robbery or a ring of counterfeiters. Nothing that should pique the interest of the FBI."

"Let me be the judge of that," Peterson said. "What do you have on them so far?"

"Embarrassingly little," Stone replied. "The murder was a professional hit. The perp knew what he was doing. Morrison was executed at another site. We have no bullet, no fingerprints. And the victim is a bit of an enigma. Other than a driver's license and his car plates, we have nothing on him, no employer, no family. His address turned out to be a boarding house in Chicago where no one remembers him. It's like he didn't exist."

"That's because he didn't exist." Peterson reached into the briefcase beside his chair and pulled out a yellow folder. He removed an eight-by-ten glossy and tossed it on the table. "That's your murder victim. His real name was Michael Tasson."

Stone picked up the picture. The man in the picture was in his early thirties. Beside him in the picture were his wife and two young daughters. They were formally dressed, obviously a studio portrait.

"You knew him?" Stone asked.

"Eleven years now. Ever since he graduated from the academy. Good family man. His wife is devastated."

Stone set the picture back on the table. He had no further desire to look at the smiling faces. Why does it always have to be a family man? "I take it he was working undercover?"

Peterson picked up the picture, placed it back in the folder, and returned it to his briefcase. "Mike had been working undercover for three months. We know an organized drug syndicate is working out of Cade County and has been for the last five or six years. Not large by big city standards of course, but still significant. They specialize in cocaine and marijuana smuggled in from Canada. It isn't hard. The Coast Guard's busy keeping recreational boaters from killing themselves. The drug cartels have discovered it's easier to smuggle drugs into Canada than Florida. Then it comes down from Canada by boat. Cade County appears to be the hub. From Cade County they ship the drugs to Milwaukee and Chicago for a tidy profit. Apparently, they also make Methcathinone somewhere in Cade County for the local trade."

"That's what killed the Pippin boy," Stone said. "Did Tasson uncover any leads before they killed him?"

"He was getting close," Peterson replied. "He was posing as a drug buyer from Chicago. He made several purchases, but the sellers always wore black ski masks. They executed all transactions in writing. Then they burned the notes at the conclusion of the purchase, leaving no physical evidence. We wired Tasson on several occasions, but with no one talking other than Tasson, there was nothing to record."

"Sounds like you made as much progress as we have." Stone sat back in his chair and looked his friend in the eye. "I assume you want something from the Cade County Sheriff's Department. What can we do for you? Keep in mind our resources are limited."

"We have no proof, but we think Eric Kampe is involved in the organization—possibly the mastermind. He assaulted the Higgins girl because she stumbled onto his drug stash. Rape was an afterthought. The wooden crates she mentioned in her testimony were probably filled with cocaine. Unfortunately, Sara Higgins became a loose end who could have opened the entire can of worms. The drug cartel couldn't let that happen. She was supposed to die. That was clearly Kampe's intent; he left her for dead. She would have died, if your deputy hadn't found her when he did. She's one lucky girl. Levi, Kampe's dangerous. He's not afraid to kill. It wouldn't surprise me if he'd still prefer the Higgins girl dead. I'd keep an eye on her."

"We have her under surveillance…as much as we can with our limited resources. One of my deputies is dating her. That gives us a high profile."

"Anyway," Peterson continued, "Kampe is out on parole, and we have reason to believe he wants back in the business. He's not the only one involved, but currently he's the only one we can identify."

"We've reached similar conclusions," Stone said. "The only hard evidence we have is Kampe's phone number on a lottery ticket found in Matt Pippin's wallet. That's pretty weak."

"He had Kampe's phone number? They've been so security conscious, that's a bit out of character."

"Everyone slips up sooner or later. There's no other reason for Pippin to have the phone number. As far as we know, they weren't friends. We found it on the body. I thought that would provide enough circumstantial evidence to buy a warrant for a wiretap and a homing device on Kampe's car. Unfortunately, Judge Madalinski felt otherwise and turned down both requests. He's usually tough on drug dealers. His decision surprised me."

"I have to take the blame for that," Peterson said. "I asked him not to issue the warrant."

"I assume you had a good reason?"

"The FBI tapped his phone as soon as he got out of the slammer. It hasn't produced much. Kampe makes few calls. The only people who call him are telemarketers. At least we think they are. We haven't ruled out coded messages from presumed telemarketers."

"I suppose you have a homing device on his vehicle too?" Stone asked.

"No, that's where you can help us. A homing device requires extensive manpower, three eight-hour shifts a day. The FBI doesn't have that kind of manpower in the Upper Peninsula, and I don't think your department has either."

"We had planned to monitor it sporadically," Stone confessed.

"Peterson reached into his briefcase and produced a brown paper bag. From the bag, he removed a black box with a four-by-four inch video screen. It reminded Stone of an oversized Palm Pilot.

"This is state of the art," Peterson said. "The Bureau's been using them a little over a year. Two days ago one of our technicians attached a monitor to Kampe's car. The homing device you were planning to use sends out a radio signal that is located with a direction finder. The device we attached works with GPS. That stands for Global Positioning System."

"I know about GPS. We aren't that backward in the U.P."

"Sorry, I tend to lecture when I get going. Anyway, the vehicle's position is digitally sent through the cellular phone system and picked up on this baby." Peterson handed the device to Stone as if he were sharing a treasure. "This works no differently than the navigational systems in those fancy cars."

"I wouldn't know, Stone said. "I drive a Ford."

"Turn on the device with this button." Peterson pushed a button, and the monitor glowed green. Stone could see an image with roads crisscrossing against the green background. "This isn't real-time. It's a stored image for demonstration purposes only. Pushing these buttons zoom in and out. See this line?" Peterson pointed to a red line that ran parallel to several of the roads. "That's the path taken by the vehicle in question. Move the cursor over any portion of the line, and it gives the time and date when the vehicle passed that point. It's all stored on a small memory card similar to the memory cards used in digital cameras. With proper documentation, we can use it as evidence in court."

"That's better than anything we have," Stone admitted.

"Someone has to recharge the battery daily. It also works best if this receiver stays in the same cell phone area as the vehicle it's monitoring. We don't have anyone in Cade County who can monitor the tracking device on a daily basis."

"So, you want one of my deputies to monitor this contraption?" Stone asked.

"No, I want you to monitor it. It's a need-to-know only basis. Your deputy tells his girlfriend; his girlfriend tells a neighbor; and pretty soon everyone knows. We already lost one agent due to loose lips. No, this has to be hush-hush."

"You know I have to have one of my grandkids come over to program my VCR."

"It comes with a manual. It's in the bag." Peterson returned the tracking device to the brown paper bag and pushed it across the table.

"Wow, this really is cloak and dagger stuff! Do I get a secret decoder ring too?"

"Trust me, FBI work is more boring than you think," Peterson replied. "Levi, Kampe killed a good friend of mine. This is personal. I want to catch Kampe and nail his carcass to the barn wall. Killing a federal agent is a federal crime. Michigan doesn't have the death penalty; the federal government does. I plan to be there when they inject that potassium into his stinking veins. I want to watch him twitch as the poison flows through his body. Like I said, this is personal."

If Stone were Peterson's supervisor, he would have removed him from the case. When things get personal, good cops make bad decisions. "How do I relay the information to you," Stone asked.

"Place the memory card in a properly labeled evidence bag. We'll have a courier pick it up once a week. If you see anything suspicious, give me a call. You have my number."

"Let the phone ring three times, hang up, then call back and let it ring twice?"

"Levi, you've been watching too many old Humphrey Bogart movies. Now days caller ID tells us who you are and where you're calling from, and a voice analyzer tells us how many times you've cheated on your wife in the last thirty days."

"It'll be a boring phone call." Both men laughed. "I have to get going," Stone said. "My wife thinks I'm at the eye doctor's. Now I have to go home and explain to her that I'm senile and the appointment is really next week."

It was just past two when Stone arrived at his office. He found it irritating how easy it was to convince Laura he had mixed up his appointment dates. She must think he was actually getting senile. The truth was his memory was no longer as sharp as it was in his youth; like everyone else his age, he had his share of senior moments. Fortunately, retirement was not far off.

Stone went into his office and shut the door. Taking a key from his key ring, he unlocked the right upper desk drawer. The drawer was almost empty except for his nine-millimeter pistol strapped in a waist holster. The gun came out every six months when he qualified on the pistol range. As county sheriff, qualifying with the pistol was optional. He mostly drove a desk, not a police cruiser. Still, he took personal satisfaction in consistently having the highest qualifying scores in the department. He never told anyone, but he always practiced the night before. Stone placed the tracking device next to his pistol. It had already picked up Kampe's signal. The car was sitting patiently in Kampe's driveway. Stone locked the drawer and returned the key to his pocket.

## 13

Jane looked out her tree house window, taking care not to damage the cardboard walls. The sky was a dark azure-blue with only a few white, puffy clouds to occasionally obstruct the sunlight. As were the skies in all her dreams, it appeared to have been hand-painted with acrylics, the blue being so intense. The surrounding jungle was a dense green, crisp and lush, the way Jane liked it. Closing her eyes, she could see parrots, toucans, and birds of every color fluttering from branch to branch. All the colors were bright and vivid; she allowed no pastels in her jungle kingdom.

Even the water in Harley Lake was intensely blue, far bluer than any lake had a right to be. Jane liked intense colors. It was her dream; she could make it any color she wanted; she could control the color palette. The water remained calm and peaceful without a single ripple to mar the tranquility, but Jane knew the tranquility was an illusion. Treachery lurked in the shadows. From her perch in the tree house, Jane could see dark, sinister eyes barely protruding above the water. The eyes, olive green in color, were eight inches apart. The crocodile had to be fourteen feet in length. It was a dangerous creature, but Jane was safe in her tree house, and she had Tarzan to protect her.

Down below, a sudden movement caught Jane's attention. A fawn was walking through the tall grass. The white spots on the fawn's back were beginning to fade with approaching maturity. It was Tiger. Jane called down to Tiger. The fawn looked up in acknowledgment and then returned to feeding on the tall grass.

Tarzan and Jane had rescued the fawn after a lion killed its mother. Tiger now followed them wherever they went. Tiger was always welcome in Jane's imaginary jungle kingdom.

It had been a good summer, and Jane wished her enchanted dream would last forever. Life was as it should be, simple and carefree. She took a deep breath, allowing the fragrant aroma of the tropical flowers to fully stimulate her nostrils. It was a sweet, pleasant smell. Jane closed her eyes to savor the moment, but she was aroused from her meditation by high-pitched warning calls from the jungle birds. Jane had heard such sounds many times before. It could mean only one thing: There was an intruder in her jungle.

Jane looked out the tree house window, searching for the source of the alarm. Off to her right, a twenty-foot python slithered through the trees not more than fifty feet away from the tree house. Its eyes, embedded in an otherwise black head, glowed brilliant yellow with fiery-red irises. This cannot be. This was her jungle, her dream. She didn't allow snakes in her jungle kingdom. Tarzan would come and make it go away. But where was Tarzan? She couldn't see him. "Tarzan?"

The serpent, its eyes now fixed on Tiger, crept toward the grazing fawn. "LOOK UP, TIGER, LOOK UP," Jane yelled, but Tiger ignored the danger lurking high above him. He was unaware of the snake stalking him. The snake's motion was almost imperceptible. Slowly it moved from branch to branch. Closer and closer it came, its red tongue darting here and there.

"Tarzan, where are you?" She would have to protect Tiger until Tarzan arrived. Grabbing the rope that hung from a branch high in the tree, Jane swung down to the ground. "Come on, Tiger, we need to hide." The snake, now less than thirty feet away, hissed at Jane. She was interfering with its meal. Jane tugged at Tiger's neck, but Jane was only seven-years-old. Tiger weighed almost as much as she did. "Come on, Tiger."

Jane pushed Tiger down the trail. Up ahead a large rock wall blocked the pathway. Where had the rock come from? she wondered. Why hadn't she seen it before? A metal door embedded in the rock offered entry into the interior of the massive rock. The door was partly open as if an invitation. Jane stepped inside. "Come on, Tiger. We can hide in here." But Tiger refused to enter the darkened chamber. It looked too dark and ominous for a frightened fawn. Jane turned back to get Tiger, but the door slammed shut, encasing her in total darkness, black upon black. She couldn't even see where the door had been. It was as if the door had never existed. She could no longer even feel the wall, and all she could see in the darkness was a pair of eyes that glowed brilliant yellow and had fiery-red irises. It was the serpent. She had locked herself in the darkness with the serpent. Jane tried to run, but her legs wouldn't respond. It was like running in chest-deep water. "Help me, Tarzan." She tripped and began to fall. "Tarzan, where are you? Eric, I need you." She was falling through the air, falling into deeper darkness. "Eric, please help me." It was no longer a beautiful dream. It had become a nightmare. She didn't know how long she had been falling or how far she fell. But she had fallen into another dark chamber, still alone with no means of escape. Staring at her were the yellow eyes with red irises. They glowed out from the black head of the serpent. As she stared at the eyes, the black head morphed into the head of a man wearing a black ski mask. The eyes still glowed yellow, the irises still fiery red. She was now seventeen, her name no longer Jane; she was now Sara.

The man with the black ski mask came after her. Sara backed away until her spine pressed against wooden crates. The man grabbed her, ripping at her clothing, tearing them from her body. "Please don't hurt me," she said. But the man began beating her with a black baseball bat, hitting her in the face, arms, and chest. Sara fell to the floor, naked and cold. She could feel blood dripping down her face. "What do you want from me," she asked, but she knew the answer. Sara's right arm was broken, her ribs hurt with each breath, and her head throbbed. She lay naked on the concrete floor unable to offer any further resistance as he came to her. She was his for the taking.

Sara awoke covered with sweat as she had three other times that week. Her heart pulsated wildly within her chest, and she was hyperventilating. The dream appeared so real. It was hard to believe it was only a dream. She looked into the semi-darkness of her bedroom expecting to see glowing yellow eyes with fiery-red irises, but nothing stared back at her. Sara reached toward the nightstand, moving her hand around until she felt cold steel. She wasn't sure if she was capable of using the gun, but it gave her comfort knowing it was there. In the daytime, she kept the gun locked in a cupboard, out of her daughter's reach; but at night, it rested on her nightstand fully loaded.

Light from a quarter moon filtered through the open window penetrating all but the room's darkest shadows. A breeze rippled the lacy curtains hanging alongside her window. Sara studied each shadow, assuring herself that nothing ominous lurked within. Only after she had exorcised all boogeymen from the room did she release her grip on the pistol.

Sara was about to return to sleep when it occurred to her. Her muscles tensed. She grabbed for her gun and pointed it in front of her using both hands as Cory had taught her, ready for any assailant. She wanted to believe she had left her bedroom window open, but she knew she hadn't. Someone had opened her window and could still be in her house. If someone were in the house, he would quickly discover this was no dream. Her gun was real, the bullets were lethal, and she was in control.

In bed, she was safe. The mattress protected her back, and with the moonlight coming through the open window, she would see anyone advancing toward her in plenty of time to shoot. She had no doubt she could shoot if the need were to arise—kill if she had to. But she couldn't remain in bed; she had her daughter to protect. She would never forgive herself if she let anything happened to her daughter. Other than the rustling of the wind through the curtains, she heard nothing but silence. Sara rechecked the shadows, finding no threat. What she couldn't see was the area around her bed, the area low to the floor. Someone could be hiding there, waiting for her to leave the safety of her bed, so he could pounce on her. Sara placed her feet on the floor with her gun pointed downward, ready to shoot anyone or anything hiding under the bed that might grab her leg.

Unlocking the safety on her pistol, she headed toward the bedroom door. It was partially open. She couldn't remember if she had closed the door before she climbed into bed. Sara left the lights off to avoid warning any intruder of her presence. She paused at the edge of the living room only long enough to grab her phone. Lifting the receiver to her ear, she began dialing 911 but stopped when she heard no dial tone; he had cut the phone line. Moonlight filtering through the picture window partially lit the living room. Seeing no one, Sara searched for her purse. She still had Holly's cell phone in her purse. She was to return it in the morning. She found the purse lying on the sofa where she had left it. Sara grabbed the purse and moved toward her daughter's bedroom, pressing her back against the wall while covering her front with the pistol. The thick-carpeted floor absorbed any noise from her footsteps, but it also provided stealth for her stalker. She slipped into her daughter's room and quietly closed the door behind her. Then she switched on the light.

"What's the matter, Mommy? Is it time to get up?"

"Nothing's wrong, honey," Sara whispered. "I just wanted to be close to you." Sara opened her purse and pulled out the cell phone. He may have cut the phone lines, but he overlooked the cellular phone. Holly loaned it to her so she could keep in touch with the sitter when playing tennis. Sara listened for a dial tone, and then dialed 911.

It seemed like hours, but only twenty-one minutes by Sara's watch when she heard a car driving up her driveway. Red and blue lights flashed through the bedroom window.

Moments later someone rapped on her front door. "Sara, it's Cory. Are you all right?"

Cory's voice provided momentary relief. She was no longer alone; help had arrived. But she now heard footsteps in the hallway, not muffled footsteps of a timid person, but heavy footsteps, footsteps of someone confident or even arrogant. The intruder was in her house, and he was between Cory and her. She held her daughter tightly with her left arm and pointed her pistol at the bedroom door. If he entered, she would shoot him. She no longer had doubts about her ability to kill. He would never harm her again.

The door to Sara's bedroom opened and then shut, as the intruder methodically searched for her. Where was Cory? Why wasn't he breaking down the door to rescue her? The footsteps were coming her way. Sara let go of her daughter and grasped the pistol with both hands. She checked to ensure that the safety was off; it was. When he opened the door, she would shoot. There was no way she could miss at this distance. The footsteps stopped outside the bedroom door, hesitating for what seemed an eternity.

She could shoot through the door and maybe hit him, but she might only get one shot. She had to be sure. The doorknob turned and the door slowly opened. Sara pointed the pistol to where she estimated the assailant's chest would be.

"Are you okay?" Cory asked.

Sara, her hands still pointing the gun at the doorway, began to tremble. "Cory...I almost shot you." Sara's inner strength melted away, her confidence gone. She began to cry.

Cory cautiously walked over to Sara and gently deflected the loaded gun away from him.

"What's happening, Mommy?"

"Let me reset the safety," Cory said. Sara passed the gun to Cory. "Can you tell me what's going on?" Cory asked.

Sara, still sobbing, pulled her daughter into her arms. "Someone came through my bedroom window and broke into our house."

"Did you see him?"

"No, I had the bedroom window closed; and when I woke up, it was open."

"Wait here, I'll check the house." Cory returned Sara's gun after engaging the safety.

"Why are you crying Mommy?"

"Mommy's just happy to see Cory. Everything is all right." It was partially true. Her daughter didn't need to know the full truth. There was no need for her to live in fear.

Sara regained control of her emotions. It wasn't like her to fall apart. It displayed a weakness she couldn't allow to happen again. She was back to her normal self when Cory returned.

"I checked the house. Everything appears normal. The bedroom window's open, but you could have left that open yourself. There's no evidence of forced entry."

"I'm sure I closed it," Sara said. But had she, she wondered.

"You also left the front door unlocked. I walked right in. You need to be more careful."

"I'm sure I locked the front door before I went to bed. What about the phone? He cut the phone wire. Let me show you." Sara led Cory into her living room. She picked up the phone and held the receiver to her ear. There was no dial tone. "See," she said, passing the phone to Cory. Cory held the phone to his ear and then followed the cord to the wall socket.

"Here's your problem. No one cut the wire. It was just disconnected from the wall socket. Your daughter must have disconnected it."

"I didn't break the phone, Mommy."

It had seemed so ominous. Sara now wondered if her imagination was getting the best of her. Her dream placed her in a delusional frame of mind. Even the most sinister plot would have appeared plausible. She had lost control of the situation. In her zest to ward off evil, she had become evil. She almost killed Cory.

"Mommy, I didn't break the phone."

"That's okay. Don't worry about it. I think it's time for you to get back into bed. Maybe you can sleep with Mommy tonight, as long as we don't make it a habit."

"Okay, Mommy."

Sara didn't want to admit it, but she was the one who didn't want to sleep alone. "Cory, I guess I owe you an apology. I think I overreacted. I'm sorry."

"Don't apologize. That's what we're here for. I work the night shift. If no one ever called me, it would be a very boring night. Are you going to be okay?"

"Yes, I'm fine. I just need to be more careful about locking the doors at night. I need locks on the windows too. Thanks again for stopping by."

"I'll make a point to drive by your house more frequently." Cory headed toward the front door. "Be careful with that gun. I don't want anyone getting hurt."

"I will." Sara locked the door after Cory left and then secured her pistol in the cupboard. She wasn't sure if she would ever take it out again. She couldn't live with herself if she killed an innocent person.

Sara shut the bedroom window. Tomorrow she would place locks on the windows. Now she needed sleep. Her daughter was already snuggled in her bed.

"It's been an exciting night," Sara said with a smile, trying to minimize any emotional trauma the night might have caused. Sara walked around to the vacant half of the bed. On the nightstand where she normally laid her gun was a white envelope. It hadn't been there when she went to bed. She would have noticed it when she placed her pistol on the nightstand.

Sara opened the envelope. The contents were written in the familiar stick letters, all formed with small straight-line segments, like all the other letters she had saved in her dresser drawer.

*You didn't leave town. Now I must kill you. I could have killed you tonight, but I didn't. You will still die, but not before I'm done with you.*

He had been in her bedroom and hovered over her while she slept. After he left the note on the nightstand, he unplugged her phone and causally strolled out the front door leaving her door unlocked.

"Mommy, are you coming to bed?"

"Yes, Mommy is coming to bed. I think we'll leave the bedroom light on tonight."

# 14

Sara awoke with a throbbing headache. She had remained awake for three hours after Cory left, mostly out of fear; but, eventually, somnolence overcame her fear, and she had fallen asleep. Now she was paying dearly for those three hours of lost sleep; her headache was a powerful reminder of that fact.

After the surreal events of the previous night, it was hard to distinguish between dream and reality. At what point had the dream ended and reality begun? If it hadn't been for the note on the nightstand, she would have declared the entire episode a ghastly nightmare. She would have forced it from her memory—or at least tried to. She looked again at the note in her hand; the note was very real and its meaning unmistakable.

He was toying with her, playing with her mind, knowing she couldn't notify the police—not without revealing the truth. That she wasn't willing to do. Many times she had considered going to the police, but each time she had rejected it. She had to protect her daughter. At least that was how she rationalized her behavior.

"Mommy, I'm hungry."

Fortunately, the events hadn't affected her daughter. She was wide-awake and full of energy. "We're just having cereal this morning." Sara set out some cereal bowls and placed a pitcher of milk on the table. "Pick out the cereal you want from the cupboard."

After they finished breakfast, Sara placed the dirty cereal bowls in the kitchen sink for future washing. Considering the previous night's adventures, some household projects were more urgent than washing breakfast dishes. At least school was out for the summer, and she had the entire day to fortify her house. Unless she ran into unforeseen problems, she should have locks on all the windows by nightfall. Then anyone wishing to enter her house would have to break in, and the noise would provide sufficient time to switch off the safety on her pistol.

"Hey, Twinkle Toes, I'm going to take a shower. You can watch TV if you want."

"Okay, Mommy."

Sara searched her dresser drawer for clean underwear. In the corner of the drawer, bound with a rubber band, sat the stack of letters. Why had she kept them? she wondered. She knew why she kept the sleeping pills. At one time that had been her escape hatch for use after she had exhausted all other resources. She no longer counted the pills. With her daughter to consider, the pills were no longer an acceptable option.

Sara stepped into the bathroom and let her pajamas fall to the floor. She stood in front of the mirror, staring at her naked body. The plastic surgeons had done an adequate job on her face; although some scars were still visible. The most hideous scar was on her right upper arm just below the shoulder where the surgeons pinned her broken humorous. There was another ugly scar on the right side of her chest where they inserted a chest tube to re-expand her collapsed lung. With minimal effort, she could find a multitude of smaller scars. At one time she had been an attractive girl, but no more. No one would ever consider her scarred body sexually desirable.

Sara turned on the hot water and stepped into the shower stall. This was not an appropriate time for self-pity. Until now, she had been reacting to events, never controlling them. If she were to survive, she needed to go on the offensive. Her defense could also use some attention. She needed a cell phone on her nightstand next to her gun, and she needed a cell phone of her own. She couldn't rely on having Holly's phone. During the day, the cell phone had to be within reach at all times. The phone was her link to outside help; and that, as evidence by the events of the night, could be twenty minutes away.

Sara dressed in work clothes and brushed her hair. Her daughter was already dressed in blue jeans and her favorite flannel shirt; although, her hair was a mess. "Come over here and let me see if I can do something with your hair."

"Okay, Mommy."

Sara sat down on the couch, allowing her daughter to crawl onto her lap. The girl's long hair bristled with angry snarls, but after a minor struggle, Sara had them under control. The hair now hung down in two long braids. "That looks good enough. Now we need to drive to the hardware store and see if we can find some locks for the windows."

"Can we stop at the library and get some new books?"

"I suppose so, and don't forget your coat. It's a bit damp this morning."

Sara unlocked the cupboard and placed her gun in her purse next to the cell phone. It was a violation of state law, since she didn't possess a concealed weapons permit. That she wouldn't confide with Cory. Unless she had to use it, no one would discover the gun without a search warrant. If she had to use it, the legal penalties would be the lesser of the two evils.

A storm front had dumped a fair amount of water during the early morning hours, leaving behind a damp mist. Patches of dense fog lingered in some of the lower lying areas as well as around the rivers and lakes of which there were many in Michigan's Upper Peninsula. It was typical U. P. weather.

Sara backed her Ford Taurus out of her driveway and headed south on County Road 587. At one time the road had been a seasonal logging trail and as such meandered aimlessly through the woods with little apparent purpose. The surrounding woods had been clear-cut thirty years ago, and the second-growth trees were approaching maturity. It would soon be time for the loggers to return. Sara hoped they would wait a few more years. The road would never be the same after the loggers clear-cut the area.

Except for four-lane highways, the official speed limit in Michigan was fifty-five, but residents of the Upper Peninsula considered that only a recommendation. People drove at whatever speed they thought was safe and comfortable. Sara preferred sixty-five on straight sections, of which there were few, and a bit slower on the curves. Today, with the patches of dense fog and the puddles of water on the road where her Taurus tended to hydroplane, she remained cautious. Sara pressed on her brakes as she approached one of the curves. The pedal sank halfway to the floor before the car responded. She made a mental note to have her brakes checked.

"Mommy, I have to go potty."

"We just left home. Why didn't you go at the house?"

"I didn't have to go then."

At times her daughter could be so precocious; she had yet to start school but could already read simple books. At other times she acted like a typical five-year-old. "Hold on as long as you can, honey. We're almost to Kampe's Korner. We'll stop at Grandpa's."

"I don't know if I can wait that long."

Without conscious effort, Sara found her speedometer pushing past fifty-five. She could handle that on the straight-aways, but they were approaching a curve. Sara took her foot off the accelerator and applied the brake. The brake slowed the car, but the engine continued at its previous pace—the accelerator was stuck. Sara pushed harder on the brake pedal until the smell of burning brake liner filled the car. She couldn't stop the car; she couldn't control the car; she couldn't even slow it down. When the brake pedal hit the floorboard, the car—no longer restrained by brakes—surged ahead. Sara glanced at her speedometer. She was going sixty. She squeezed her foot behind the gas pedal and pried up, hoping that would free up the accelerator. The pedal lifted easily but failed to slow the car. She tapped on the pedal. Perhaps that would jar it loose. It only increased the acceleration. Her speedometer was pushing toward seventy, with the sharp curve fast approaching. Sara crossed to the other lane seeking the inside of the curve. At least there was no oncoming traffic. The car skidded sideways through the curve, returning the vehicle to its proper lane.

She now had a half-mile of straight road ahead of her, but the next curve was sharper than the last, if she remembered right. There was no way she could negotiate that curve at seventy miles per hour, not on a wet road.

"Mommy, you're going too fast."

"I can't help it, honey. The car won't stop." This was why he hadn't killed her during the night. He didn't need to. They were going to die just like he promised.

"Mommy you're going too fast."

"The car won't stop."

"Turn it off."

"I can't turn it off. It's stuck." Why couldn't she turn it off? She wondered. If she didn't stop the car within the next few seconds, the car would leave the road and crash into the trees. They would be dead before any help arrived. Sara reached down and turned off the ignition. The motor immediately ceased, locking the steering wheel. She turned the key to accessories, freeing up the steering wheel. Sara still had to wrestle with the wheel to keep the car on the road. Without power steering, the car maneuvered like an obstinate farm tractor plowing through soft soil. At least the car was slowing down, but it was still going too fast to negotiate the curve.

The car should have an emergency brake, but she had never used it. Since her car was an automatic, and she had never found the need. Sara tried to remember where it was located. On most new cars, it was a foot pedal near the sidewall. She probed with her left foot while wrestling with the steering wheel. Finding what she hoped was the emergency brake, she pushed hard with her foot. The car slowed as she entered the curve. Pulling the steering wheel hard to the right, Sara forced the car into a wide curve—too wide for the tight curve of the road. The car slid off the road and then plowed through the thick brush before coming to a stop just short of the woods. It would have hit a large maple if the emergency brake hadn't reduced its forward momentum.

Sara slumped over the steering wheel and cried. No matter what she did, he was always one step ahead of her. She had been lucky today, but good luck couldn't last forever. Eventually, he would kill her and perhaps her daughter as well, and she was powerless to stop him.

"Mommy, I didn't have to go potty that badly."

"That's okay, honey. Kampe's Korner is just down the road. The car needs to be fixed, but I think we can walk to Grandpa's house from here."

The light mist had subsided, although the gray, overcast skies left the impression that a drenching downpour could commence at any time. The church parsonage was a half-mile farther down the road; but at this time of the day, her father would be next door in church office. Motivated by a five-year-old's full bladder, they reached the church just as the light sprinkle turned into a heavy downpour.

As she expected, Sara found her father sitting behind his desk under the watchful eye of his wife who looked on from the vantage point of her framed picture. His reading glasses were riding low on his nose, and he appeared to be engrossed in a leather-bound book. Sara assumed it had some erudite theological significance. His concentration was so intense he hadn't even noticed when Sara entered the room.

"Hello, Papa."

"Sara, how did you sneak in?"

"It wasn't hard. You seemed really intrigued by your book."

"I've been reading *Meditations of Saint Augustine*. Occasionally, I get this uncontrollable urge to read what the great theologians of times past had to say. They can be very articulate, but I'm afraid they don't have any better understanding of the universe than theologians of today."

"When you get the universe figured out, let me know," Sara said. "I have more than passing interest in that subject myself."

"Where is my favorite granddaughter?"

"She's in the bathroom. We were on our way into town and needed to make an emergency pit stop. That's one of two reasons we stopped by."

"She's just like her mother. We would just get you bundled up in your snowsuit and boots when you'd have to go to the bathroom. It never failed. You said you had two reasons?"

"My car broke down a half-mile north of here. I was wondering if I could borrow the church mini-van for a couple of days."

"The Lord is always encouraging us to help stranded travelers in need, even if we aren't Samaritans. I don't think He'll mind if you borrow the church van." Retrieving the van's keys from his desk drawer, he tossed them to his daughter. "It's got our church logo on the sides. If you drive around town, it'll be good advertising. We won't need the van until Sunday."

"Thanks, Papa." Sara gave her father an unexpected hug, almost knocking his reading glasses from his nose.

"For a hug like that you can have my personal car too." Higgins readjusted his glasses. "What's wrong with your car? Do you need a tow truck?"

"The brakes gave out. I've already called Rasmussen's Auto Repair on my cell phone. He said he could pick it up later today but won't get around to fixing it for a couple of days."

"Brakes giving out sounds serious. I take it you were able to stop the car?"

"We ran off the road, but I don't think we did much damage to the car. It was scary. As they say in the movies, my whole life flashed before me. It was a quick reminder that I'm not immortal."

"You never know when the Lord's going to call you home. One must always be prepared."

"That's something else I want to talk to you about." Sara paused a moment to collect her courage. "If anything ever happens to me, I want my daughter well cared for."

"You know I'd take good care of her."

"I know that, Papa. But you're not as young as you used to be. You could be dead or incapacitated before she becomes a teenager."

"What do you have in mind? We don't have any close relatives."

"The hospital placed Eric's name on the birth certificate. That makes him the legal father. If he would want to adopt her, I don't want you to stand in the way."

"Do you really mean that?" Higgins took off his reading glasses to better study his daughter.

"Yes, Papa, I do."

"That'll raise some eyebrows."

"I don't even know if he'd want to, but I know he would make a good father. I know he would."

"Sara, you still love him, don't you?"

"I don't know, Papa. Life is so confusing."

"A couple of days ago, I talked to Eric and I think he finds life just as confusing."

"You talked to Eric?"

"I took over a plate of your mother's chocolate chip cookies. He's a neighbor. It's only proper that I welcomed him home."

"What did you say to him?"

"I gave him the same advice I gave you, and bears repeating. Sara, you got me more confused than ever, but you know right from wrong. Use your best judgment. Follow your heart and the Lord will lead you down the right path.

# 15

Sara turned off her headlights two miles from the farmhouse. If she kept to the center of the road, the parking lights would shed sufficient light on the aspen lining the road to ensure safe passage. She didn't expect any oncoming traffic at one-thirty in the morning. Reasonable people were home safely tucked in their beds, hopefully dreaming pleasant thoughts. But she wasn't concerned with reasonable people. If by chance an oncoming car were to approach, she would turn on her lights and drive past her house, becoming just another car heading toward some unknown destination farther down the road. The van provided security as long as she kept moving.

A half-mile from her house, she switched off the parking lights and eased her foot against the brake pedal, further slowing the van. The woods would soon dissipate into an open field where, even at a significant distance, the casual observer would notice the parking lights. Sara didn't wish to flaunt her arrival. The road wound around several sharp turns, but Sara knew them well. This was her road. She traveled it daily, although without lights, it remained a challenge. She slowed to five miles per hour until the forest gave way to an open field, as she knew it would. Light from a sliver of a moon now reached the road, providing a faint outline of its boundaries. She increased her speed to fifteen miles per hour. When the farmhouse came into view, Sara reached into her purse and pulled out her pistol, setting the gun on the seat beside her. It was unlikely she would need it, but it gave her courage—and she needed courage. She was no match for his strength; that she had learned from experience. The pistol made a great equalizer. It leveled the playing field. Normally she wouldn't have left the gun in the open; tonight, with Rory asleep in the back of the van, she would make an exception.

The house was dark with no cars in the drive—she found no surprise there. Everything looked normal, but if he were waiting for her at the house, she didn't expect him to leave a light on. This wasn't Motel 6. He was a man of infinite patience, willing to wait the entire night in the dark if need be. Darkness was his friend, and he used it wisely. But what Sara had to do also had to be done in the dark. With a bit of luck, their paths wouldn't cross. If they did, her gun was ready, and she was a good shot. Cory had taught her well.

Sara pulled up to her mailbox and opened the cover. She removed the contents and placed them on her lap. With a small penlight cupped in her hands to reduce the scattered light, she checked the return addresses on the envelopes. None was from Oregon. She returned the envelopes to the mailbox; it was best if no one knew she had checked her mail.

Sara shifted into reverse and backed up twenty feet. Then she turned left and slowly drove down her driveway. Half way down the drive, she veered to the right, heading toward the barn. At one time there had been a road of sorts leading to the barn door. Now vegetation covered the drive, although the ground underneath remained flat. Grass and other vegetation scraped the undersurface of the van, as Sara drove toward the barn. It was a poor place to get stuck or have the van breakdown. The last thing she wanted to do was leave the van in the open where anyone could see it. As an afterthought, Sara punched the automatic door lock on the van and heard the click as the doors locked in unison. She didn't know why she hadn't thought of that earlier. Simple mistakes like that were unacceptable. The stakes were too high.

Sara braked the car to a stop ten feet from the barn doors, picked up her gun, and cautiously stepped out of the car. She was not excited about using the barn, but she couldn't leave the van where someone could see it from the road. She wasn't even sure she could open the barn doors. Fortunately, the barn leaned away from the double doors; otherwise, the doors would have swung into the ground. Sara pulled on one of the doors, but it failed to budge. Tucking her pistol under her belt, she wrestled the door with both hands, and it gave way with a groan. How far away could that be heard? she wondered. The other door, with its rusty hinges, likewise gave way only under duress.

The inside of the barn was unbelievably dark. Even her penlight failed to penetrate to the far walls, but she saw no obstacles just inside the door. That was her only area of concern. Sara drove the van into the barn and turned off the engine. The sudden silence was overwhelming, and the darkness was absolute. With the lack of moonlight, she could barely see the steering wheel. Gun or no gun, there was no way she was blindly stepping out of the van into that darkness. She momentarily turned on the parking lights. With her eyes already adjusted to the dark, that provided sufficient light to illuminate the empty barn. The only signs of life were a couple of well-fed rats that scurried along the barn's support beams. She always had a morbid fear of rats. That alone was almost enough to consider aborting her task, but she needed food and clean clothes. She couldn't live in her sweatshirt and jeans forever. A hairbrush would also be nice. Her hair had become a tangled mess. She was not fond of ponytails but had resorted to one for convenience. If nothing else, it kept the hair out of her face.

Sara stepped out of the car with a gun in one hand and a penlight in the other. She decided not to lock Rory in the van. If he came after Rory, a locked car door wouldn't stop him; and if she needed to leave in a hurry, she couldn't waste time fumbling for the keys to the door. The same applied to the barn doors. She could shut them, but from the road, only the shadow of the barn was visible. No one could tell if the doors were open or closed. She had to be ready for a fast exit. Her errands shouldn't require more than two or three trips at the most. With Rory being such a sound sleeper, she was unlikely to awake and find Sara gone.

Sara turned off her penlight and stood in the doorway of the barn. She saw many shadows, but none was moving. Other than crickets chirping away as if all was well, there was total silence. Sara approached the farmhouse. The front door was locked, as it should be. A walk around the house revealed no open windows— no evidence of forced entry. But that was meaningless, since she still didn't have locks on the windows. Sara unlocked the back door, took her pistol off safety, and entered the house. The kitchen was as she had left it earlier in the morning. The dirty breakfast dishes sat in the sink waiting for someone to wash them; they would have a long wait. Rory's box of cereal lay undisturbed on the counter; no one had thought to put it back in the cupboard. Eventually, the cereal would provide a treat for some lucky field mouse. Sara walked through each room armed with penlight and gun until she was sure she was alone. After she had cleared all the rooms to her satisfaction, she returned the gun to safety and stuck it under her belt.

She returning to the kitchen and filled two grocery bags with canned goods and anything they could eat without cooking. She added several bowls, paper cups, silverware, and a can opener. In less than five minutes she was back at the van with enough food to last several days. One more trip for some clothes, and they'd be gone. She shined the light on the back seat; Rory was still asleep.

The second trip took longer than she had anticipated. She had to sort through dresser drawers, closets, and laundry baskets to find everything they needed, all by penlight. Unlike the groceries, she had to be more selective to ensure they had clothing for various needs and a variety of weather. Rory's favorite flannel shirt was still in the basement on top of the dryer where she had left it with the other freshly washed clothes. She had planned to fold them and put them away in the afternoon. If it hadn't been Rory's favorite shirt, she would have left it. She didn't relish a trip to the basement in the dark.

Sara opened the basement door and, with pistol again in hand, forced herself down the stairs. She didn't expect to find him in her basement. If he were in the house, he would have made his presence known by now, but the steps lacked risers, and the thought of a hand reaching through to grab her ankle was unnerving. She seldom used the basement, even in daylight. She stored a few infrequently used items in boxes and had some winter clothes hanging from hooks attached to overhead pipes; but for the most part, she only used the basement for washing clothes. The previous owner installed the washer and dryer in a small recess along the south wall. Louvered doors cordoned them off when not in use. Sara opened the doors, grabbed Rory's flannel shirt, as well as some towels, and ran back up the basement stairs.

She had the laundry basket filled to overflowing. That should provide them with plenty of clothing. They might have to wear the same clothes several days several days in a row, but she could live with that. Her farmhouse, pleasant as it had been, was now history. She would never return. Her father could handle the sale of the property. She might have to return to sign over the deed, but that would be it. She was leaving Cade County with no regrets.

Sara locked the van doors, tucked her pistol away in her purse, and backed out of the barn. There was just enough room in front of the barn to turn the car around and head for the road, as long as she didn't back up to far. That would have placed her in a ditch. Boldness was now overcoming apprehension, and she turned on her parking lights to facilitate turning the car. Sara strained her neck to see out the back window. With her concern about escaping from the farmhouse, she didn't notice as she backed out of the barn. She didn't notice as she turned the steering wheel hard to the right to swing the rear of the van around. She didn't notice as she shifted into forward. Only when she pointed the van toward the road did she notice. She looked back at Rory. Rory was gone!

Sara stepped on the brake bringing the van to a halt. Her first response to the situation was to cry. She was losing control again, but that assumed she at one time had control. She needed to pull herself together, and fast. Sara remained behind the wheel, her hands trembling, while she contemplated the possible explanations. None of them was good. Perhaps Rory awoke and climbed out of the car. That was the best scenario, probably the most likely. If he were here, he would have come after her, not Rory. He was never shy in the dark.

Sara returned to the barn with penlight in hand. "Rory?" Sara heard noises here and there, but each time she shined the light at the noise, all she saw were well-fed rats. A search of the barn revealed no evidence of her daughter. Sara looked at the farmhouse through one of the open slats in the barn wall. A light was shining from Rory's bedroom window. Rory had walked to the house and crawled into bed. Sara sighed in relief. It was so logical when she thought about it. If Rory woke up in the van, why wouldn't she walk to the house?

Sara was halfway to the farmhouse when Rory turned off her bedroom light. The house disappeared in the darkness. As tired as she was, the thought of crawling into her own bed and sleeping through the night was tempting. Was her paranoia getting the best of her? There was no reason to believe he would return tonight. He had to assume the alterations to her car were effective, and she was lying dead in some hospital morgue. That scenario had not been far from reality. No, she had to stick to her plan. She had underestimated him too many times. She wouldn't always be lucky, if you could call the last five years of her life lucky.

Sara entered the house through the back door, using her penlight for guidance. The light was beginning to dim. Only a small circle of light illuminated the area in front of her. She had spare batteries in the car, but that didn't help her now. She walked across the kitchen toward the hallway and Rory's bedroom. She was halfway across the kitchen when a pull on her ponytail yanked her head backward. Pain seared through her scalp. Before she could react, an arm came down hard on her face. She assumed the liquid dripping from her nose was blood. If her nose were broken, it wouldn't be the first time. The arm slid farther down her face and then tightened in a hammerlock when it reached her neck.

"This time you die, bitch." The voice coming from behind her was whispered and muffled. It had been five years, but she still recognized the voice. She would never forget that whisper. She had heard it too many times in her dreams to forget. Sara reached back for his face, but he was out of her reach. The few times she was able to make contact, it was at the extreme of her range of motion, and she couldn't generate any force. The best she could do was scratch him. That might be annoying but it didn't mount a significant defense. His arm tightened around her neck. She became light-headed, as the chokehold cut off oxygen to her brain. She tried to remember the moves she had learned in her college self-defense course, but her thoughts were confused. She remembered how to block an attack with a knife, and how to break a chokehold from a man attacking from the front, neither of any value. She tried to poke at his eyes, but his head was unseen, and he easily dodged all such attempts. The chokehold was not only cutting off circulation to the brain, but it was beginning to crush her windpipe. She couldn't breathe. She lifted her right foot and kicked backwards aiming at the knee. A low groan confirmed she had hit a sensitive spot. The arm around her neck fell, allowing Sara to turn around. Another kick, this time to the groin, sent her assailant to the ground.

Sara stumbled and fell. She got up only to stumble again. On the second try she stayed on her feet. Even with her brain still cloudy, she knew she had to run. She had to put distance between them. Sara flipped on a light switch, but the room remained dark. He had turned off the power. The penlight now emitted only the dimmest of light. Sara bounced off the walls in the hallway and fell. Reaching up she found the handle to the basement door. Without thought or plan of action, she opened the door and headed down the wooden stairs. Once her mind began to clear, she realized that was a poor decision. The basement was an open area used only for storage and washing clothes. She could hide behind some of the storage boxes, but that wouldn't provide cover for long. Wooden crates hadn't protected her five years ago. There was no reason to believe they would protect her now.

The only other option was the recessed washroom. She could hide behind the louvered folding doors. For no rational reason that she could think of, Sara ran toward the washroom. She opened the folding doors and climbed onto the dryer. There was barely sufficient space to sit on the dryer and dangle her feet in front of her when she closed the louvered doors. If nothing else, she would be in a position to run if he discovered her. She might take him by surprise when he opened the door.

Sara heard doors opening and closing above her. Her assailant was methodically searching the house. It was only a matter of time before he searched the basement. Sara turned on her penlight to survey her surroundings, but found no weapons. Nothing she could swing or throw. All she had was an open box of laundry detergent setting on the washer. Why hadn't she brought her purse? With the cell phone she could have called the police. Cory would have been here in twenty minutes, maybe less. That was still a long time, but it would have given her hope. Or if she had her pistol, it would have been an even match, perhaps in her favor.

Blood dripped freely from her nose, soaking her sweatshirt with blood. More ominous was the pool of blood on the floor beneath her dangling feet. Had she left a trail of blood? It would be hard to see by flashlight in the dark, but once he knew she was bleeding, he would concentrate on following the trail. Sara was hoping the intruder, when not quickly finding her, would assume she had escaped through the front door. The basement door opened, dispelling that fantasy. He was walking slowly, following the trail of blood that would lead to her hiding spot in the laundry room. Sara looked through the louvers, watching her assailant's flashlight beam as it flashed around the room.

For the most part, the beam concentrated on the floor with its telltale droplets of blood. Then the light sprayed on the louvered doors. Horizontal strips of light illuminated the interior. He wouldn't be able to see through the louvers, but he had to know she was there. The light became brighter. She could hear heavy breathing on the other side of the door. This was it. This was the end.

A hand covered with a latex surgical glove opened the doors and her body became suffused with light. Some of the light reflected back, revealing ominous eyes peering through a black ski mask. It was the same hateful eyes she had seen five years earlier, as well as in her nightly dreams. She hated those eyes. They stared at each other for a moment, but only a moment. Sara was the first to react. She threw a handful of laundry detergent at his face, aiming for those spiteful eyes. The assailant immediately dropped his flashlight and grabbed his face. A piercing moan confirmed the detergent had reached its intended target. Sara pushed off from the dryer on which she had been sitting and rammed her head into his chest, knocking him to the floor. She grabbed his flashlight and smashed it against the concrete floor. It was her house. She could maneuver better in the dark than he could.

She found the stairs where she knew they would be and quickly climbed to the basement door; it was open. She shut the door and latched it. The latch was cheap, a simple hook and eye screw she had placed on the door to keep Rory out of the basement. Latching the door was a worthless gesture. He could easily break through the door, but it made her feel good just the same. For good measure, she tipped over the kitchen chairs, hoping he would trip over them in the dark.

With a bloody right hand on the hallway wall, Sara felt her way toward Rory's room. She opened the bedroom door. A soft light from the crescent moon filtered through the bedroom window, revealing a motionless object lying under the covers. Was Rory still alive? The thought that he might have killed Rory crossed her mind. If he had, she would return with her gun. He would pay for it. Sara pulled back the covers, and Rory awoke.

"Thanks for carrying me in from the car, Mommy."

He had carried Rory into the house and had used her as bait. "That's okay, Honey, but we need to return to the van." Sara scooped Rory into her arms and headed toward the back door. Detergent in the eyes would be painful, especially without water to flush them out, but it wouldn't incapacitate him forever. She had to hurry.

Sara heard him coming up the steps as she exited the back door. There was no way she could outrun him, not while carrying her daughter. If she had enough lead-time, she would make it to the van. If not... But he had to be still in the house; she could hear him swearing as he tripped over the kitchen chairs. His pain and discomfort gave Sara some personal satisfaction. Perhaps he would break his neck. She reached the van without looking back. She couldn't do anything different even if she did see him running after her. Sara pulled on the van's panel door; it was locked. She had only unlocked the driver's door. Sara set her daughter down on the hood of the van and ran to the driver's side. She pushed down on the automatic door lock button, but it wouldn't work. Inserting the car keys into the ignition and turning it to accessories solved the problem, and she heard a reassuring click as the doors unlocked. The panel door now opened without problems. Sara laid Rory on the middle seat.

"Where we going, Mommy?"

"We're going for a short ride, Honey."

Sara ran back to the driver's seat and locked the doors. She felt a sense of relief when the doors click shut. They had made it.

Sara shifted the van into drive and headed down the driveway. With no further need for secrecy, she turned on the headlights. Standing in the driveway thirty feet in front of her was the man with the black ski mask. He couldn't stop them now. Sara stepped on the gas and pointed the van directly at her assailant. It would damage the van if she hit him, but it would be worth it. The man with the ski mask calmly raised his left hand and fired two shots into the windshield of the approaching van.

# 16

Levi Stone keyed the lock to his desk drawer and removed the GPS tracking device. Much to his surprise, maintenance of the device had been far simpler than he had expected; so simple even an old county sheriff could comprehend the operation. Stone removed two AA rechargeable batteries from the back and replaced them with a fresh pair, placing the old batteries into the battery charger.

This was the end of the first week, and he needed to download the stored data onto the data card for the FBI. He didn't relish the task. According to the manual, it should be a piece of cake, but Stone still approached the project with a degree of trepidation—every piece of cake came with a price. He inserted the data card Peterson had given him, appropriately labeled with time, date, and signature into the machine. *Save* and *cancel* buttons immediately appeared in the right lower corner of the screen. Stone assumed that was a promising sign. Crossing his fingers, he pushed the *save* button and held his breath. A horizontal thermometer began filling with black while above it *downloading* ominously flashed across the screen. When the thermometer was completely black, a non-flashing *download complete* replaced the flashing *downloading*.

Stone removed the data card and placed it in the envelope marked evidence. Hopefully, the FBI wouldn't be too disappointed with the data. From what Stone had seen, Kampe made two trips to the hardware store and one trip to the lumberyard with a side jaunt to the grocery store. For the most part, his car had remained in his driveway. Stone didn't find that surprising. Except for that yellow dog, Kampe didn't have a friend in Cade County to speak of. His social life had to be non-existent.

Stone licked the seal and immediately regretted his actions; it tasted terrible. Why can't they make a better tasting seal? Next time he would delegate that task to Laura, assuming the civil liberties people didn't declare that cruel and unusual punishment. Stone walked to the outer office.

"Laura, someone from the FBI is dropping by to pick up this evidence envelope. Make sure he signs for it."

"Sure, Chief...by the way, Ryan Rasmussen just called. He wants you to stop by the shop sometime today."

"Did he say what he wanted?"

"No, he said it was important and that he would have to show you."

"I don't suppose we could send a deputy?"

"He specifically asked for you."

"No rest for the wicked. I guess I could stop by on my lunch break."

Ryan Rasmussen was the best auto mechanic in Cade County. After graduating magna cum laude from Michigan Tech with a degree in mechanical engineering, he accepted a high-paying job in the downstate auto industry. It didn't take long for Rasmussen to become jaded by the micromanagement and the fast pace of Detroit's city life. After two years of disenchantment, he returned to Cade County to start his own auto repair shop. He took a cut in pay, but at least he was his own boss. Detroit's loss was Cade County's gain.

Rasmussen was working under the chassis of a Ford pickup when Stone arrived. At least Stone assumed it was Rasmussen. All that was visible were a pair of oil-stained boots and the lower half of some very faded jeans.

"Is that you down there, Ryan?" Stone heard an indistinguishable grunt, which could have passed for either yes or no, leaving it still unclear as to the ownership of the legs. Moments later, Ryan Rasmussen rolled out from under the truck on a mechanic's equivalent of a skateboard.

"Hi, Chief. Been expecting you."

Rasmussen wiped his hands on a rag that was dirtier than his hands, and then walked over to a vehicle with its hood up. Stone assumed he was to follow. "You know how the throttle on a car works?"

"Sure, I step on the gas pedal, and the car goes faster. I drove all the way over here on my lunch break for you to ask me that?"

"It's a bit more complicated than that," Rasmussen replied, unfazed by Stone's sarcasm. "Let me turn the car on for a second." Rasmussen turned the key in the ignition, and the car came to life. "See this lever?" Rasmussen pointed to a small arm extending up from the end of a quarter-inch diameter axle. Connected to the tip of the arm was a wire cable. "When you step on the gas, the wire cable pulls on the lever causing this axle to rotate, forcing more gas into the engine." Rasmussen manually pulled the lever to prove his point, and the car gave out a roar. "Let up on the gas pedal and that spring coiled around the axle pulls the lever back, returning the engine to idle."

"That's an interesting concept to know. Now I won't have to bring my car in for repair. I can fix it myself." Stone assumed there was a point to the discussion but was becoming impatient with Rasmussen's drawn-out lecture. He had little interest in mechanics and had no desire to spend his lunch break learning the intricacies of how a throttle functioned.

"Three days ago I got this call from Sara Higgins. She said her gas pedal stuck at full throttle and then her brakes gave out. I picked up her car, but didn't get around to repairing it until this morning. It wasn't hard to find her problem. The wire spring on the accelerator was broken, which prevented the throttle from returning to idle when she let up on the gas pedal. With the car going full speed, she naturally stepped on the brakes, but that was like braking down a long mountain road. Her brakes eventually gave out."

"So far, I don't think she's broken any laws."

"I didn't think much of it at first either, until I found something strange." Rasmussen walked over to a mint-green Ford Taurus and opened the driver's door. "See anything unusual about her seat belt?"

"Looks normal to me," Stone said.

"Look at the receptacle on the driver's side."

"Still looks normal," Stone said. "Why don't you tell me what you're driving at?"

"The plastic housing is faded. It's a lot older than the other seat belts, not original equipment."

"That's terrible. Now, I will have to write her a ticket."

"Try connecting the seat belt."

Stone inserted the seat belt into the receptacle and heard a click.

"Now give it a pull."

Stone tugged on the belt, and it easily pulled loose from the receptacle. "Are you saying someone purposely replaced the seatbelt with a faulty latch?" Stone asked, all sarcasm now gone.

"Makes you wonder, doesn't it? It got me wondering too, so I took a closer look at that faulty spring under a magnifying glass. Look at the broken ends of the spring." Rasmussen passed the spring and the magnifying glass to Stone.

"Tell me what I'm looking at."

"See those ends. They're beveled on both sides like the roof of a house. The spring didn't break due to structural fatigue; someone cut it with wire cutters. And that slippery texture you feel on the spring is paraffin."

"So what's the significance of the paraffin?" Stone asked.

"Paraffin is amorphous, not crystalline."

"Can you explain that in terms a simple county sheriff can understand?"

"Sorry, I forgot chemistry isn't required curriculum in the criminal justice program."

"Well I don't have a degree in mechanical engineering if that's what you're driving at."

"Water is a crystalline substance and has a specific melting point. It's solid at any temperature below thirty-two degrees and liquid at any temperature above it. An amorphous substance like wax doesn't have a melting point. As it heats up, it simply gets softer and softer until it gradually turns into a liquid. Whoever cut the spring covered the cut end with liquid wax. As the wax cooled, it glued the spring to the shaft and the spring was functional. Since the entire assembly sits on top of the motor, the wax warmed up when the car warmed up, and the spring failed a few miles down the road."

"Are you saying someone tried to kill Sara Higgins?"

"Not someone...Eric Kampe."

"Hold on a minute. Unless you have his fingerprints on the faulty spring as well as a signed confession, it's a tad premature to be getting out the lynch rope. I have to admit what you have is interesting, but that's all it is. At this point, it's circumstantial. There might be a simple explanation for the broken wire. Sara might also have an explanation as to why one seat belt is older than the others."

"I would be inclined to agree," Rasmussen said. "If that were all, but there's more." Rasmussen pulled a lever on the wall, and a hydraulic left began elevating the Ford Taurus off the floor. He released the lever when the car was above their heads. "See this bleeder?" Rasmussen pointed to a nut at the convergence of the brake line and the wheel. It's used to bleed air out of the brake line."

"I suppose now I'll get a lecture on brakes."

Rasmussen ignored the comment. "There's one at each wheel. Kampe open all four valves. After Sara pumped the brakes a few times, all the brake fluid leaked out and the brakes failed."

Stone, finding little interest in the brakes, wandered to the back of the vehicle. "What's this?" he asked, pointing to the underside of the gas tank. "It looks like an empty toilet paper roll taped to the gas tank with duct tape."

"Don't touch that or we'll be barbecued. That's more circumstantial evidence. I'm sure Sara has a logical explanation for that too."

"And that looks like a large firecracker...I suppose you know the purpose of this contraption?" Stone asked.

"If you look inside the toilet paper roll, you'll find a D-cell battery with a wire soldered to the back of it. When the car comes to a sudden stop, the battery slides forward in the tube, coming to rest against that metal plate at the front of the tube completing an electrical circuit. The current flows through some fine steel wool, which Kampe wrapped around the fuse of the firecracker. And that's not just any firecracker; it's an M-80, more powerful than a cherry bomb. When the electricity goes through the steel wool, it'll heat up like the filament in a light bulb. That will ignite the fuse of the M-80. Within seconds, there will be a hole in the gas tank bigger than your fist."

"You think that would work?" Stone asked.

"The mechanics are sound. Sara drives down the road, and the engine heats up melting the wax. The car accelerates uncontrollably. She panics and slams on the brakes. The car momentarily slow down until the brake fluid bleeds out, and then the car accelerates again. She wouldn't be able to slow down at the corners and would eventually leave the road at a high speed and hit a tree. Her seat belt would fail to secure her to the seat. That alone would probably kill her when she hit the steering wheel. If not, the sudden stop would send the battery flying forward causing the gas tank to explode. All that would remain would be charred bodies inside a burned-out wreck. No one would find the broken spring or check the status of the brake's bleeder valves. The toilet paper tube, steel wool, and firecracker wouldn't survive the fire. You might find some wire or the battery on the ground, but who's to say that wasn't litter left on the ground prior to the accident. An investigation would reveal Sara wasn't wearing her seat belt; the car left the road at a high speed; and with no skid marks, the investigators would assume she didn't apply the brakes."

"And I would declare it a suicide," Stone said.

"She was lucky she to stop the car without setting off the bomb. Chief, I think you have the makings of a perfect crime. Kampe learned more than how to make license plates in prison. We don't need the likes of him in Cade County, and if you don't do something about Kampe, others will."

"What do you mean by that?"

"Jack Pippin's got people worked up. I hear they plan to burn Kampe's house to the ground this time. Maybe then he'll take the hint and leave Cade County."

"You can spend big time in prison for arson, Ryan. You have your wife and Lily to think about. What would happen to them while you're doing time?"

"I didn't say I'd get involved, but don't expect me to shed many tears when his house does burn to the ground."

Stone took in a deep breath and let out an audible sigh. This was quickly getting out of control. He had enough problems finding the people responsible for killing Michael Tasson and Matt

Pippin. He didn't need self-appointed vigilantes roaming the streets and burning down houses.

"You said you talked to Sara Higgins?" Stone asked.

"Three days ago when she called to have me pick up her car. I tried calling her this morning, but she wasn't home."

"Apparently the plan wasn't all that great if she's still alive."

"Kampe had one serious flaw in his plan—he underestimated his victim."

"How's that?" Stone asked.

"She didn't panic. Kampe assumed she would react like a blond bimbo. Sara was my daughter's kindergarten teacher. She's anything but a bimbo. Most people, male or female, would have panicked when the brakes gave out and the car accelerated out of control. She had the composure to turn off the ignition and engage the safety brake. Definitely not your typical bimbo."

Stone had to agree on that point. Sara Higgins was a survivor. She had proven that during her fight for survival in the hospital.

"How many people know about this?" Stone asked.

"At the moment, just you and me."

"Keep it that way, and don't touch anything. I'm declaring this a crime scene. I'll be sending someone over to take pictures."

"What if Sara calls for her car?"

"I'm heading out to her place now. If she calls before I get there, tell her to hold tight."

Stone's lunch hour deteriorated into a Big Mac, greasy fries, and lukewarm coffee—thanks in part to Stella's notorious lawsuit. He felt a bit hypocritical for eating while driving since he was quick to criticize anyone else who ate or used a cell phone behind the wheel; but time was essential, he rationalized. Two homicides in Cade County were a tad excessive for one month. He needed to find the Higgins girl before Eric Kampe or whoever was trying to kill her had a second chance.

There was sufficient evidence to convince a jury that someone was trying to kill Sara Higgins, but nothing to implicate an individual—except for Eric Kampe, no one had a motive. No one else would enjoy or profit from her death. He would have to keep Kampe on a very short leash.

If the GPS surveillance system was accurate, which Stone had no reason to doubt, Kampe had driven into town two times during the last week. At no time had he gone close to the Higgins's place, at least his car never did.

Stone re-set his trip odometer when he drove past Kampe's house. It registered just over four miles when Stone turned into Sara Higgins's driveway. It was a fair distance, but not insurmountable. From what Stone had heard, Kampe ran farther than that every morning. He could have run to Sara's house with a fanny pack filled with tools, sabotaged her car, and returned to his house in time for a good night's sleep. Stone found the scenario plausible, but speculation would never convince a jury.

Stone drove his car to the end of the driveway and placed it in park. There were no other cars in the driveway; but then, he hadn't expected to find any. He had just impounded Sara's car, and it was too early in the day for visitors. Stone mentally sized up the house through his rolled-down window before exiting his vehicle. The house gave the impression of being vacant. It was too quiet. Usually, a patrol car parking in someone's driveway can produce a variety of reactions; silence was not one of them.

Stone walked over to the front door and knocked several times without receiving any response. That came as no surprise either. Obviously, no one was home. No house with a five-year-old in residence could be this quiet. The drapes to the front window were open providing a full view of the living room. Several magazines lay neatly stacked on an end table, and a large, leather-bound book, which Stone assumed was a Bible, sat perfectly centered on a glass-covered table in front of a worn, but tasteful, brown sofa. Sara was a tidy housekeeper, almost obsessive/compulsive. There was nothing out of place to suggest foul play. Stone twisted the doorknob and gave it a shove. The door was locked, apparently with a sturdy deadbolt. A cursory examination revealed no evidence of forced entry. Stone then checked the windows one by one as he worked his way toward the back of the house. At the rear of the house, Stone found a garbage can enclosed in a screened box to keep out inquisitive wildlife. Stone was too old and set in his ways to be considered wildlife, but he was still inquisitive. He lifted the lid to check out the garbage, finding nothing he would consider fresh. That could be meaningless, Stone tried to convince himself. They could have eaten out. Sara had left the back door closed but unlocked, typical of the Upper Peninsula mentality. She of all people should have known better. Stone considered going inside, but decided against it. Technically, without a search warrant, it would be breaking the law. Stone was not one to break the law, although he had no problems bending the law to the extreme if the situation warranted it. He might reconsider his decision later.

Stone returned to his car and backed out of the driveway, stopping at the mailbox. A good cop is a nosey cop, and Stone was one of the best. He opened the mailbox and found it stuffed with letters and bills. The newspaper holder attached to the same post held three newspapers. Sara hadn't been home since her car failure. She also hadn't called about her car in three days. That was not a good sign. Stone hoped there was a logical explanation for her absence, but if he were unable to find that explanation, and quickly, he would be forced to declare Sara and her daughter missing persons.

Stone drove back down the driveway to the farmhouse. The untouched mail and accumulation of newspapers demanded a more in-depth investigation. He couldn't legally enter the house, but he could evaluate the premises. Stone began walking around the farmhouse in enlarging circles. He wasn't sure what he was looking for, but he definitely didn't want to find any freshly turned dirt. Thirty minutes of searching left him fifty yards from the house with nothing to show for it other than a snowshoe hare he had flushed from its hiding spot.

Looming in front of Stone was the old weathered barn, leaning precariously at a forty-five degree angle. It appeared ready to collapse at any moment. Stone counted the reasons he shouldn't search the barn and easily came up with a dozen. He could only think of one reason why he should search it: because he was sheriff of Cade County.

Stone stepped into the barn through an open slat and waited for his eyes to adjust to the light. The floor of the barn was concrete, although it was covered with a half inch of dirt that had accumulated over the years. Stone wondered how much of it was dirt and how much was old manure from cattle long since gone to that happy pasture in the sky.

Other than some old, rusted-out farm equipment that might fetch a fair price at an antique auction, Stone found nothing to suggest human activity. There was broken glass from vintage beer bottles, testament to clandestine parties in years past. Stone was about to leave when he noticed several candy wrappers and empty Barq's Root Beer cans scattered over by the far wall, none showed signs of aging. Stone picked up one of the cans; according to the label, the bottler filled the can in April. Whoever left the mess had done so in the last two months. Someone had also removed a board from the wall, which provided an unobstructed view of the farmhouse.

Stone pushed open one of the doors to exit the barn, allowing sunlight to enter. Only then did he notice the fresh tire tracks heading into the barn. Why would Sara or anyone else store a valuable piece of property in a barn that could collapse at any time? Some wheeled vehicle had also pressed down the grass in front of the barn; that had to have been in the last several days. Stone followed the tire tracks toward the road. Halfway down the drive, he noticed two small metallic objects reflecting in the sunlight. Stone knelt down to pick them up: nine-millimeter pistol shells—a little heavy for shooting rodents.

Other than the accumulation of mail and fresh litter in the barn, there was little to suggest a crime had been committed; spent cartridges were a dime a dozen in the U.P. Without a car, Sara might be staying with her father. That was only logical. But why hadn't she checked on her car? Why hadn't she checked her mail?

Stone headed back to Kampe's Korner with more questions than answers. Hopefully, Sara's father would be able to shed some light on her whereabouts, but the feeling in his gut did not exude optimism.

Don Higgins was planting spring flowers in front of the church when Stone drove into the parking lot. He was wearing his broad-brimmed hat, which had become his trademark over the years. Several flats of spring flowers lay at his side, hardly the appearance of a distraught parent. Perhaps Stone was over-reacting. Stone tried to banish that grim feeling from his gut, but it refused to budge.

"Hello, Don," Stone said as he approached the pastor. Stone and Higgins had been friends for countless years, and addressing Higgins other than by his Christian name would have been an insult. "Nice day for planting flowers."

"Don't thank me, Levi. It's the man upstairs who has given us this beautiful day; although, I did suggest it to him. And what brings you out to Kampe's Korner this afternoon?"

"I would like to talk to you for a few minutes if I may."

"It'll be my pleasure," Higgins said as he labored to get up off his arthritic knees. "Is the discussion concerning your profession or mine? Or is this perhaps social in nature?"

"I'm hoping this will be entirely social," Stone replied, "but I'm afraid it might concern both our professions."

"In that case, let's retire to my office where we can discuss it over a friendly cup of coffee." Higgins washed the dirt off his hands with a garden hose and wiped them dry on his pants before leading Stone toward the church office.

Higgins poured two cups of coffee from the office coffee maker he kept at the ready for such situations. "I hope you like decaf," he said. "That's the only kind I make anymore. Otherwise I can't sleep at night. Please sit down."

Stone sat in a chair facing the large desk, placing his coffee cup on the desktop after he had taken a sip. "It's good coffee."

"Thank-you." Instead of sitting behind his desk as Stone had expected, Higgins pulled up a chair beside Stone. He placed his broad-brimmed hat on his desk and wiped the sweat from his balding forehead. "Now, what can I do for you today?"

"I'm trying to locate your daughter and thought you might know where I can find her."

"You tried her house?" Higgins asked.

"I just came from there."

"The last time I saw her was three days ago. Her car broke down, and I loaned her the church mini-van. Is she in any trouble?"

Stone paused to collect his thoughts before proceeding. He had been hoping the pastor would provide a logical explanation for Sara's absence. This didn't appear to be the case. "We have reason to believe someone may want to harm your daughter. It also appears your daughter as well as your granddaughter has been missing for up to three days."

Higgins closed his eyes for what seemed an eternity. Stone wondered if it were a moment of prayer or just meditation. Either way, it was not the reaction Stone had expected. Only when

Higgins opened his eyes and exhaled did Stone realize Higgins had been holding his breath.

"Levi, this may come as a shock to you, but what you tell me doesn't come as a surprise; although, I have been praying daily that this would not come to pass. Something sinister happened five years ago, something that has not been exposed to the light of day. It is something Sara won't even share with me, but I know it causes her to live in constant fear."

Stone looked into the pastor's eyes and saw the sadness within. Don Higgins was the shepherd who was always there to comfort his flock when they were in need, but who is there to comfort the shepherd? He had lost his wife and now his only daughter and grandchild were missing and, for all Stone knew, probably dead.

"Do you have any idea what's going on or where she could be?" Stone asked.

"Her best friend is Holly Sutherland, but if there were any danger, that would be the last place Sara would go. She wouldn't want to place her friend in any danger. As for what's going on, I haven't a clue. I do believe that, whatever it is, Eric Kampe is deeply involved. I'm not sure if he's the problem or the solution. I do know he's a very troubled young man."

"Do you have the plate number for the mini-van?" Stone asked.

"It's a light blue van with the church logo on the side, license number ODV-H18. Let me write that down for you." Higgins scribbled the information on a scrap of paper and passed it to Stone. "Levi, I'm not one to ask favors from others, but I'm begging you. They're all I have left in the world, all I have to live for. Please find them for me." The face of Don Higgins remained stoic, showing nothing of the fear and pain within until his eyes began to water and eventually overflow. Tears flowed down both checks. He made no attempt to brush them aside.

"Don, you have my word. I'll do everything in my power to bring them back safely; we'll leave no stone unturned. When I came here I said it might involve both our professions. It wouldn't hurt if you put in a few good words to the man upstairs from your side of the fence."

"I do that on a daily basis, but God has no fences. I'm sure he would listen to you as quickly as he would me."

"Think he'll listen to a mediocre Catholic?"

"I have no doubt. Man made religious denominations, not God. And, Levi, I would hardly classify you as mediocre."

Stone stood up to leave. "I'm heading over to Kampe's house. I'll let you know if anything turns up."

* * *

The Kampe residence was four doors down from the Presbyterian Church. Stone approached the house slowly and then turned into the drive, parking behind Kampe's car. It was hard to believe the car in front of him was sending information to his desk drawer back at the office.

Stone, hearing some human-generated sounds, followed them to their source in the back of the house, where he found Eric Kampe working on the entryway. It appeared almost finished. Kampe had done a decent job for someone with limited experience. "Nice job on the repair," Stone said.

"Thank you." Eric's reply was cold, nothing more than a response to Stone's comment. Eric stood in the doorway offering no further dialogue.

"I'd like to talk to you for a few minutes," Stone said. "May I come in?"

"Do you have a search warrant?"

"Do I need one?"

Eric paused for a moment. "No, I guess not. Come in." Eric stepped aside, allowing Stone to enter and led him to the living room where Stone sat down in the recliner. Eric remained standing to discourage a prolonged visit. Tiger sniffed at Stone's feet and declared him a friend after Stone scratched him behind the ear.

Stone then leaned forward in his chair to obtain a better feel for Kampe. Stone was normally good at sizing up a man, but this twenty-three-year-old standing in front of him was an enigma. He could have passed as an electrical engineer or a medical student. The way he spoke and his confident air gave the impression of intelligence. He was the type fathers would enjoy having their daughters bring home. But some people aren't always as they appear to be, and this rapist almost killed Sara Higgins. That would be sufficient to tarnish any medical student's résumé.

Kampe's disposition had not changed appreciably since Stone's last visit. He still had that intense anger and bitterness, but was it enough to kill? He had no reservations five years ago when he beat Sara Higgins to within inches of her life. That happened under the influence of drugs—not premeditated. What he had done five years ago was an impulsive crime, an act of sadistic lust, a sign of teenage immaturity. Stone assumed that had all changed. Kampe had graduated from one of Michigan's toughest academies: Marquette Branch Prison. Whatever he did now would be neither impulsive nor juvenile; it would be cold and calculated. There would be no mistakes or half-measures. Tampering with Sara's car was a premeditated and calculated act of hatred. The angry man standing before him was fully capable of such an act.

Since it was a hostile confrontation, Stone proceeded directly to the point. "Mr. Kampe, can you tell me what you've been doing over the last several days?"

"Are you my parole officer now?"

"If need be, I can have him come over and repeat my questions."

"If it really matters, I've been repairing the back entryway, which your law-abiding citizens destroyed." The sarcasm in Eric's voiced was not lost on Stone. "I can show you the proper building permits if you so desire."

"That won't be necessary. How many times have you left your house?"

"I wasn't aware I was under house arrest, so I went to the hardware store a couple of times. I've been to the grocery store, and every morning I run a few laps around the lake. Do you mind telling me what this is all about?"

Stone ignored the question. "When is the last time you talked to Sara Higgins?"

"I haven't seen her since the trial. Is that a problem?"

"You haven't seen her or talked to her in the last three days?"

"I already answered that question. Do I need a lawyer?"

"Sara Higgins has been missing for three days. You won't need an attorney if you had nothing to do with her disappearance.

If you are involved, you'll need a damn good one. You won't get off easy this time. You'll be staring at natural life, no parole."

"I'll say it again. I haven't seen Sara Higgins since the trial. She can be rotting away in some ditch—food for maggots and ravens—for all I care. In fact, I hope she is."

Stone wondered if the comment was a veiled reference to the booby-trapped car. That information he hadn't released to the public. Only the perpetrator would have known about it. On the other hand, if he were responsible for Sara's disappearance, he would have known the tampered car had failed to kill her.

"If you have no more serious questions, I have work to do." It was obviously the end of the discussion.

"Thank you for your time, Mr. Kampe. We'll be in touch."

"I don't think so. We just had our last conversation. Anything else you need to know, you can ask in front of my attorney." Eric walked the chief to the door and watched him back his car out of the driveway.

# 17

"Hey, Amy, how about another pitcher of beer." Jack Pippin waved an empty pitcher at the waitress washing glasses behind the bar. It was the third pitcher of the evening, and even divided five ways, that was pushing the limits of sobriety. None of the men at the table with Pippin was drunk by legal standards, but they all had sufficient alcohol flowing through their veins to distort their judgment.

"Coming at cha." Amy Rasmussen purposefully filled the pitcher only two-thirds full from the tap and carried it to the thirsty men at the rear of the lounge. It was late afternoon and the bowling lanes were idle, but a few of the regulars were nursing beers in the lounge before heading home for supper. Except for Jack Pippin and the four men sitting with him at the back table, the patrons had elected to straddle barstools.

Amy set the pitcher of beer in the center of the table and policed up the empty pitcher. "More pretzels?" Three pretzels were all that remained in the bottom of the basket.

"Can't have too many pretzels," one of the men said.

Amy grabbed the pretzel basket. "If you guys are driving, you need to indulge more on the pretzels and less on the beer. I wouldn't want anything to happen to any of you guys...I'd miss the tips." The men laughed.

"We have no intention of getting drunk," Pippin patted Amy on the rump, something he would have considered repulsive had it not been for the alcohol. "We got some work to do tonight."

Pippin waited until the waitress was out of earshot, and then turned to the men at the table. "So, are you guys with me?" He was met with silence. Pippin looked at the men one by one, finally focusing on Tom Stevens. "Tom?"

Tom Stevens returned Pippin's gaze for a moment and then lowered his eyes and massaged both sides of his head with his fingers as if to mollify some perceived discomfort. He had consumed enough beer to justify a hangover, but that wouldn't begin until morning. "I don't know about this, Jack," he finally said. At twenty-eight, Tom Stevens was the youngest of the group and had yet to develop the standard beer belly typical of Tamarack's middle-aged men. His skin was deeply tanned and his arms muscular. Logging will do that to you. "I think we should let the cops handle it. Isn't that's why we pay them the big bucks?" It was a rhetorical question. He didn't expect an answer, and no answer was forthcoming. "This could get us in a lot of trouble," he said to fill in the silence.

Pippin refilled his beer mug from the fresh pitcher. "Tom, you don't have any kids, but my wife tells me Kathy's expecting…It's going to be a boy, right?"

"No, it's a girl."

"You want to raise your daughter in a community filled with drug pushers and potheads?" Pippin paused to let his words sink in. "Tom, this isn't about Matt. Matt's dead. There's nothing we can do to bring him back." Pippins eyes began to water, as they did whenever he talked about his son. "This is about your daughter…your future daughter." Pippin looked at the other men at the table. "It's about all your sons and daughters. I like Stone as much as any of you, but the ACLU has his hands tied. He can't sneeze without those liberal lawyers serving him up with a lawsuit."

"Jack, what's to protect us?" Steve Lundquist asked. "We're as vulnerable to lawsuits as the Chief…maybe more so. Those same attorneys could come after us." Steve Lundquist was not one to make impulsive decisions without a complete evaluation of the facts, a trademark of a good accountant. But the facts remained sketchy at best. "We could do jail time."

"There's a certain amount of risk in everything we do, but someone has to have the gonads to take action," Pippin replied.

"We had a nice community until those bleeding-heart liberals gave Kampe a parole. Since he's been out, we've had two drug-related murders. Matt's death wasn't a suicide, despite what the coroner said. It was a cold-blooded murder. Kampe sold him drugs knowing the drugs would kill him. I call that murder. Anyone here think otherwise? If so, I want to hear it." Pippin paused waiting for a reply. He was greeted with silence. "Steve, we have to do this. We have to protect our kids."

Lundquist took a sip of beer and carefully placed the mug back on the table. It was a stalling tactic, but it bought him time to select his words. "Jack, you know we feel for you. We really do. Matt was a good boy, and I agree with you. What Kampe did was nothing less than murder. But, as you said, we have our own kids to think about. I don't want Pat raising our kids by herself while I'm rotting in prison on an arson charge."

"You think the county can find twelve people who'll convict us for running a rapist out of town?" Pippin looked at the four men sitting around the table. On that point, they were in agreement.

"Jack...there have been four murders this month—not two." Karl Schmidt played with a broken pretzel. It was the same pretzel he had been toying with for the last ten minutes. The men waited for Schmidt to elaborate, but he continued tormenting his pretzel.

"Karl, what do you mean there's four murders?" Pippin asked.

"I'm just saying there have been more than two murders this month." Schmidt flipped the pretzel to the side, no longer finding it of interest, but his eyes remained focused on the spot where the pretzel had previously resided. "I'm not supposed to say anything.... It could get my son in trouble. Luke sometimes helps out at Rasmussen's auto repair." Schmidt raised his gaze to look Pippin in the eye. "He says Kampe planted a bomb on the car belonging to the Higgins girl. For some reason, the bomb failed to explode; but as my mother used to say, it's the thought that counts. Ryan found it while repairing her car. Chief Stone wants to keep a lid on the information...so you didn't hear about this from me."

"The bomb didn't kill her?" Pippin asked. "You said there were four murders."

"There have been four murders. No one's seen the Higgins girl or that kid of hers for three days. Kampe got to them. Jack, they're as dead as your son."

Silence descended on the table as each man searched his soul for answers. Any lingering doubts concerning the pending course of action resolved with Schmidt's revelation. Sara Higgins was an exceptional teacher. Her students adored her. She had survived a brutal rape and still made something of her life. That alone was enough to earn the community's respect.

"Is everyone onboard with this?" Pippins asked, breaking the silence. Each man nodded in the affirmative. "We'll need gas cans. Shotguns only—no rifles. Pellets can't be traced."

"We only burn down the house," Stevens said. "No killing. I don't care what he's done. I won't go for any killing."

"Not unless we have to," Pippin replied.

"Any more beer or pretzels?" Amy asked.

"Pippin looked at the four men at the table. "I believe we're about done. Everyone knows what to bring?" The men nodded. "We meet at Kampe's Korner at ten. It'll be dark then."

Pippin turned to Amy. "Put this on my tab. Tonight's my treat."

* * *

"Hey, Chief, you got time for a visitor?"

Stone looked through the open door of his office. Amy Rasmussen was standing in front of Laura Weatherdon's desk fidgeting with the seam of her waitress uniform. Her presence at the police station was clearly making her uncomfortable.

"For Amy, I'll make time. Come on in, Amy."

Stone pulled a chair over to the side of his desk. "Here, Amy, have a seat." He didn't return to the chair behind his desk until Amy was comfortably seated.

"And to what do I own the honor of this visit? Can I get you some coffee?"

"No, thank you."

"Hopefully, none of my boys gave you a speeding ticket. If they did, I'll have to talk to them about that." It was only idle chatter. Everyone knew Stone didn't play favorites. A ticket was a ticket. He never interfered with the judgment of his deputies.

"I wish it were that simple. My husband told me about Sara's car."

Stone's smile evaporated. "I was hoping Ryan would keep that quiet for a few more days."

"If people find out, it won't come from me or my husband. But what I have to say is somewhat related." Amy paused—her attention now drawn to a small stain on her uniform. Whatever she had come to say was not easy. Stone waited for her to continue. "Chief, you have a problem."

"There's never a shortage of problems around here," Stone said, trying to lighten the atmosphere. "Which problem are you referring to?"

"I'm probably overreacting, but I think Jack Pippin and some of his friends are going to burn down Kampe's house tonight."

Stone didn't like what he was hearing, although it came as no surprise. Pippin could be impulsive, and it was inconceivable he would take the loss of his son lightly, but Stone had been hoping Pippin would only vent his anger verbally.

"I assume you have evidence to support your conclusion?"

"No. Nothing like that. I wasn't even sure if I should come. It's more of a gut feeling."

Stone had been in the business too long to ignore gut feelings. They were right more often than not. "Go on."

"Jack Pippin and four other men were in the lounge this afternoon. They did some heavy drinking—maybe too much. It was approaching the point where I didn't feel comfortable serving them any more. They thought they were having a private conversation, but when men have too much to drink their voices get louder. I didn't hear much of the conversation, but they mentioned Eric Kampe several times. When they were paying the bill, Jack told everyone to meet at Kampe's Korner at ten. I called my husband at the garage, and he suggested I come here." Amy looked down at her purse, signaling the end of the discussion. She had nothing more to say. Coming in had not been an easy decision, but it was over. Her conscience was clear.

"I want to thank you for coming," Stone said when it was clear she had nothing more to offer. "Ryan gave you good advice."

"I don't want to get them in trouble," Amy said. "They're good people."

"I know."

"I wouldn't shed a tear if lightning struck Kampe's house, and the house burned down with him in it. He either burns now or waits for hell. It still makes me sick when I think of what he did to Sara." Amy dabbed at her eyes with Kleenex from her purse. Stone hadn't been aware Amy and the Higgins girl had been that close, but judging from their ages, they could have been classmates in school.

"Can you stop them without arresting them?" Amy asked. "They haven't broken any laws, have they? It's only talk."

"I'll talk to them. There's no law against venting steam, but if they start any fires, we'll have to press charges."

Amy got up to leave. "I'd appreciate if my visit here wasn't made public."

"You were never here." Stone walked her to the door. "Amy...thanks for coming. You've been a great help."

"I hope you're right, Chief."

Stone closed the door behind her. It took a lot of courage to do what Amy did. Stone wished more citizens were that courageous.

"Laura, who's working the western side of the county tonight?"

Laura checked her schedule book. "We got Logan Koski working until midnight, and then Cory Kramer takes over."

"Get ahold of Koski and tell him to meet me tonight on M-28 one mile east of Kampe's Korner. I'll need him there by nine. And tell him to bring the Stinger." Stone grabbed his jacket. "I'm going out and get a bit to eat. This could be a long night."

* * *

Chief Stone parked his car on the shoulder of M-28 facing east and turned on his emergency roof lights. An approaching car, seeing the lights, slowed to a crawl and then timidly drove past; flashing red lights brought out the paranoia in everyone. Ten minutes later, Logan Koski pulled up in his police cruiser and parked on the opposite shoulder. Laura had given him a short briefing, which lacked many essential details. She assumed Stone would fill in the gaps. Koski rolled down his window.

"Hi, Chief. What's up?"

Stone climbed out of his car and walked over to Koski.

"Turn your car around facing east and park on the shoulder opposite my car. And turn on your light bar; it makes us look like real cops."

Without comment, Koski made a tight U-turn and parked on the opposite shoulder. With a flip of a switch, his emergency lights flooded the periphery with alternating red and blue light. The flashing lights on both sides of the highway were bound to get people's attention. Stone opened Koski's passenger door and claimed shotgun. He adjusted the seat backward to accommodate his large frame and then placed a brown shopping between his legs.

"I brought the coffee and donuts. It's been a while since I've been on a stake-out, but if I remember right, coffee and donuts are essential equipment." Stone reached into his grocery bag and pulled out a thermos and two Styrofoam cups. A second foray into the brown bag produced a white sack filled with pastries.

"Does Lois know about the pastries?" Koski checked out the forbidden fruit. There was a wide assortment of decadent goodies, none of which could be deemed low calorie.

"I try not to bring my work home. What happens at work stays at work. Consider that an order." Stone reached into the bag and selected a jelly-filled roll.

Koski selected an austere donut with a slight coating of cinnamon and sugar. "Ya know, Chief, I'm not a wizard at math, but every time I count it up there are five of them and only two of us. How you plan on playing this?"

"We screen everyone heading west. I assume Pippin and his friends will be coming in a convoy of three or four cars; numbers give them strength. When we see them, we turn on our headlights. They won't be able to see behind the lights where you will be standing. They'll have no idea how many men we have. That'll make them nervous. You have the Stinger?"

"It's in the trunk."

"Throw that across the road when you see them. It should extend fifteen feet if I remember right. Our cars are blocking the shoulders, and the Stinger will puncture the tires of anyone who tries to push past on the road."

"You ever used the Stinger?" Koski asked.

"No, but it looks good when the TV cops use it."

Stone grabbed another donut from the bag. He justified his
indiscretion by picking a smaller specimen. It was still slathered
with icing.

"I want you behind one of the cars for protection. No sense
both of us getting killed. They may have shotguns, but I don't
expect they'll use them. If you have to shoot, use your shotgun and
aim one or two yards in front of their feet. The pellets will ricochet
into their lower legs. That'll get their attention without causing
serious damage."

It was ten minutes past ten and two donuts later when Koski
saw the two pickup trucks and an SUV heading in their direction.

"They're late."

"No one's ever on time in Cade County." Stone stuffed the
last of his donut in his mouth and brushed the crumbs from his
clothing. "I think it's time to get out the Stinger."

Koski opened his trunk and removed a pump shotgun from its
case and loaded it with five shells. Then he opened the black case
containing the Stinger. It only weighted nine pounds but it
stretched to fifteen feet and contained one hundred and ten hollow
spikes. The spikes could deflate a tire in fifteen to twenty seconds.

While Koski was throwing the Stinger across the road, Stone
turned on the headlights of the two squad cars and switched them
to high beam. The on-coming vehicles slowed to a stop twenty feet
from the roadblock. Six people emerged from the vehicles; they
had recruited an additional man.

"Howdy, boys." Stone walked into the wash of the headlights.
As usual, he was unarmed. He assumed heavy artillery only
escalated tensions. His policy had served him well over the years.
"The road's closed to traffic. You'll have to turn around."

Jack Pippin was the first to speak. "We have no grudge with
you, Stone. We just need to mosey on down the road a ways."

"Can't let you do that. The bridge between here and Kampe's
Korner is out."

"There's no bridge between here and Kampe's Korner."

"I would have sworn that was where Laura said the bridge was
out."

Stone walked over to one of the pickups. "There's a shotgun
in the cab. You boys going do some hunting?"

"You might say that," Pippin replied.

"It looks like a shotgun in the SUV too." Stone checked the back of one of the pickups, finding several gas cans. "Hunting season is over. This is June."

"The season on varmints never closes."

"Jack, I believe you're right. You guys definitely know your hunting rules. I'm sure you also know in Michigan all guns have to be in a case or broken down when transported in a car. I do believe you guys have broken the law." Stone pantomimed sniffing the air. "I believe I also smell alcohol. I think someone may have been drinking." Stone turned toward the patrol cars with their circling red lights. "You guys have any breathalyzers handy?" He carefully addressed Koski in the plural.

"Chief, a couple of the boys here just happened to have them ready to go," Koski replied. "Want us to start checking people out?"

Stone rubbed his chin as if in deep thought. "If we start writing citations for DUI and transporting firearms improperly, that's a whole lot of citations. And it looks like some opened alcohol containers in those cup holders. It'll take us half the night to do all that paperwork. Hey, Deputy Koski...how we doing on tickets for the week? Are we getting close to our quota?"

"I'm not positive, Chief, but it's got to be pretty close."

Stone turned back to the men. "There you have it. If you guys wanted to turn around and head for home, we could call it an evening and pretend this never happened. It sure would save me and the boys a lot of paperwork."

Stone was met with silence. The men looked at Jack Pippin for guidance. Pippin didn't appear willing to back down. Stone mentally reviewed the options. In a mob situation, never go for the leader. That only gives the mob strength. It's better to peal away the followers layer by layer like an onion until only the leader is left. That was how it worked in theory.

"Look," Stone said. "We know why you men are here and what you plan on doing. We all feel for Matt's untimely death. It should never have happened, and I apologize for letting it happen on my watch, but this isn't the right way to go about it. Laws have to be respected. What you plan to do is bigger than a few open beer cans in a cup holder. You could do hard time."

Stone turned to Tom Stevens. "Tom, I hear Kathy's expecting. What is it—a girl? My wife tells me you're going to name her Annika. That's a pretty name. Too bad you won't be there for the delivery. Maybe Kathy can hold up some pictures to the glass at the state pen's visiting room. In five to ten years you might be able to hold your daughter."

Stone walked over to Steve Lundquist. "Steve, you got a couple of kids in high school—girls, I believe. What're they going to tell their friends during the trial? In a small town like Tamarack, the trial's going to be big news. It'll be the talk of the town."

Lundquist looked over at Pippin. Even in the flood of the headlights, the strain in Lundquist's face was palpable. If Stone could break even one person, the rest would crumble; but again, that was only theory.

"Jack, I'm sorry. I can't do this." Lundquist lowered his gaze to avoid Pippin's eyes and then quietly climbed into the cab of his pickup. One by one, the others followed suit and drove away, leaving Jack Pippin standing alone; the onion had been pealed revealing only a broken man. Pippin wore a three-day-old beard and his shoulders sagged under the weight they bore.

"Levi, he was only seventeen. He wasn't even old enough to vote."

Stone placed a hand on Pippin's shoulder. "I know, Jack, but this won't make things right. Vengeance only provides short term relieve, but the guilt will last forever. I can't give you details, but we're a cat's whisker from arresting him. We have to be sure we have sufficient evidence to may the charges stick. I don't want him walking after the trial."

"Just arrest Kampe. You won't find twelve men or women in Cade County who won't convict that rapist."

Pippin turned and headed for his truck.

"Jack, I can have Logan give you a ride home…. We'll bring your truck around in the morning."

"I'm fine. I just need some time alone."

Stone watched Pippin's taillights disappear down the road. Stone wasn't sure he would have acted any differently if it had been his son lying in the morgue. This wasn't the fun part of his job. Stone felt an urge to eat another donut.

"Are we really that close to an arrest?" Koski asked.

"I haven't told anyone yet, but this morning I was out to the Higgins place. I found two nine-millimeter casings out by the barn. They were lying on newly bent grass and couldn't be more than a day or two old. We have two missing persons and two shell casings. This is now a homicide investigation. If we can obtain a search warrant and find Kampe's gun, we might be able to match it to the casings. The firing pins leave a distinctive mark. Tomorrow I'm also getting a search warrant for the Higgins farm. I want it torn apart inside and out. My guess is we'll find the bodies somewhere on the premises. You working tomorrow?"

"Tomorrow's my day off, but if you need help, I can put in some overtime."

"Can you meet me at the Higgins farmhouse at ten?" Koski nodded in the affirmative.

"Pippin was right about one thing."

"What's that?" Stone asked.

"You could charge Kampe with sole responsibility for the Holocaust, and the good people of Cade County would find him guilty."

"You may be right, Logan, but it's our responsibility to ensure that doesn't happen."

18

Logan Koski was leaning against his police cruiser when Stone pulled into the driveway. Stone brought his Ford Explorer to a stop behind Koski's car and placed it in park. Unless he needed a police radio or a partitioned back seat, he preferred the familiarity and extra legroom of his personal vehicle.

"Did you get the search warrant?" Koski asked.

Stone stepped out of the SUV and patted the document in his breast pocket. "Since Higgins is officially a missing person, Judge Madalinski is giving us free rein." Stone walked to the back of his Explorer and popped the hatch. He retrieved two black cases. One was for the Polaroid camera; the other was the evidence kit. It contained latex gloves in a variety of sizes, specimen containers, and an assortment of forensic chemicals.

"I snooped around the outside while I was waiting for you," Koski said. "Nothing much of interest. The mailbox is full, and she has four days' worth of newspapers. I knocked on the door, but no one answered."

"Well, let's go have a peek inside. The backdoor was unlocked yesterday."

Stone peered through the window in the back door. Finding nothing changed from his previous visit, he put on latex gloves, opened the door, and stepped into the kitchen. The farmhouse was small, but the Higgins girl had turned it into a cozy home. Except for some cereal bowls in the sink and an opened box of Cheerios on the counter, the kitchen was tidy. The kitchen chairs were lined up around the table with military precision, and the floor was spotless. Stone was relieved to find no foul odor. It Sara and her daughter had been killed four days ago and the bodies left in the house, the stench would be overwhelming.

"Logan, why don't you take the basement. I'll do the ground floor. We'll do a quick walk through and then we'll regroup and take the house apart room by room. I'll let you have the camera and evidence kit. You're better at that stuff anyway."

Koski took the two bags, hung their straps over his shoulders, and headed for the basement stairs while Stone headed for the bedrooms. The larger bedroom had adult clothes in the closet. Stone assumed that bedroom belonged to Sara. The double bed was neatly made, not to military standards, but far better than Stone would have done it. Lying on top of the bed were four empty clothes hangers. Considering the tidiness of the rest of the bedroom, they appeared out of place. Stone found nothing in the room to suggest violence. The second bedroom was noticeably smaller. A small throw rug with *Winnie the Pooh* in the center covered the hardwood floor beside the bed. Unlike the other bedroom, the bedding was pulled back as if someone had slept in it, but it was not violently torn apart. On the left side of the bed was an end table with several children's books scattered across the top. Stone picked up the top book and flipped through the pages. It was *The Cat In The Hat*, a favorite of his kids when they were growing up.

"Chief, can you come down to the basement for a minute."

Stone set the book aside and headed for the basement. Koski was at the bottom of the stairs holding a damp mop and a spray bottle of Luminol.

"What ya got, Logan?"

Without comment, Logan sprayed the mop with Luminol. The mop gave off a bluish glow.

"There's blood on the mop."

The test was disconcerting, but not definitive. Luminol combined with the iron in hemoglobin to phosphoresce. Unfortunately, the Luminol combined with any iron, not just iron in blood.

"It could be iron in the water." Stone did not want it to be blood. Blood was never a good sign in a missing-persons case.

Koski walked over to the dryer and sprayed the floor. It too gave off a bluish glow. He sprayed a path from the dryer to the steps and small smudges of blue emerged to form a line leading to the stairs. Cleaning had removed all visual evidence of blood, but not the microscopic traces.

"Chief, I'm willing to bet a month's salary the forensic team will confirm this is blood."

That was another bet Stone was not willing to make. Luminol had its limitations, but a pattern like that was almost definitive. Another drawback of Luminol was timing. The blood could be a month old or four days old. Stone hoped it wasn't the latter.

Two hours of diligent searching failed to find the smoking gun, but then it didn't turn up any dead bodies either. Stone found a stack of threatening letters in a dresser drawer. They were undated, but the top note was likely the most recent and also the most ominous. *Leave town and don't come back or I will have to hurt you and your daughter* leaves little to the imagination. Stone returned the letters to the dresser. There was enough evidence to declare the farmhouse a crime scene. He would have the State Police send in their forensic team for a more thorough examination. That could take weeks to get a formal report. If the Higgins girl and her daughter were still alive, which was now doubtful, they didn't have weeks. Stone placed *Do Not Enter* signs on both doors and walked Koski back to the cars.

"Well, Logan, what's your take on the story? What do you think happened here?"

"I've come up with two stories. Which one ya want?"

"Why don't you give me the *Cliff's Notes* version of both stories."

"In the first scenario, it is evening four days ago before the newspapers began to accumulate. The daughter is already in bed. Higgins receives the death threat and panics. She packs some emergency clothes and leaves the hangers on the bed in her haste. She scoops her daughter out of bed, tosses her into the church mini-van along with the clothes and a few cans of tuna fish, and disappears into the sunset. Now she's lying on the beach somewhere in Acapulco sipping piña coladas."

"And the second scenario?"

"Same time frame. The daughter is in bed, but this time the Higgins girl is in the basement washing clothes. Kampe walks in through the unlocked back door. He finds Higgins in the basement and beats the snot out of her with his handy-dandy black baseball bat. She escapes and tries to flee leaving a trail of blood up the stairs. He catches her outside and gives her the *coup de grâce* with a nine-millimeter. He goes back and drags the terrified kid over to her mother's dead body and then he shoots the kid in the head. He then buries the bodies in the woods five miles from here where we will never find them. The rain we had two days ago washes away the blood and all that remains on the grass are the nine-millimeter shell casings you found. Kampe goes back into the house and mops up the blood, thinking he's removed all traces of the homicide."

"I like your first scenario better."

"Me too."

"How do you explain the blood and shell casings in the first scenario?"

"I can't."

# 19

Eric finished stretching his hamstrings and headed down the bike path. The morning was unseasonably cool, and dense fog hovered motionless over Harley Lake like loose fluffs of cotton candy. Somewhere—beyond that fog—the sun was rising, but it wouldn't burn off the fog until mid-morning. Undeterred by fog or cool weather, Tiger ran ahead, pausing now and then to mark a tree.

Cool temperatures were conducive to running, but Eric was in no mood to appreciate the cool weather. Cool weather did not ensure cool temperaments. No matter how hard he tried, Eric could not push Stone's accusations from his mind. He was not normally quick to anger, but he was reaching his limits. Cade County was his home. This was where he grew up. This was where his childhood memories had their birth; but as long as he stayed in Cade County, he would remain the modern-day Jesse James, blamed for all misdeeds, large or small. The more he thought about Cade County the less it had to offer. His parents were dead, and other than Rory, he had no friends in Cade County. He had no future in Cade County.

Motivated by pure hatred and anger, Eric increased his pace until he was no longer running; he was sprinting, pushing his body to the limit. His lungs ached with pain, but he could endure pain; pain was good; pain was therapeutic. He pushed on, placing distance behind him. But no matter how fast he ran, he couldn't outrun Chief Stone or Sara Higgins. He could think of nothing else. At the far side of the lake, when his body refused to endure further pain, Eric slowed to a jog. Finally, he stopped to catch his breath. He leaned forward, bracing his palms against his knees while his heart and lungs labored to catch up with his muscles.

"Tar Zan, Tar Zan."

Eric turned just in time to catch Rory as she jumped into his arms. "Hey there, Rory. Haven't seen you for a while. What are you doing on this side of the lake? Your sitter will have a fit when she can't find you."

"Mommy and I are camping."

"That sounds like a fun."

"Hello, Eric…or should I call you Tar Zan?" Sara stepped out of the woods but came no closer. Normally an impeccable dresser, her clothes were wrinkled, and sweat-smeared grime covered her face. She had her snarl-filled hair tied back in a ponytail, and caution had replaced her usual air of confidence.

"Hello, Sara." Eric lowered Rory to the ground. He had planned to confront Sara, but not like this. He wanted to confront Sara on his terms and on his schedule. She had taken him by surprise. "Rory's your daughter?"

"You didn't know?"

"How was I to know? Rory is so loving and honest—there's nothing in her character to suggest she was your daughter." Eric hoped Sara appreciated the coldness in his response.

"I suppose I deserved that."

"Rather careless of you to let your daughter associate with a convicted felon, a certified sex offender."

"Mommy, this is my friend Tar Zan."

"Rory, why don't you and Tiger run off and play while Tar Zan and I talk." Sara waited until Rory was out of hearing. "You'd never do anything to hurt Rory."

"How do you know that?"

"I know you inside and out. You aren't capable of hurting anything. I was the one who had to pith your frog in freshman biology. You couldn't even kill a frog."

"I've changed. I've been to prison."

"You may think you've changed, but you haven't. Everyone knows what you did for that yellow dog of yours. And I know why you named him Tiger. Eric, you haven't changed one bit. The biggest lie is the lie you tell yourself. It's not nice to lie."

"Where have I heard that line before? You're definitely Rory's mother, but it's too bad you never listen to your own sermons."

Eric and Sara stared at each other like a pair of alley cats sizing up each other before a fight, neither one willing to betray any emotion; their faces remained stoic.

"I can't blame you for hating me," Sara finally said. "I have no doubt I will rot in hell for what I did."

"Then why did you do it? Why did you lie?"

"I don't know...I was scared. You had always been there when I needed you. You were always the strong one. I always counted on you. When you weren't there... I blamed you for letting it happen...I hated you...I hated the world. I wasn't thinking right. He said he would beat me and rape me again if I didn't do it." Sara's dispassionate façade began to crumble. Five years of sequestered emotions burst past the mental barricade she had erected, and her eyes began to water. "Oh, Eric, I'm so sorry I hurt you."

"Who was it? Who did it to you?"

"I don't know. If I knew, I could've told the police. He wore a black ski mask and only whispered. He left a threatening note at the hospital. It was on my dinner tray. He has to be someone from around here. Someone people trust. Without a name or a description, going to the police would have been useless. People said I had a strong will to live, but I wanted to die. I so badly wanted to die, but the doctors wouldn't let me. I have pills in my dresser. I could have done it. I've considered it many times. If it hadn't been for Rory, I would have done it. It would have been better for everyone if I had. I felt so cheap and degraded. My face was disfigured; no one would ever love me again." Sara wept openly. She tried to wipe away the tears with her shirtsleeve, but it only smeared the dirt on her face. The tears continued to flow.

"Did you really think my love was that shallow?" Eric asked, his face still cold and expressionless. He did not intend to make it easy.

"You didn't see me, Eric. You can't imagine how disfigured I was before the surgeries."

"I saw you every day." Eric's expressionless face turned to anger. "Sara, I was at that hospital every stinking day. I held your hand for hours. And when you came out of the coma, they said you wouldn't see me."

"Eric, I'm so sorry." Sobbing uncontrollably, Sara fell to her knees, her face in her hands.

"You could have gone to the police. You still can…assuming you have some spine. They're looking for you, by the way. They think I'm responsible for your disappearance."

"At one time I had a signed confession in my dresser drawer that completely exonerated you. I came close to mailing it several times."

"Why didn't you? Couldn't find a post office?"

"It would mean perjury and obstruction of justice. I could have done prison time."

"So you let me do prison time instead?"

"I had Rory to think about. There's no one to care for her if something happens to me. My father's getting old. That's why I'm here. He's still out there, Eric. He tried to kill me. He'll try again if he gets the chance. The hospital put your name on Rory's birth certificate. Eric, you're Rory's legal father. I know I have no right to ask this of you, but if something were to happen to me, if he should kill me, would you take Rory? I know you would make a good father. You have every right to hate me. But please don't hate Rory. She had nothing to do with what I did." Sara tried to regain her composure. She wiped away her tears, but fresh tears replaced the old.

Eric looked down at the quivering figure before him. He now had Sara where he wanted her. She was vulnerable. He could inflict pain upon pain and exact his revenge. This was what he had dreamed about every day he was in prison. He could make her pay for what she had done. But when he looked at the pathetic figure in front of him, he experienced no joy. He felt neither love nor hate, only pity. "What makes you think he's trying to kill you?"

Sara took the note from her shirt pocket and handed it to Eric. "He broke into my bedroom while I was sleeping and placed the note on my nightstand. Then he tampered with the accelerator and brakes of my car. He almost killed us."

Eric studied the note. All the letters were written in a block style to prevent identification. "This was written by a woman. All the i's have small circles above them instead of dots. That's something a woman would do."

"He RAPED me, Eric. Trust me, he's male."

"Why would he want to kill you?"

"In case you haven't noticed, Rory has blond hair and blue eyes; neither of us does. If we stay in the area, people will begin to talk. A DNA test will prove you aren't the father, and the case will be re-opened. Don't you see? He can't allow that to happen. That's why he has to kill Rory and me. I've applied for a teaching job in Oregon. They said I have an excellent chance of getting the job. I'm expecting a contract in the mail any day. Rory and I have been hiding in the woods, but I check my mailbox every night. I just hope the contract comes soon. We're running out of food, and I don't know how much longer we can hide without someone seeing us. If something happens to me, would you take Rory? I no longer care if I die. It would be better for everyone if I were dead, but someone has to care for Rory. I have no close relatives. Eric, I'm begging you. She's as vulnerable as that orphaned fawn. She deserves a chance at life just like that fawn did."

"Whether or not you die makes no difference to me; however, it will to Rory. I'll help you get to Oregon. After that, you're on your own. I never want to see you or hear from you again. I'm only doing this for Rory. Is that clear?"

"Thank you, Eric. That's all I can ask. When I get to Oregon, I'll have a hospital take a DNA sample from Rory and send it to Chief Stone along with a signed confession. That'll exonerate you. Then you can go on with your life. I'm hoping they won't find it worthwhile tracking me down in Oregon."

"You're jumping the gun. In case you haven't noticed, this isn't Oregon, Toto. We'll have to get rid of that van before someone discovers it. A bright blue van with church logos on the sides is hard to hide. Then we need to find a place you can stay."

"Can we stay at your house?" Sara asked. "It'll only be for a day or two. We'll stay out of your way."

"That's the first place the police will look. And whatever you do, don't call me on the phone. The police probably have my phone tapped. My father has a hunting camp at the end of

Witticker Road. It has two bedrooms, a shower, and a small kitchen. You'll be safe there. There should be canned goods in the cupboard. Right now, you need to stay out of sight. I'll meet you here after dark with some milk, cereal, and bread. That along with the canned goods at the cabin should get you through the next few days. We can't use my car. The police are watching it. They'd become suspicious if it's not in my driveway."

"How will we find your camp?"

"I'll drive you out there in the van and then return the van to the church. We can't leave any vehicles at the hunting camp. If someone drives by, the place needs to look deserted."

Eric whistled and Tiger came running back, along with Rory. "You need to stay off the bike path. People will be using it once the fog burns off. I'll meet you back here at nine tonight."

"Thank you, Eric."

"Don't thank me. I'm doing this for Rory. She needs a mother. She's a good kid, Sara. You've done a good job raising her."

Eric walked the rest of the way around the lake. Running relieved frustrations, but he preferred walking when he needed to think. The late-night rendezvous wouldn't be easy. He was sure the police had him under surveillance. The question was how tight was the surveillance? In a rural setting, it's difficult to stake out a house from a parked car without being seen. Most likely, they were periodically driving past his house to ensure his car was in the driveway. In that respect, he would not disappoint them.

Eric did his grocery shopping early and randomly added the special provisions to his regular groceries. The police were unlikely to check his purchases; if they did, they would find a normal shopping list. Next he stopped at the video store to pick up a movie. If the police were watching him, it wouldn't hurt to have them think he was spending the evening watching a movie. They could see the flicker of his TV from the street. That should pacify any surveillance team. He would be back before the movie ended. Eric spent fifteen minutes selecting the movie he would never watch. He settled on *The Shawshank Redemption*, a movie about an ineffective police force and a corrupt prison system where the inmate eventually comes out ahead. He had seen it before, but felt the plotline would be poetic if the police were to check his selection.

At a quarter to nine, Eric inserted the DVD into his TV and adjusted the volume louder than he would normally have desired. He turned off all his lights except for those in his living room; he didn't want any light escaping when he opened the back door. He stuffed the groceries into a backpack, all except the bread. That he would hand carry. At ten minutes to nine, Eric and Tiger slipped out the back door.

He carried a flashlight, but didn't use it until his house was out of sight. Most of the time, Eric was able to follow the path without the flashlight. He used it sparingly when large oaks blocked out the starlight. Five minutes into the walk, Eric stepped off the trail and waited quietly under the trees. Only after he was assured no one was following him did he continue on his way.

Tiger found Sara and Rory first, wolfing out a friendly greeting. Eric would have preferred a silent, less-friendly greeting. He flashed the light in the direction of the noise and found Rory on her knees with her arms around Tiger's neck. Tiger was licking her face.

"Where's the van?" Eric asked.

"Follow me." Sara, using her penlight, led them down a narrow trail frequented only by fisherman, her discomposure of earlier now gone. After a hundred yards, the trail widened into two parallel ruts. The van was parked off to the side, hidden in the darkness. Unless someone were to walk up to the van and see the church logo, it would appear to be a fisherman's van.

"Give me the keys," Eric said, "I know the way to the camp."

Sara gave Eric the keys without comment and climbed into the front passenger seat while Rory and Tiger took over the rear of the van. Eric tossed the backpack filled with groceries into the back corner.

"Here's some candy bars." Eric gave one to Sara and threw two in the back for Rory and Tiger to share. The candy bars were quickly devoured.

Eric climbed into the driver's seat and inserted the key. "You have bullet holes in your windshield."

"And you wonder why I think he's trying to kill us? He was at my house two days ago and took a couple of shots at me."

"Are you hurt?"

"No, I guess not...except for a nose bleed. He tried to strangle me, but I escaped and made it to the van. When I turned on the van's lights, he was standing in the driveway right in front of me. I aimed the van at him and stepped on the gas. Then I bent down in the seat. That's when he tried to shoot me. I think we both missed our targets. My father's not going to be happy when he sees the holes in his windshield. And I got blood all over his front seat."

Eric turned on the lights and drove the van out of the woods. It would cause less suspicion than maneuvering without lights. In the darkness, no one would see the church logo, and the headlights would ruin their night vision. The turnoff to Witticker Road wasn't far. They wouldn't traverse any well-lighted intersections that would illuminate the logo on the side panel, and with some luck, they might make it to the hunting camp unseen.

Ten minutes later, Eric turned left onto Witticker Road. It was a gravel road used seasonally by owners of the cabins located at the end of long, dirt driveways. No houses or cabins faced the road. Since it was neither hunting nor tourist season, they encountered no oncoming traffic. Four miles farther down the road, the trail would terminate in a small cul-de-sac only large enough to make a "U" turn. Just before the cul-de-sac, Eric turned off Witticker Road onto a narrow driveway that gave the impression of limited use. Tree branches brushed simultaneously against both sides of the van.

A hundred yards from the road, the drive opened into a small clearing. Starlight outlined a small cabin. It was primitive and rustic, the type of residence men not only tolerated, but enjoyed.

"What did your parents use the cabin for?"

"The cabin comes with forty acres of woods and swamp. My father and some of his cronies used it for deer hunting. At least that was their cover story. I think it was mostly to get away from their wives and play cards. In the summer we came here for the peace and quiet. There's a good hiking trail, and a small stream to the north has some good-size brook trout."

Eric drove up to the back door and parked such that the van's headlights illuminated the back of the cabin. Sara climbed out and opened the side door for Rory and Tiger. They were both eager to stretch their legs.

A heavy-duty Yale lock secured the back door. Eric keyed the lock and opened the door. The flood of his flashlight revealed a small kitchen. It had a musty smell, not a surprise since no one had used it since deer season. Eric pulled a lever attached to the electrical panel box and flipped a wall switch. Overhead fluorescent fixtures suffused the kitchen with light.

"It's not fancy," he told Sara, "but it beats living in a van. It has electricity and flush toilets. I'll light the water heater, but it'll take an hour before you'll have hot water for showers."

"This is beautiful. I don't know how to thank you."

"Don't…I'm doing this for Rory."

"What's with the trap door?" Sara pointed to a panel of wood attached by two rusty hinges to the center of the kitchen floor.

"That's a root cellar." Eric pulled up on an iron ring, and the trap door opened. A long wooden ladder extended into the darkness. "People used to store potatoes, turnips, and other vegetables in root cellars to keep them fresh through the winters."

Sara looked into the darkness. "I hope I never have to go down there. It looks awful spooky."

"It's empty. No one's used it for years. If you really had to get into the root cellar, there's another entrance from the outside—a lean-to shed door with steps. Trust me; the root cellar has little to offer. You can look around while I get the groceries from the van. Some of groceries need to be refrigerated."

Sara opened the refrigerator and found it warm. She reset the thermostat and a soft hum filled the room as the motor kicked in. Like the rest of the cabin, the refrigerator had a musty smell.

"Everything will need cleaning," Eric said when he returned with the groceries. "That'll give you something to do. You shouldn't spend any time outside where people can see you." Eric set the groceries on the counter. "I hope you like gas ranges."

"I'm more used to electric, but we haven't eaten a hot meal in three days. We'll make do with what we have."

Eric opened the cupboard doors. You have lots of canned goods…beef stew…tuna fish…and here's some instant rice. With the additional groceries I bought, you should be able to survive in style for a week or more."

"I'll reimburse you for any food we eat."

Eric ignored the comment and walked into the living room, which was an extension of the kitchen. Only the edge of a well-worn rug covering the living room floor established the demarcation between the two rooms. Like the kitchen, the living room was rustic—and dirty. Dusty sheets covered the furniture. Sara removed a sheet from the couch. It was dark blue with lighter blue floral patterns—definitely selected by a woman. A fireplace constructed of stone added a homespun atmosphere. A stack of kindling wood along with some split logs of sugar maple sat next to the fireplace, proof that the fireplace was functional and not just an ornament. The two bedrooms were small but adequate. The bare mattresses sagged in the middle from years of use.

"Sheets and blankets are in the dresser drawers." Eric pointed toward the dresser.

"I never knew your parents had a cabin out here."

Eric offered no reply and began unloading the groceries. He had no desire for idle conversation with Sara. The sooner she was out of his life the better. He placed the fresh milk and orange juice in the refrigerator. The refrigerator was still warm, but it would cool fast.

"I probably bought more food than you need, but I don't know when I can return."

"It's a nice cabin," Sara said, "although the bars on the windows make it feel like a prison."

"If you really want to get the feeling of a prison, try locking yourself in the bathroom for five years. That's what a real prison feels like. If it make you feel any better, my mother didn't like the bars either, but we had so much vandalism my father thought it necessary. You'll get used to them in a day or two. You won't even know they're there. Did you check the cupboards?"

"There are plenty of canned goods," Sara said. "More than we'll need."

"I don't know how clean the dishes and bowls are. No one's used them since November. I got you some dish soap. I wasn't sure if there would be any here. I haven't been here in years. You got milk, orange juice, and hamburger in the refrigerator. There's a tub of ice cream in the freezer compartment in case you want a snack. Rory prefers her ice cream with chocolate syrup. That's in the refrigerator."

"We'll do fine," Sara said.

"I'm leaving Tiger with you. He's not much of a watchdog, since he likes everyone, but he'll bark if anyone approaches the cabin. I put dog food in the cupboard for him. He likes lots of chocolate syrup on his ice cream." Eric scratched Tiger on the head. "He's a bit spoiled and sleeps on my bed at home. You might have to lock him out of your bedroom unless you want him in bed with you."

"It's only for a day or two. We'll do fine. But I should call Cory and let him know I'm all right. I don't want the police thinking I'm missing."

"I wouldn't do that. The more people you tell, the more likely that anonymous 'friend' of yours will find out. Remember, keeping your whereabouts unknown is why you're here. How are you going to explain your presence in my cabin to the police?"

"I know you don't like Cory, but he's only doing his job. He can be discrete."

Eric didn't dignify the comment with a reply. He didn't trust anyone with a badge.

"Anything else you need?"

"No, we're fine."

"I need to get going. I have to be back before the movie ends. If you need to get ahold of me, call on your cell phone. Let it ring once and hang up. Do that twice. It takes caller ID two or three rings to identify the caller. I'll call you back from the pay phone at the store."

Eric drove the van toward Kampe's Korner. He had no good plan for returning the van. The gas station flooded Kampe's Korner with light, and there was always traffic, even at this time of the night. Someone was bound to see the van. Only one option came to mind, and that was risky. Just before Kampe's Korner, Eric turned off the road and headed toward the bike path. It hadn't rained for several days, and the ground was dry and hard. Eric drove the van across an open field and onto the bike path. He turned off his headlights, using only the parking lights for navigating. Luckily, there were no late-night strollers on the path, and the church parking lot was void of people. Eric parked the van in its reserved parking spot and wiped his fingerprints off the steering wheel and door. Then he left the keys in the ignition and walked home. His movie was just coming to the end. He hoped it had been a good movie.

## 20

Sara waited until the van's taillights disappeared around the bend in the driveway before opening a can of tuna. She was famished; but didn't wish to provide Eric with the satisfaction of knowing that. She couldn't remember the last time tuna fish smelled this good. She had skipped several meals to ensure Rory had plenty to eat. Until now, she hadn't realized how significant those sacrifices had been.

A patina of dust covered the bowls in the cupboard, begging for a thorough cleaning. That presented a major affront to Sara's sense of tidiness, but she pushed such thoughts aside. She only washed the bowl she needed; the rest of the dishes would have to wait until morning when she had more energy.

"Hey, Twinkle Toes, you want a tuna sandwich and some chips?" Sara added Mayo from the jar in the refrigerator. "If you do, wash your hands."

Both Rory and Tiger arrived at the dinner table ready to eat. Rory's hands were clean up to her wrists. Sweat-smeared dirt still covered her forearms and face. It would take a good tub soaking to remove that much dirt.

"Can Tiger have a sandwich too?" Rory asked. Tiger looked up, waiting for a reply.

"Tiger has his own food." Sara opened a can of dog food and placed it in a bowl on the floor, and then passed a tuna fish sandwich to Rory along with some chips. Too exhausted to maintain a conversation, they ate in silence. The Spartan conditions they had endured while living in the van had robbed them of quality sleep and their sleep-deprived bodies now refused to function. Tonight would be different. They would sleep in real beds with real pillows and with real food filling their stomachs. They finished their sandwiches and washed them down with two-percent milk fresh from the carton. Sara would have preferred skim milk, although the extra calories wouldn't hurt them. Tuna and chips made a crude evening meal, but then Sara was famished, and it was almost bedtime. She had neither the time nor the patience for such niceties as preparing a well-balanced dinner. Tomorrow morning she would prepare a hot meal, perhaps pancakes. She had discovered a box of pancake mix in the cupboard along with an unopened bottle of syrup. Rory was fond of pancakes.

"Bed time," Sara proclaimed after they consumed the last of the potato chips. "I'll let you pick your bedroom."

Rory and Tiger checked out the rooms and settled on the smaller of the two bedrooms after a few trial bounces on each of the beds. The northern pike mounted on the wall of the smaller room was the deciding factor. The pike's mouth gaped open as if preparing a vicious attack on a yellow fishing lure that the taxidermist had mounted in front of the fish. The large mouth with its multitude of sharp, pointed teeth encouraged the creative mind. To a five-year-old with a vivid imagination, the fish became a ferocious sea serpent waiting to be slain. Tiger had no comment.

After tucking Rory into bed, Sara sank into the living room recliner. The stress of the last three days was catching up with her. That and her lack of sleep were converging into a horrendous headache. She had never experienced a migraine but wondered if a headache of this magnitude would qualify. It couldn't get any worse. It felt like someone was piercing her brain through her eye sockets with a pair of red-hot pokers. A cursory search of the premises produced a half-empty bottle of aspirin from the medicine cabinet above the bathroom sink. She took three.

The cabin was a major improvement over the van, providing beds, food, and hot water for showers. Being at the end of the road also eliminated any passing traffic. To most of the world, she and Rory no longer existed, having dropped from the radar screens of friend and foe alike. Soon people would notice and begin looking for them. Eric said the police had already listed them as missing persons. The seclusion provided security, but it didn't justify having the police expend valuable man-hours in a fruitless search.

Sara retrieved her cell phone from her purse and dialed Cory's apartment. He worked nights, and wouldn't be home, but she could leave a message on his answering machine. He occasionally checked his machine from his cell phone. Sara chided herself for not memorizing Cory's cell phone number. Then she could have called him direct.

The answering machine kicked in on the fifth ring. "Hello, Cory," Sara said at the end of the beep. "This is Sara. I just called to let you know I'm alive and well and staying at a cabin at the end of Witticker Road. If you hear this message before eleven o'clock, please give me a call on my cell phone. You have my number. Otherwise, I'll call you in the morning." Sara hung up the phone. She wasn't optimistic about Cory checking his answering machine before eleven o'clock, not that there was anything critical she needed to tell him. She just needed to talk to someone. Cory was tactful. He could terminate the police search without excessive questions. As far as the police knew, she hadn't broken any laws.

Sara returned the phone to her purse and took out her pistol. She had been unable to lock up her gun while living in the van and had removed the bullets for fear Rory might find the gun. Darkness was now a bigger fear. That was when her tormentor crawled out of his hole to perform his evil deeds. If he were to try again, he would find her ready. Sara reloaded her pistol, ensured it was on safety, and returned it to her purse.

Then Sara thumbed through an old Sports Illustrated magazine and half-heartedly read some of the articles. She should be sleeping, but she would sleep better after talking with Cory. At least that was the argument she offered in defense of staying awake. Perhaps she should come clean with the police. Her father would care for Rory if she had to do jail time. In the end, that could be less stressful than living her current lie. She looked at her watch: it was ten to eleven, making it unlikely Cory would call. It had been wishful thinking on her part. She would have to wait and talk to him in the morning. Now she needed sleep.

Sara checked the doors. There were two entrances to the cabin. The front door was solid oak with a bronze-colored stain that had faded over the years. It appeared as old as the cabin. The upper half had been fitted with a half panel of glass. Like the other windows in the cabin, decorative iron latticework covered the glass to discourage intruders. The ironwork was tasteful, but still induced claustrophobia. A deadbolt secured the door. No one would be breaking through that door without specialized equipment.

The back door, which entered into the kitchen, was constructed from unstained oak. Unlike the front door, it lacked an iron grill over the half-panel window. The door was newer with fewer scuffmarks. Most likely, Eric's father had replaced the door after he had added the bars to the windows. Sara secured the deadbolt.

As an afterthought, she flipped on the porch light. A bare, yellow, light bulb to the left of the door illuminated a fifteen-foot hemisphere around the door. Beyond was darkness. Other than the tall, unkempt grass, there was nothing to see. She turned off the light. It was ten minutes past eleven. Cory wouldn't be calling tonight. It had been unrealistic to expect him to call, but Sara still felt disappointed.

Sara found several towels in a bathroom cupboard. They smelled musty but otherwise appeared clean. After three days without a shower, she would have considered a dirty horse blanket perfectly acceptable. The shower stall was Spartan. The white enamel was chipped at the corners, and a large teardrop-shaped rust ring surrounded the drain. But the water was hot. That was all she cared about.

Sara dropped her clothes to the floor and stepped into the stream of hot water. The only available soap was small and dried with dark cracks running the length of the bar. The soap couldn't be any dirtier than she was, Sara decided. She and the soap could clean up simultaneously.

Sara scrubbed her body clean and rinsed off the lather. She remained in the stream of hot water and let her muscles relax. Tomorrow would be Rory's turn. Tonight, there was no one with whom she needed to share the hot water, and the moist heat drenching her naked body felt too good to forego. She didn't know if it was the aspirin or the hot shower, but her headache was gone. Tomorrow would be an even better day.

Ryan should have her car fixed by noon—if not already repaired. Cory could give her a ride to the garage to pick it up. She could tell Cory the cabin belonged to a friend and leave it at that. If the contract was in her mailbox as she expected, she could be driving toward Oregon by late afternoon, long before her stalker had time to react. She would return for her belongings after she had secured an apartment.

Sara stepped out of the shower and toweled herself dry. In the van, she had slept in her clothes; tonight she would wear pajamas.

Sara peeked into Rory's bedroom. Rory was asleep and sprawled across the double bed. The yellow dog was lying beside her with his head resting on her tummy. Rory had become attached to the dog. Perhaps she should get Rory a dog once they were settled in Oregon.

Sara rechecked the doors. Both were locked as she expected. At the back door she turned on the outside light. The only sign of life was a moth circling the yellow light. Sara flipped off the light, grabbed her purse with her cell phone and pistol, and headed for her bedroom. Tired as she was, she didn't look forward to sleep. Sleep invited nightmares. Sleep was when the man in the black ski mask became real and inflicted pain with his black baseball bat. Sara placed her pistol on the nightstand next to her bed, turned off the lights, and then slipped between the sheets.

Despite Sara's apprehensions, sleep came quickly, and she sank into a deep, dreamless slumber while her body tried to recover from the three days of sleep deprivation. The body can only endure so much abuse before it shuts down, and Sara had been approaching that limit. Eventually, as her body recovered, she rose into REM sleep where the blackness of deep sleep yields to the vivid videos of the inner mind. Sara found herself on a sandy beach. Tall birch trees lined the water's edge creating a perfect reflection on the calm water. Yellow butterflies fluttered above the surface of the water, dancing from one spot to another with the grace that only a butterfly can master. In the water's shallows, a multitude of black pollywogs swam in random directions, the purpose of their haste known only to them. Was this Harley Lake? She didn't know. The lake was placid with hardly a ripple to mar the surface. A mother duck with a clutch of small ducklings swam along the shoreline. An old man was sitting on a bench throwing breadcrumbs to the ducks. He was wearing a broad-brimmed hat that Sara had seen so many times before. It had to be her father. Yes, it was her father. "Hello, Papa," she said, but he didn't answer. Couldn't he hear her? He looked so sad. Tears were rolling down his cheeks. He was crying. Sara had only seen him cry once before. That was when her mother died. Did someone die? Was she dead? "I'm over here, Papa. I'm not dead. I'm still alive. Why can't you hear me?" The old man fed the last of the breadcrumbs to the ducks and got up to leave.

In the distance, Sara heard an animal barking, and the ducks began to scatter. A wolf was after the ducks. "Papa, you must protect the ducks. You can't leave now. A wolf is after them. The ducks trusted you. You have to help them." The wolf was getting nearer. The barking sounded so close. It was as if the wolf were beside her.

The fog of the dream began to dissipate, but the barking did not...It was Tiger. Not knowing if it were a dream or reality, Sara reached for her pistol. As she lay in bed, a wave of light panned across the ceiling, announcing the arrival of a car. Sara couldn't see her watch, but it had to be the middle of the night. Perhaps it was a couple of lovers seeking a secluded spot for a romantic tryst.

Pointing her pistol toward the ceiling, Sara climbed out of bed and headed toward the front room. The illumination from the kitchen's digital clock cast sufficient light to see shadows of the furniture, but nothing more. Tiger, no longer barking, stared at the back door. "You hear something out there, Tiger?" Sara looked out the windows but saw no evidence of headlights or car. They could have turned around and left. Tiger gave out a low growl. "We have to keep the lights off and be very quiet," Sara whispered to Tiger. "We want them to think no one is here." Sara knelt down beside Tiger and placed her arms around his neck to comfort him or was it to comfort her?

She waited quietly for fifteen minutes according to the digital clock in the kitchen. Tiger remained tense but ceased his barking. Without further lights or sounds, Sara began to relax. No one knew they were here. And no one could have followed them in the dark without using their headlights. Sara would have noticed that. Whoever had driven by had not been seeking them.

Sara stood up and walked over to a window, but all she could see was darkness. The overcast sky prevented any starlight from penetrating the night. Tiger, illuminated by the light from the kitchen clock, continued staring at the back door. "What's out there, Tiger?" Sara whispered. She walked over to the back door and peered through the glass, her forehead almost touching the pane of glass. She couldn't see anything in the darkness. If it were a couple of lovers parked by the cabin, turning on the porch light would encourage them to seek privacy elsewhere.

Sara flipped the light switch, and yellow light flooded the area around the back door. A man with a black ski mask stared back at her. He stood in front of the door inches from Sara's face. His left hand tightly gripped a pistol. Swinging the barrel of his gun, he smashed the light bulb, and disappeared in the darkness.

Sara backed away from the door, her pistol held firmly with both hands as Cory had taught her. She pointed it at the back door, aiming at chest level. The doorknob began to turn, and the intruder gave a push on the door, but the dead bolt held firm. Sara pointed the gun at the noise and pulled the trigger. The sound of shattering glass followed the muzzle blast from Sara's pistol. Sara fired again and heard a low-pitched, guttural groan followed by silence. She was tempted to empty the gun at the intruder, but decided to conserve her bullets; what bullets she had left in the gun were all she had.

"Mommy, what are you doing?" Rory, still half asleep, stumbled toward Sara. "I heard noise."

Sara knelt down and scooped Rory into her arms. "Tiger and I were playing a game, Honey. We're sorry we woke you." Sara leaned back against the wall, facing the back door. "Tiger and I are going to sleep out here tonight. You can join us if you want." Rory laid her head in Sara's lap and within seconds was back to sleep.

With the window shattered, the intruder could easily unlock the deadbolt from the outside. But that would make noise, and Sara was sure she would hear even the slightest noise. She would be ready for him. Leaning against the wall, hidden in the shadows, she would be difficult to see. She would see him first, and that would be all the advantage she would need. This time she would empty her gun. There would be no second chance. It would be him or her.

Sara set her gun down beside her and placed her right arm around Rory's waist. Rory slept with the innocence of a child. She and Eric had been just as innocent when they skinny-dipped in Harley Lake so many years ago. Why do children have to grow up? Sara placed her left hand on Tiger's back and messaged his shoulder muscles. Tiger snuggled against her left side, pressing against her thigh. It was a comforting feeling. Sara was considering a dog for Rory. Perhaps she was the one who needed a dog.

The night was again quiet, but it had been quiet before. Sara continued watching the back door. She was prepared to stay up all night if need be. She could nap in the daylight. Nothing ever happened in the daylight. The sun was streaming through the window when Sara awoke.

# 21

Eric flipped through the channels with his remote, pausing at any vaguely interesting channel before moving on. After the third cycle through the channels, he punched off the TV and set the remote on the end table; nothing piqued his interest. For the first time in his life, he was lonely. During his childhood there had always been Sara. In the overcrowded prison system, with no privacy, lonely would have been a blessing. In contrast, the solitude and isolation he felt upon parole came as a welcome relief. Like a city dog turned loose in the woods, he had savored that moment. He had enjoyed that freedom, but no more.

Eric thumbed through the magazines in the rack beside his chair. They were mostly his mother's magazines, which were promoting the latest fashions in kitchen remodeling or offering suggestions on how to excel at rock gardening; he had no subscriptions of his own. Finally, he settled on one of his father's old *Sports Illustrated* issues. He enjoyed sports, but had no interest in the real or perceived scandals of the participants. He didn't care who was divorcing whom or which star deserved the highest salary. After a few minutes of flipping pages, he returned the magazine to the rack.

For his own sanity, he needed to leave Cade County. His parents were dead, and he had no relatives in the area. He had nothing to keep him here. The local residents obviously weren't going to accept him into the community. The demolished entryway was testimony to that. He would never make friends in Cade County.

Eric walked into the kitchen and placed a cup of water in the microwave. He set the timer for a minute. Two cans of dog food sat on the kitchen counter next to the microwave. Tiger had enough food for two days, but needed more. Eric would have to take the dog food with him on his next visit to the cabin. He missed Tiger. Tiger was his only reliable companion. In the beginning, he had only wanted to nurse the dog back to health. He intended to find a good home for the dog after the dog had fully recovered, but Tiger had other plans, and leaving his newfound home was not one of them.

The buzzer on the microwave beeped. Eric added a teaspoon of instant coffee to the hot water and stirred it with a spoon. He found some leftover butter pecan ice cream in the freezer and placed half of it in a bowl. Normally, Tiger would have eaten the other half. Tiger had been gone less than twenty-four hours, and already the void was palpable. Even running wasn't the same without Tiger. Eric took a sip of coffee, finding it too hot. He added a small amount of cold water.

Eric cleaned up the entryway after he finished his ice cream and coffee. That killed another hour. Except for tiling the floor, the entryway was finished. It looked better than it did before the bomb. The floor tiles were on special order but wouldn't arrive until the following week, leaving nothing further Eric could do on the entryway. Eric placed the broom and dustpan in the closet, and then remembered he hadn't gotten yesterday's mail. In the confusion following the meeting with Sara, he had forgotten.

Eric walked out to his mailbox. Surprisingly, it was still standing. A personal mailbox is normally the target of choice for hate groups. Perhaps the good citizens of Cade County had found it unworthy of their attention and elected to demolish his entryway instead. Eric found an assortment of bills, advertisements, and unsolicited applications for credit cards in the mailbox. Having no friends, he didn't expect any personal mail. One of the letters listed the courthouse as its return address. That would be from the sheriff's office. He had requested a copy of the police report. Lisa Harding, his State Farm Insurance Agent, wouldn't process his claim without the report. Apparently, insurance companies were reluctant to pay claims on bombed-out houses without additional details.

Eric tossed the mail on the kitchen table. Then he sat down on a stool and picked up the letter from the sheriff's department. Before he could sell the house and leave Cade County, he had to settle the insurance claim. He had to resolve all such issues before he left, since he wouldn't be returning to Cade County.

Eric opened the envelope and scanned the enclosed document. It was a standard department form with several areas of white space where Officer Cory Kramer had penned in his findings. His penmanship was deplorable—he should have been a doctor. All the letters slanted backwards, typical of a left-handed writer. But what caught Eric's eye was not the penmanship; it was the "i's." Above each "i" was a perfectly formed circle.

Eric stared at the document in disbelief, but the more he thought about it, the more sense it made. Why hadn't he considered that possibility? He would have to warn Sara, although in her present state of mind, she might assume he had added the circles to the report. If she did, it would be her own undoing. At this point, Eric no longer cared.

Eric had been avoiding the cabin for fear the police, or even worse, Sara's stalker might follow him to the cabin. It never occurred to him that they were one and the same. He felt obligated to warn Sara about Cade County's corrupt police department. What she did about that information was up to her. He would be leaving Cade County with a clear conscience.

Eric grabbed some women's magazines for Sara to read and headed for his car. No vehicles were in sight when he backed out of the driveway. He had expected a police tail. That apparently was not the case. Stone and his boys were getting lax, not that it really mattered. With the limited traffic, it was impossible for the police to follow someone who did not wish to be followed, and Eric did not wish to be followed. At Kampe's Korner, Eric turned north, heading toward Witticker Road. Eric monitored his rearview mirror; no cars were in sight. The overcast sky and low ceiling made any attempt to follow him from the air fruitless.

Eric stopped at Sara's farmhouse to check her mail. If the teaching contract were in her mailbox, she could be heading for Oregon by mid-afternoon. It was a risky decision. The farmhouse could be under police surveillance. With binoculars, the police could easily watch him from the comfort of the house. Eric was counting on the county not having the manpower or financial resources for twenty-four hour surveillance.

The farmhouse appeared quiet, as it would be if it were under surveillance. No cars were in sight. That too was meaningless. Eric sorted through the mail. The mailbox was large, but still full with five-days-worth of mail. A large brown envelope looked promising. It was too thick and heavy for routine junk mail. Eric looked at the return address. He had never heard of the town, but the state was Oregon. That had to be her contract. Eric placed the envelope on the seat next to him and headed for the cabin.

# 22

Levi Stone parked his car in a parking space reserved for police and grabbed his briefcase. He had forty-five minutes before he would be meeting Floyd Carter, the County Clerk, to discuss the following year's budget. Stone's current projection put his department fifty thousand over budget. He would have to do some fast-talking to keep his department from unraveling. There would have to be significant cuts; but he hoped he could avoid cutbacks in personnel. That would be a disaster. Covering all of Cade County was impossible even with the current staff.

Stone walked through the front door of the courthouse and punched two on the elevator panel. He could cancel the new Kevlar protective vests, but could he live with himself if one of his officers were killed or injured because of a budget cut?

"Morning, Laura," Stone said as he entered the department's outer office. Laura started her day at six in the morning, way too early for Stone's temperament. He was lucky if he arrived by eight. He did frequently work late into the evening, Stone rationalized. "Can you get me the cost breakdown on the Kevlar Protective Vests? I'm going to need it for my meeting with Floyd Carter."

"I canceled your meeting with Carter."

"You canceled my meeting with Floyd Carter?" It was unlike Laura to cancel a meeting with the County Clerk without consulting him first. "We have to nail down next year's budget."

"I told him you'd be too busy this morning."

Stone looked at his secretary, waiting for the other shoe to drop. She was more than a secretary and frequently made executive decisions in his absence, although not without good reason.

"Reverend Higgins called a couple of hours ago," she said. "He found the church van in the parking lot this morning, but no sign of his daughter. There were two bullet holes in the windshield."

Stone felt a sinking feeling in his gut. It was not as if it was unexpected. Normal people don't disappear for five days without a good reason. The two bullet holes in the van Windshield were adequate reason.

"We'll need to have a forensic team go over the van."

"I sent the team out hours ago."

"And?"

"Only a preliminary report at this time. There was blood on the seat. That'll take several days to fully analyze, but the blood type is O positive, same as Sara Higgins' blood type. I believe we still have samples of Sara's DNA from the assault. I'm hoping the DNA won't match, but I'm not optimistic. They found plenty of fingerprints, as you would expect. Some belonging to a child. Most of the prints were from the back of the van. The steering wheel and front seat were wiped clean."

"Did you run a make on the fingerprints?" Stone asked.

"One matched Eric Kampe's right thumb. They found it on a candy wrapper. The forensic team also found a sack filled with empty cans. The fingerprints on the cans were a match for Sara Higgins. The good news is the inside of some of the cans were still moist. They hadn't had time to dry out. The forensic team thinks Sara was still alive two or three days ago."

Stone walked into his office without comment and set his briefcase on his desk. Someone was trying to kill Sara Higgins, and now he had proof Kampe had been in contact with her. Sara had been missing for—what was it now—five days? He had feared the investigation would deteriorate into a search for human remains. He had no desire to explain that to Sara's father. At least it now appeared he hadn't killed them outright.

"Want me have one of the deputies pick him up?" Laura asked.

Stone gave the question a moment of thought. Sometimes the perpetrator can be intimidated into a confession, but Kampe had done time in prison. He wouldn't intimidate easily. "No, we don't want to tip our hand too early. We still have no proof a crime was committed. No one stole the van. Pastor Higgins loaned it out legally, and we have no dead bodies to confirm a homicide, although the bullet holes and blood on the seats are not very reassuring. No, we can find him if we need him. If we keep a low profile, he might lead us to the crime scene. Can you get me the Higgins file again?"

"It's on your desk, Chief."

"Thanks."

The file was lying on his desk next to his briefcase. He didn't know how he had overlooked it. Stone flipped through the pages until he came to Kampe's psychological profile. The shrinks had declared Kampe a low risk for violence unless under drugs. Was he back on drugs? Stone wondered if the old profile was even valid. Kampe had spent five years in maximum-security. That can do a lot to a man, and the changes are not always for the better. Prison didn't always make kinder and gentler people.

Stone picked up the stack of eight-by-ten glosses. The pictures were ugly, and after five years he still found them repulsive. He needed to look at such pictures periodically to remind as to why society needed people like him. The real question was why society needed people like Kampe. Stone hardly recognized Sara from the picture. The entire right side of her face was caved in. The muscles to her right eye were ruptured, and the eye pointed off to the side. It was a wonder she regained sight in that eye. The picture of her chest revealed a large laceration across her right breast with deformities of her right ribs. A tube protruded from her chest. The doctors said that was to expand the collapsed lung. Stone studied the pictures for a moment and then reached for the pictures of her extremities. Her right forearm was broken. The bones were protruding through the skin. Why hadn't he noticed it before: all the injuries were on the right side? Sara sustained her injures while defending herself. Stone had been in unpleasant situations before, but he never experienced the dread that was now descending over him. He only hoped his suspicions were wrong.

Searching through the folder, Stone found Kampe's personal and statistical information sheet. At the top were mug shots of Kampe in front and profile views. At the bottom were his fingerprints. Stone read through the statistical information: age 18, height 6' 1", weight 180, hair brown, eyes brown, *right hand dominate*... He had sent the wrong man to prison. Because of his incompetence, an innocent man had spent five years in prison.

"Laura, get me all the information we have on Cory Kramer's whereabouts on the day of the rape: radio traffic logs, traffic citations, anything you can find. And this request is confidential, even within the department." No one ever questions why a hero is in the right place at the right time. Stone had been as guilty of that oversight as anyone. Kramer had no business inside the city of Tamarack. They have their own police department.

"Chief, here's a photocopy of the radio log." Laura handed Stone a sheet of paper still warm from the copy machine. "Just the usual traffic, but nothing from Cory. I couldn't find any traffic citations he had written during that time period. He must have had a quiet night until the rape. Is there something in particular you're looking for?"

"No, this is fine, thank you." Stone added the copy of the radio log to the Higgins file. If the Higgins girl had falsely testified against Kampe and sent him to prison for five years, that could be sufficient motive for revenge, but was Kampe capable of murder? Not according to his psychological profile, assuming the profile was still valid.

Stone unlocked his desk drawer and pulled out his GPS locator. The triangular shaped cursor, signifying Kampe's car, was no longer in the driveway. It was slowly moving north on Witticker Road. Stone had only been on that road a few times. If he remembered right, it went nowhere. "Laura, there is one more thing you can get for me," Stone yelled out to the outer office. "See if you can find a plat map." Stone pushed the reverse button on the GPS locator, and the cursor marched backwards toward Kampe's Korner, pausing momentarily at what Stone assumed had to be Sara's farmhouse. Don Higgins was right about one thing: a lot more happened five years ago than was presented at trial.

"Here you go, Chief." Laura passed the plat book to Stone. "If you find any cheap lake-front property, let me know."

Stone flipped through the pamphlet until he came to the section, which included Witticker Road. As he expected, most of the land belonged to a large paper company that invested in forestland for its pulpwood. A few small parcels were under private ownership. A forty-acre plot at the end of Witticker Road had Kampe printed on its center. Ward Kampe was an avid deer hunter. He must have had a hunting camp on the property. It was isolated, making it a good place for a murder, but a bad place to dispose of the bodies. Kampe must know the police would eventually search the camp. And why was he driving back to the cabin? He had five days. Surely, he would have disposed of any bodies by now. What if they weren't dead? What if Kampe was holding them hostage at the cabin for some kind of sadistic revenge? That would be risky on his own property...unless they weren't hostages. What if he were protecting them? Stone looked at Kampe's psychological profile again as if it could give him insight into the mind of a man who had unjustly served five years in maximum security.

"Laura?"

"Yes, Chief."

Stone walked out to the outer office. "You still think love is a stronger emotion than hate?" Stone had talked to Kampe several times over the last couple of weeks. He had no doubts concerning the sincerity of Kampe's hatred for Sara. It had been intense.

"Without a doubt, Chief. At the end of the day, love always wins."

"I sure hope you're right."

"How's that?"

"Because it's getting close to the end of the day."

Laura looked at her watch. It wasn't even noon.

Stone returned to his desk and removed his pistol from the drawer. He attached the holster to his belt and checked to ensure the gun was loaded: it was. "I'll be out of the office for awhile. You can reach me on the police radio if you need me."

In all the years Laura had worked for Stone, she had never seen him carry a gun except on his way to the pistol range. "You want me to call for backup?"

"No," Stone said after a moment of thought, "This is something I have to do myself. It wouldn't hurt to have Koski patrol the northwest corner of the county in case I do need back up. I'll be at the end of Witticker Road." Stone put on his suit coat to cover the pistol on his right hip and walked out the door.

## 23

Sara awoke with a headache. The few hours of sleep she obtained during the night had done little to alleviate her sleep deprivation. At least now she knew where to find the aspirin. Superimposed on her headache was the guilt over the sleep she had gotten; she hadn't intended to sleep at all. What if he had returned during the night? She would be dead. And it wasn't just her; the man was sick and capable of killing a five-year-old without remorse.

Sara placed her pistol in her lap while she contemplated her next move. She wasn't in eminent danger. The sun was shining through the broken window, and she could hear birds chirping in the background. If anything, it was a beautiful day. There was nothing to suggest the intruder was still lingering around the cabin. He had shunned daylight in the past; hopefully, today would be no different. She may have hit him with her second shot. That was when he ended his pursuit. The thought of a dead man outside her back door was unsettling, but that was preferable to having him outside the back door and not dead.

Sara looked at her watch. It was almost eight. Cory should be home from work. Sara dialed Cory's apartment number, but got no response, not even a dial tone. Sara checked the display on her phone. A slash superimposed over a graphic picture of a battery glared up at her from the phone's display—her battery was dead. She was fortunate the battery lasted long enough to call Cory's answering machine the previous evening. Why hadn't she thought to bring the battery charger? If she hadn't been a pastor's daughter, this would be an appropriate time to swear. For some reason that thought struck her as funny, invoking a childish, almost hysterical giggle. She was getting slaphappy.

At least Cory knew where to find her and would call when he got home. He would surely investigate when Sara didn't answer. Maybe he was already on his way to the cabin. Guarding the door while she waited for Cory to arrive was currently her only prudent option.

A half-hour passed with no sound other than the susurration of Rory's heavy breathing. Rory, curled up by Sara's right side, had her head resting in Sara's lap. At least Rory was getting some sleep. Tiger was well entrenched on Sara's left side, pressing against her thigh with no intention of yielding additional turf. From his occasional movements, Sara assumed he was awake. Sara gently massaged his shoulder muscles. "Thank you, Tiger." Tiger looked up for a moment and then placed his chin back on his front paws and closed his eyes.

Sara stretched her leg in response to a cramp. She had been sitting on the hardwood floor most of the night, and her body was beginning to protest. In addition to the leg cramp, her tailbone felt permanently embedded in the wood floor. She couldn't wait forever for Cory, and Eric said nothing about returning today. Spending another night in the cabin was not an option; *he* knew she was here. If someone didn't arrive soon, they'd have to walk to the nearest inhabited building. That would be a long hike. She hadn't seen many driveways on the way in. She assumed most of the driveways she had seen led to seasonal hunting camps, and this wasn't hunting season.

"Mommy, I'm hungry." Rory sat up and stretched. Her snarl-filled hair hung down over her face. "Can we eat breakfast?"

"In a few minutes. Maybe we can have pancakes." Sara slipped her right hand under her pajama tops to hide her pistol. It was best if she didn't have to explain the reason for the gun's presence to Rory. "Why don't you get dressed while Tiger and I have a look outside?" If there were a dead body outside their door, Rory didn't need to see it.

Rory headed toward her bedroom. Tiger got up to follow, but Sara held him back by his collar. "You don't think I'm going out there by myself, do you, Tiger?" Sara slipped into her slippers and headed toward the door. "Come on, Tiger." Tiger followed with neither enthusiasm nor reluctance.

Shards of window glass covered the floor by the door, making Sara wonder if she should have Tiger follow her; she didn't want him to get glass slivers in his paws, but neither did she wish to venture out alone. Sara looked out the shattered window but found no corpse on her doorstep. She wasn't sure if that was a good sign or not. A dead body would have ended her ordeal. Sara unlocked the dead bolt with her left hand while the pistol in her right hand protected her front.

Sara opened the door and discovered more broken glass lying on the four-by-four-foot concrete apron in front of the door. Multiple red spots lay splattered over the glass. Sara bent down to touch one of the spots with her finger; it felt sticky and appeared to be blood. If she had shot him, had he crawled off to die or was it a minor wound? He came by car, but she didn't see any cars near the cabin.

Sara let Tiger run ahead while she walked around the perimeter. In their haste of the previous night, Tiger hadn't had the opportunity to mark his territory and was now making up for lost time.

After making a complete circle without finding anything more sinister than a garter snake, Sara convinced herself that no villains were lurking in the immediate area; how long that would last, she didn't know. Sara left Tiger outside to finish exploring the area and returned to the cabin. He would be her point man. She assumed he would bark if someone were to approach the cabin.

Sara found a broom and dustpan in a closet and swept up the broken glass. Then she removed the remaining shards of glass still imbedded in the window frame. She would have to reimburse Eric for the damages.

"Can we eat now?" Rory asked.

"Let me change clothes first, and then you and I are going to make a big batch of pancakes."

"Can Tiger have some too?"

"I don't know if dogs like pancakes; but after last night, he can eat anything he wants. He's earned his keep."

Sara threw on a sweatshirt and some jeans. This was not the appropriate time to worry about the fashion police. After breakfast she would have Rory take a shower, and then she needed to work on those snarls in Rory's hair. After five days, they appeared unmanageable. Hopefully, the hairbrush she found in the bedroom would be up to the task.

Sara mixed the pancake batter and was about to pour some on the griddle when she heard Tiger bark. She pulled the curtain aside and looked out the kitchen window. A blue Ford was coming up the driveway; that would be Cory. She had hoped to avoid police involvement, but after last night she could use a shoulder to lean on, any shoulder. She couldn't tell him everything, but she would have to explain the greater portion of her dilemma. She preferred to have that discussion when Rory wasn't around. The less Rory knew about what happened, the better. It was a nice day. Rory and Tiger could play outside.

"Hi, Cory, come on in," Sara pushed open the back door to let Cory in. "You're just in time for pancakes."

"Found your message when I got off work." Cory was still in uniform, although he was driving his own car, not a police cruiser. "You OK?"

Sara wrapped her arms around Cory's neck and gave him a hug. Under normal circumstances she wouldn't have been that spontaneously affectionate—not with Cory. Cory was a great friend, but she had never felt the right chemistry for a romantic relationship. This morning her need to be held transcended chemistry.

Cory cringed as Sara tightened her arms around him. "What's wrong?" Sara backed away, wondering if she had been too forward.

"Got a sore shoulder. A drunk hit me with a tire iron last night." A dark stain spread across his right shoulder.

"You're bleeding."

"Damn, this is the second shirt I've had on. I thought the bleeding had stopped."

"Take your shirt off. Let me look at it."

"I've got a pressure dressing on it. It'll quit bleeding in a minute."

"Shouldn't you see a doctor?" Other than the brief moments the previous week at the farmhouse, Sara had never seen Cory in uniform. He looked formidable with his gun and nightstick attached to his utility belt. Someone would have to be severely impaired by alcohol to take on Cory.

"I'll see a doctor later. I wanted to check on you first." The stain over Cory's right shoulder didn't appear to be spreading.

"What happened to the drunk?"

Cory pulled the nightstick out of the ring that secured it to his utility belt. "I gave him an attitude adjustment with Old Betsy here." He waved the nightstick a few times for emphasis.

*The room was dark but Sara could still see the whites of his eyes peering out from behind the black ski mask. They eyes were sinister and filled with hatred. "Please don't hit me," she said, but he still struck her, hitting her naked body in the arms and ribs. He raised his black baseball bat to hit her in the face. The bat was long and slender and of uniform diameter. No, it wasn't a black baseball bat; it was too thin...it was a policeman's baton, a nightstick!*

Sara backed away from Cory and reached for her purse, her hands trembling with fear. Standing before her was her monster, the demon who had tormented her night after night in her dreams. This was the person who had beaten her close to death, destroying forever her relationship with Eric. He was now devoid of ski mask, but he was just as dangerous, just as evil. Sara reached into her purse and pulled out her gun. This time she would kill him. She would use every bullet in her gun until she was sure he was dead. Cory's nightstick came down hard on Sara's wrist, and her gun slid across the floor. A second blow hit her on the right arm just below the shoulder and knocked her to the floor. She rolled away from her demon and sprang to her feet. She wouldn't allow it to happen again, not if she could help it. She grabbed an empty vase and threw it at Cory, hitting him on the left shoulder. He only laughed.

"I should have killed you," he said. "You were supposed to die, you know. You would have died if it hadn't been for those damn doctors." Cory moved toward her, his nightstick held high over his shoulder. "This time I'll do it right. There'll be nothing left for the doctors to fix."

Sara searched for other objects to throw. Finding none, she kicked at Cory's groin but hit his right knee instead. Cory dropped the nightstick and grabbed his knee. She had hit a sensitive spot. It had to be the same knee she had kicked at the farmhouse.

"Bitch!"

Sara looked over at Rory who was watching from the doorway to her bedroom.

"Run, Rory, Run. Hide in the woods."

Rory remained frozen in fear. Her only exposure to violence had been Roadrunner and Wylie Coyote. She found it incomprehensible that anyone would purposefully hurt another person. Tiger danced around angrily barking at all participants.

The knee pain didn't incapacitate Cory for long. He charged at Sara, his shoulders low to the ground like a linebacker in pursuit of a ball carrier. In more reflex than skill, Sara deftly stepped to the side, dodging the attack. The maneuver caught Cory by surprise. His momentum propelled him past Sara, but not before he grabbed a handful of her sweatshirt with his right hand. He grimaced as pain seared through the gunshot wound in his shoulder. The dark stain on his uniform began to enlarge.

"You're going to die, bitch!" Cory slapped Sara across the face, his ring cutting deeply into her cheek. Blood flowed profusely down Sara's face to form stalactites of coagulated blood that clung to her chin.

"Stop hitting my Mommy."

Rory kicked Cory in the leg with her bare foot. It was more insult than injury, and Cory rewarded her effort with the back of his hand. Rory fell to the ground.

That was all the incentive Tiger needed—no one hits Rory. Tiger lunged at Cory, instinctively going for the throat but catching his right wrist instead when Cory raised his arm to block the attack. The momentum of Tiger's sixty pounds hitting against his chest knocked Cory to the ground. Tiger continued his grip on Cory's wrist, violently shaking the extremity like he would a captured rabbit, his teeth tearing deeper into the flesh. Blood spurted from the wound. Cory grimaced in pain. He tried to push Tiger away, but Tiger had embedded his teeth deeply into Cory's wrist and refused to release his grip. Blood now flowed freely from Cory's injured shoulder. His muscles no longer responded at full strength, but adrenaline is a great compensator. Cory picked up his nightstick and swung blindly at Tiger, hitting him on the side of the head. Tiger released his grip and stood motionless for a moment, giving Cory time to send a second blow crashing down on Tiger's skull. Tiger staggered a few steps then slumped into a motionless mass.

Sara's right eye was almost swollen shut and blood continued to drip from her chin, but she was still alive. That would quickly change if she didn't take advantage of the diversion Tiger had created. Ignoring her injuries, Sara ran to the kitchen and began pulling out drawers. On the third drawer, she found what she wanted—a butcher's knife. The knife was large and sharp, but still had limitations. It might fend off an attack with a nightstick, but would be no match for Cory's pistol. She could run for the door and hide in the woods. If she reached the woods, he would never find her. But she couldn't leave Rory. That she wasn't willing to do. She might die no matter what she did, but she could at least die defending her daughter. Sara rushed at Cory hoping to reach him before he could draw the gun from his holster. The button-down flap on his holster would buy her a second or two. That might be all she needed.

The heavy knife was not good for stabbing, but she could use it like a machete and slash at his throat. The neck offered many large blood vessels. All she had to do was hit one of them. According to her college biology books, he would then quickly bleed to death. As she raised her arm for the attack, she felt searing pain in her eyes as if someone had inserted burning embers under her eyelids. The caustic smell of pepper spray burned in her nostrils and flowed down into her lungs causing uncontrollable spasms of coughing. Cory pried the knife from her hand. Without her eyesight, she could offer no further resistance. A strap tightened about her left wrist. She pulled back, but her strength was no match against Cory's. She rubbed her eyes with her right hand, but that only increased the burning sensation. Gradually, her vision returned; blurry at first as she peered through a stream of tears, then objects came into focus. Nylon binders, the kind police use for disposable handcuffs, bound her left wrist to a vertical water pipe that disappeared into the floor. She pulled against the binder, but it only cut into her wrist. At least he was no longer beating her. He could have killed her and be done with it. Why the bindings, she wondered.

"What do you want from us?"

Cory ignored the question. He was busy securing Rory to the same water pipe. Rory's meager resistance was even less a match than Sara's. Cory finished binding Rory to the pipe, and then picked up Sara's gun. He stuck the gun under his belt. "I trust the two of you will be here when I return?"

Sara glared at Cory. She would not dignify the question with a reply.

"You always were the defiant one. That's what I liked about you. It made the conquest so much more enjoyable." Cory walked out the back door without further comment.

Sara heard him rummaging through a storage shed. She didn't know what he was planning; but whatever it was, it wouldn't be in her best interest. He would have to kill them. She knew who he was, and he was not likely to leave loose ends. But why hadn't he killed them outright? It would have been better if he had. They were now play toys to be exploited at his sadistic pleasure. She assumed their deaths would be painful. Tiger was lucky. He lay motionless on the floor with blood caked over his right eye. Tiger's pain was over. Rory was the one Sara felt sorry for. She would soon be dead like Tiger. She didn't deserve to die so young. Sara wrapped her arms around her daughter and pulled Rory to her chest.

Cory returned moments later with a hammer, nails, and a small sheet of three-quarter-inch plywood. "You made a mess out of the door," he said. He didn't expect a reply, and none was offered. Cory covered the broken window with the plywood and secured it in place with an excess of nails.

"If you're going to kill us, why don't you do it and get it over with?"

"Kill you? I'm not going to kill you. I'm a police officer, protector of law-abiding citizens. Kampe is going to kill you. I'll naturally have to arrest him and send him back to prison. This time your boyfriend won't be getting out. If I'm lucky, maybe he'll resist, and I'll get to kill him too—all in the line of duty of course."

"You'll never get away with it even if you do kill us. There'll be autopsies and genetic testing. When they discover Eric isn't the biological father, they'll start looking a little closer at you."

Cory ignored the comment and walked over to the front door. He locked the deadbolt and then placed nails along the edge of the door to ensure it couldn't be opened from inside or out. "See this fireplace? Careless use of fireplaces cause many house fires. It can be a chimney fire that gets out of control or a spark that gets ejected onto a wooden floor or rug like this." Cory poured some lighter fluid over a small pile of kindling wood stacked in a metal tray designed for that purpose. He made sure some of the lighter fluid spilled onto the rug. "Even a carelessly lit match can cause a fire." Cory struck a match and dropped it on the firewood. It immediately burst into flames. Cory waited until the rug caught fire. "You do like barbeques, don't you?" Cory continued his monolog when he received no reply. "Do you know what fire does to proteins and DNA? It denatures them. It renders them useless. The fire will also destroy those nylon cuffs. Yes, there will be an autopsy. I will even recommend that myself when I discover your charred bodies. If we are lucky, your skull and jawbone will be intact so we can identify your remains. This is Kampe's property. When we find the padlock on the back door preventing your escape, it will be an open and shut case, murder one. They won't find twelve men or women anywhere in Cade County who won't find him guilty."

Cory dropped the hammer on the floor and withdrew his nightstick. Using the tip of the stick, he forced up Sara's chin. "Keep your chin up, my dear, and do try to stay warm. We wouldn't want you to catch cold." The fire began climbing up the wall in the far room. "I think it's getting a little too hot in here for my taste. I hope you won't find it rude if I take my leave." Cory walked out the back door and closed the door behind him. Sara heard the padlock snap shut.

"Mommy, I want to get out of here."

"So do I, Honey." Sara pulled at the nylon binder; but again, it only cut into her skin. She couldn't break it, but she could cut it if she had a sharp instrument. She looked around but found nothing within reach that would cut through the nylon strap. The closest object was the hammer lying on the floor. If she could reach the hammer, she could hit the binder against the metal pipe with the claw side of the hammer. That would chop through the strap.

Sara pushed her strap down the pipe until she was lying on the floor. Even with her outstretched feet, she was two feet short of the hammer.

"What are you doing, Mommy?"

"I'm trying to get the hammer. If we can get the hammer, I think we can get out of here." Even with the hammer, it wouldn't be a sure thing; they still had to get past the doors or the bars on the windows. Sara could find nothing she could use to extend her reach, and smoke was filling the room.

\* \* \*

Eric was a mile away when he saw the smoke. How stupid could Sara get? Burning rubbish in the trash barrel was sure to draw attention. The density of the smoke increased as Eric got closer. When he arrived in the clearing, flames were rising from the roof at the front of the cabin. He found Cory's car parked at the cabin's rear. Cory was sitting on the hood watching the fire while sipping on a can of Barq's Root Beer. Eric slammed on the brakes twenty feet from Kramer's car and shifted into park. He didn't bother turning off the ignition before exiting the car.

"You know, Kampe, I'm beginning to like this root beer," Kramer said in greeting. "You have good taste."

"Did you call the fire department?"

Kramer threw the empty root beer can on the ground. "Not yet. I thought I'd give the fire a few more minutes. I'm glad you're here. That'll make things easier."

Eric wished he had a cell phone. With no friends, he assumed a cell phone would be a worthless purchase. "Where's Sara?"

Cory pointed to the cabin with his nightstick. "In there."

"You swine!" Eric ran to the front door and found it locked. It wouldn't budge. He ran to the back door. A heavy Yale lock secured the door. He rammed the door with his shoulder, but the door wouldn't give.

"SARA, ARE YOU IN THERE?"

"ERIC...WE'RE INSIDE. PLEASE HURRY!"

Eric slammed his shoulder into the door again with no change in results.

"You looking for this?" Cory held up the key to the Yale lock.

Eric lunged at Cory. Even with his painful right arm, Cory was too agile. He hit Eric solidly on the upper arm with his nightstick and stepped aside. Cory, the veteran of many personal assaults, used his nightstick with precision, blocking all of Eric's attacks. He played with Eric like a cat might play with a mouse, while the cabin burned in the background.

\* \* \*

"Rory, lie down on the floor."

Rory curled up on the floor next to Sara. Smoke was filling the cabin; but most of it rose toward the cathedral ceiling, leaving adequate air close to the floor. That wouldn't last forever. The fire was currently confined to the front half of the cabin, although it had burned through the roof in several areas. Smoke and fumes rose through the holes, sucking in fresh air from under the back door and through cracks in the wall. The fire was spreading. They couldn't survive on air leaks forever.

"ERIC, PLEASE HELP US."

Sara listened, but heard no response to her plea for help. She couldn't believe Eric would leave them to die in the fire no matter how much he hated her.

"Mommy, I can't breathe." Rory sat up and rubbed her eyes. Her eyes were now red and filled with tears.

"Stay on the floor. The air's better there." Sara wondered how much better it really was. Curls of smoke were beginning to accumulate even at floor level. The smoke was more irritating than Cory's pepper spray. It had to be irritating Rory's lungs as well. Tiger had been lying motionless on the floor, but now sneezed and shook his head.

"Look, Mommy, Tiger's alive."

It would've been better if he were dead, Sara thought. He would have suffered less. At least he shouldn't have to suffer alone. "Tiger, come over here. Come to us." Tiger forced himself to his feet.

"Mommy, Tiger can help us. He's a CAT."

The smoke and toxic fumes were already affecting Rory's thought processing. She was no longer thinking logically. It wouldn't be long now. "No, Honey, Tiger's a dog."

\* \* \*

Eric paused to catch his breath. His arms were sore and bruised. The blows from Cory's nightstick had taken their toll. He was fast, but no match for Cory's nightstick. He couldn't get closer than two feet. Each time he tried, he paid dearly with new contusions. There was no way he could get Cory's key. It was already too late. Flames had engulfed the cabin, and Sara was no longer calling for help.

"Why did you have to kill them?"

"Loose ends, my boy, loose ends. I've earned enough money in the medicinal trade to retire in style. People needed recreational drugs and were willing to pay top dollar for them. I helped provide for their basic needs. Someone had to do it. I have the money safely stashed in untraceable offshore accounts. But I can't leave behind loose ends. I hope you understand. Loose ends always come back to haunt you. Besides, I didn't kill them. You did. You locked them in the cabin and started the fire. I tried to stop you, but you shot me in the shoulder with this gun you took from Sara." Cory pulled Sara's gun from his belt to show Eric. "I had to shoot you in self-defense. When I call for back up, they'll find Sara's gun in your scummy little hand. It was nice of you to show up when you did. Loose ends. You have to take care of loose ends. Now do you prefer I shoot you in the head or the heart? I suppose I could shoot you in the gut and let you bleed for a few minutes." Cory pulled out his service pistol.

"Go ahead, shoot."

His parents were dead. Sara and Rory were dead. Even Tiger was dead. Everyone he had ever loved was dead. He had nothing more to live for. He might as well die too.

"Go ahead and shoot me, but I hope you rot in hell."

"Let's not get testy. This is strictly business." Cory raised his gun and pointed it at Eric's chest. "So long, loser."

Eric closed his eyes and waited for the bullet that would take his life. He wondered what the bullet would feel like. Would he hear the gunshot? According to the old war movies, you never hear the shot that gets you, but that was Hollywood. Did it really matter, he wondered. He could handle the pain. It couldn't be any worse than the pain he now felt. Eric tensed his muscles in anticipation. Then he heard it. A gunshot followed by a second gunshot. You *can* hear the one that gets you, but he would never live to tell Hollywood. He took a deep breath. There was no pain. There should be pain unless he was already dead.

Eric opened his eyes. Cory was staring at him through glassy eyes, his mouth gaping open. Two wet spots on his chest were rapidly expanding. He was still clutching his gun, but his arm hung at his side. Then he dropped the gun and fell to his knees. He paused on his knees for a second before falling face down.

"You alright, Kampe?" Levi Stone stepped out of the woods, his nine millimeter now at his side.

"You should've let him kill me. Why couldn't you let him kill me?"

Stone looked at the cabin. Angry flames now engulfed the entire structure. "They were inside?" It was more of a statement than a question. Eric watched the cabin burn, offering no reply. The flames rose over forty feet into the sky. Everyone in the fire would now be dead. It was a horrible way to die. "I'm sorry" was all Stone could say.

Eric turned away from the fire, unable to look at it any more. Staying at the cabin had been his idea. They would have been better hiding in the woods. They were dead and no *what if's* would ever bring them back. Until now he hadn't realized how much he loved her. Despite everything she had done, he still loved her. He wished he had told her that on the bike trail.

Eric hadn't cried in public since he was seven, not since the first Tiger died. Now he placed his head in his hands and wept openly—not soft, silent tears, but uninhibited sobs filled with years of pent-up emotion.

"Hello, Eric."

Eric had heard that soft voice many times before. But it wasn't possible. He turned around and almost fell to the ground as Rory leaped into his arms.

"Tar Zan, Tar Zan, Mommy's boyfriend tried to kill us! He tied us up and then he set the cabin on fire. But Tiger helped us get loose. And then…and then Mommy found a hole in the floor. I climbed down the ladder all by myself. Mommy came down the ladder carrying Tiger on her shoulders. Mommy says that's how firemen do it."

Eric looked at Sara. Black soot covered her face and stained her clothes. A streak of dry blood extended downward from a cut on her cheek, and her right eye was almost swollen shut. "You got out through the root cellar? Wasn't the lean-to door locked?"

Sara, unsure of herself, maintained her distance. "It was locked, but the wooden door was old. It wasn't hard to break through with the hammer. I guess I owe you for the door as well as a broken window. But we didn't start the fire." Sara tried to smile, but her lips just quivered. She crossed her arms, placing her hands under her armpits to hide the tremors. It was hard to believe it was over, even though she could see Cory's corpse on the ground, his upper half-covered by Stone's jacket. But if her nightmares continued, was it really over? Only time would tell. Even so, she could never undo what she had done to Eric. She could never return to the life she had before the incident. That life was gone, lost forever. There was a time when Eric would have held her tightly and quelled her fears. He would have gently wiped away the tears from her face. She so badly wanted Eric to hold her again, to feel the warmth of his body. Eric shifted Rory to his left side and held out his right arm. Sara cautiously slid under the arm, and Eric pulled her to him. The barricade Sara had built up over the years began to crumble. The dam began to break and a cascade of tears sequestered behind the barricade burst forth, soaking Eric's shirt. It felt good to be home.

"Want me call an ambulance?" Stone asked. "You need to be evaluated at the hospital. Smoke inhalation can be dangerous."

"I'll take them in my car," Eric offered. "It'll be faster than waiting for the ambulance."

"Only if we stop at the vet's first," Sara said. "Tiger has first priority; he earned it." Tiger was lying at their feet. His right eye was swollen shut, and blood matted the hair on his head.

"Eric," Stone said, "I own you an apology. My investigation wasn't adequate, and I'm sorry. I think I've heard enough today to get the gist of what happened five years ago. I'll see that Judge

Madalinski clears you of all charges. DNA testing should prove you aren't Rory's father."

"That won't be necessary, Chief. The birth certificate's correct; Rory is my daughter. I've been thinking about leaving Cade County anyway, maybe moving to Oregon and starting over."

Stone looked at the cabin. The roof had collapsed and the heat was becoming unbearable. He had called the fire department. They would soon arrive, but the cabin would be a total loss. Nothing could stop the fire. "This has to be a miracle," Stone said. "I'm surprised you made it out alive."

"I'm not," Sara replied. She ran her fingers upward along Eric's spine and into his hair. "God owed me a miracle."

## Support Indie Authors

If you enjoyed this novel please find the book on Amazon.com and leave a review with plenty of stars. You don't need to purchase the book on Amazon to leave a comment. The comment only requires a line or two. Example: "Name of novel" is well written with an engaging plot. I would highly recommend reading "name of novel."

# ABOUT THE AUTHOR

Larry Buege is a former chemistry and physics teacher and a retired physician assistant. He currently lives with his wife in Marquette, Michigan along the southern shore of Lake Superior.